# Merchant

# Merchant

**Alexandra Grunberg**

Goldsmiths
Press

# MERCHANT
## DRAMATIS PERSONAE

## Venice

*The Upper Keep*
> Jessica – *a merchant of Venice*
> Abraham – *Jessica's father*
> Talia – *keeper of Shakespeare's words*
> Abby – *a mother*
> Daniel – *Abby's husband*
> Omar – *Daniel's father*
> Ruben – *Abby's youngest son*
> Chava – *a child of the Upper Keep*

*Venice Main*
> Luka – *Jessica's childhood friend*
> Andrusha – *the hero of Venice*
> Borya – *Andrusha's lover*
> Grigory – *resident pest*
> Ecrin – *resident of Venice*
> Zehra – *resident of Venice*
> Nazli – *Feral child*

*The Gangs*
> Roman – *a young gang leader*
> Cem – *a member of Roman's gang (weak for Farooq)*
> Farooq – *a member of Roman's gang (weak for Cem)*
> Sedef – *a member of Roman's gang, friend of Cem and Farooq*

Shen – *a member of Roman's gang*
Roksana – *Roman's Favourite*
Bota – *a young gang leader*
Nikita – *Bota's Favourite*
Ghanim – *a member of Bota's gang*

## Fuji

Ama – *empress of Fuji*
Shinobu – *head scribe of Fuji*
Shinku – *scribe*
Makoto – *scribe*
Etsuna – *botanist and engineer*
Mizutsuki – *Greenhouse technician*
Kazuku – *head nurse of Fuji*
Yuki – *nurse*
Sumikai – *chef*
Hirokai – *sailor, Shinku's lover*
Sora – *sailor*
Yana – *plastic runner on the gathering ships*
Masuna – *plastic skimmer on the gathering ships*
Yousuke – *plastic runner on the gathering ships*
Minato – *plastic skimmer on the gathering ships*

## Kilimanjaro

Ibada – *delegate from the Kilimanjarian council*
Fadhila – *delegate from the Kilimanjarian council*
Nen – *Fadhila's son*

**Les Alpes**
Dario – *delegate from Les Alpes*
Sofia – *Dario's ward*

**The Flood**
A monster
A mermaid

# ACT 1

## THE QUALITY OF MERCY

The quality of mercy is not strained.
It droppeth as the gentle rain from heaven
Upon the place beneath. It is twice blest:
It blesseth him that gives and him that takes.
'Tis mightiest in the mightiest; it becomes
The thronèd monarch better than his crown.
His sceptre shows the force of temporal power,
The attribute to awe and majesty
Wherein doth sit the dread and fear of kings;
But mercy is above this sceptered sway.
It is enthronèd in the hearts of kings;
It is an attribute to God Himself;
And earthly power doth then show likest God's
When mercy seasons justice. Therefore, Jew,
Though justice be thy plea, consider this:
That in the course of justice none of us
Should see salvation. We do pray for mercy.

~ *The Merchant of Venice*, Act 4, Scene 1

# Chapter 1 (Jessica)

From her perch on a balcony in the Upper Keep, far above the boulders and deceptively calm waters of the Flood, Jessica told herself there was nothing to worry about, and almost believed the lie. The fighting of gangs, Feral children, and other Venetians had echoed for three days through heavy rains. The waters churned in shades of blue and purple so dark it was hard to imagine that the riot started with one body colouring the harbour bright red. But now, the loudest sounds she heard were the muffled curses of her father, Abraham, inside the thick walls of their home. The violence only stopped when the rain stopped, the heat and humidity too heavy for people to do more than rest in the shadows.

Hopping over the balcony, Jessica saw the silhouettes of her neighbours in their windows tying back kelp knot curtains. She secured herself around a house leg in a practiced hold and her mind wandered. As well as her current errand, trading for algae blocks, she needed to retie her own curtains, and her entirely frayed knot ladder, and refill the desalinator… Her breath became fast and shallow. The wave of other pressing issues pounded against her temples: how her back teeth burned when she drank sake or ate a pickle to the point where she could not eat anything but the gelatinous algae blocks, the skin between her fingers and toes shedding into spongey bleeding cracks, the itching in her hair like crawling bugs…

*Breathe,* a memory of her father whispered in her mind.

Jessica counted each problem and breathed them out. They could wait. None of them mattered if she starved to death. Nor would they matter if anyone had seen her in the riot …

Jessica exhaled until her hands stopped shaking. She slid down the house leg. The Star of David pendant on her necklace cut into the skin of her neck and the chain caught on her wild red curls. The heavy sack tied over her shoulder bumped painfully into her hip as the pickle jars clacked against each other. But the trip downward was quick, and she soon landed with a soft thud on the boulders that led to the harbour and Venice Main beyond.

She immediately felt eyes on her. She froze, scanning the shadows. and saw three children from Roman's gang. Two boys and a girl huddled together despite the heat, wearing plastic trash washed up from the ocean. They scowled at her in drowsy contempt. Jessica's dress too was made of plastic trash but had been processed into a slick black fabric by the Fujians. The children resettled into their half-sleep and Jessica hurried out of the shadows of the Upper Keep to the open boulders. They were already hot beneath her feet.

Roman was standing near the edge of the water. Jessica avoided his warning glare as she hopped from boulder to boulder. He took care of the children the best he could in a way that made Jessica's chest ache, his effort to protect them painfully familiar. Impulsively, she gripped her necklace.

Jessica remembered standing at the base of her house leg with Luka. They could not have been more than seven or eight. His arm was around her, hiding her against a large rock. She did not remember why she was down there or why Luka had come from the Main, but she remembered feeling rain splattering against her hair, and her fear of an oncoming storm. When she looked up, drops landed on her lips. She tasted salt, and thought the world had been turned upside down, because salt water came from the ocean. But when she wiped her lips, the back of her hand smeared red and she realized blood was falling from all the houses above. The drops spotted her cheeks, her temple, and around her eyes, but she could not stop looking and listening to the noise that she thought was screaming birds because she had never heard people scream like that before. Then Luka's arm was over her eyes, and the world was shadow, and the only sound was Luka's voice in her ear:

*"Don't look, Jess, it'll be over soon…"*

Her foot slipped off the rock. Jessica gasped, catching herself before she could fall. An eel lurking beneath the waves jerked deeper into the Flood. Jessica spat into the water and leapt away from the gang, the Upper Keep, and the memory.

She followed the popular boulder path that lined the harbour, smoothed out by decades of footsteps. The two Fujian ships from the last delivery were still moored, unharmed in the riot. Jessica tried not to think about the sailors. She pushed their names, their little kindnesses and familiar faults, the ways she had seen some of them die and the ways she imagined the others had died, all out of her mind, and she hauled herself up to the steps leading to the ramparts of Venice. The sun beat down on her. Sweat plastered her dress to her skin. She stumbled on some new repairs where the ancient smooth tiles (a mosaic, her father said, that repeated geometry of faded squares of blue, white, and orange, it was a *mosaic*) were broken and replaced with rocks dried white and crusty with a layer of salt. She gave herself a moment to lean against the wall and nodded at the few Venetians venturing this way, equipped with large plastic buckets to be filled in the harbour and desalinated above. Most ignored her; a few returned her nod with a glare.

"No trade today," muttered one man to his companion, straight black hair as damp as Jessica's. "Food's already in hands and bellies."

Jessica winked though he never looked directly at her face.

"There's always a chance to trade," she said. "If someone's ready to buy, I'm ready to sell."

The man's companion spat on the ground but did not correct her. Jessica shifted the strap of her sack higher up her shoulder and continued up the steps alone.

Reaching the ramparts, she was overwhelmed by the smell of packed bodies and the growing cacophony of arguing voices. Her pulse thrummed in pleasure. She was drenched in sweat, sticky and hot, but if she closed her eyes, she could imagine she was an ordinary Venetian with straight black hair, friends waiting on the ramparts, and the ability to move freely on the Main without feeling like an intruder. But if she kept her eyes closed too long, she could hear Luka's whisper, and the salt of the sweat on her lips took on that bright red taste.

Jessica's thoughts rolled and twisted, like the meeting of two gangs, one side pulling her towards Venice Main, the other dragging her back to the Upper Keep. Her heart revolted against both options. She wanted to get out of Venice, past the horizon, to somewhere that would not make her body scream. But when she'd asked the Fujian sailor to take her away, Hirokai, the nice one with broad shoulders, he'd laughed at the idea. The distant, beckoning lands were beyond her reach, but here was a malice growing with the Venetians' hunger, and she felt it directed at her whenever she came to the Main. She needed to escape, and when Hirokai said no, she panicked.

Jessica opened her eyes and stepped onto the ramparts. Others were jostled and nudged and pushed, but everyone made room for her.

The Venetians had gathered outside the growth of towers on the side of the mountain. The buildings were like reincarnations of the long dead trees whose ancient wood formed the disaster-resistant walls constructed in layers upon layers of planks, giving credence to the popular Venetian belief among both Hindus and Buddhists that all souls will be reborn into a new form. They looked fragile, but Jessica had seen them withstand storm after storm, raging winds of hurricanes and trembling earthquakes that rocked the waters below the mountain that supported them. The layers of the buildings would shake and slide, but loose stone fillings made them flexible to natural calamities. They had not broken for centuries. It was safe inside the towers, cool in the shadows under the roofs. But before the sun became too unbearable, everyone was outside – trading, gossiping, and communing in the increasingly crowded market of the ramparts.

Jessica scanned the masses for anyone likely to help. The children were the friendliest. They did not yet understand that she was not seen as Venetian on the Main. A few were gathered in a small group learning Diplomacy from a boy not much younger than Jessica. She remembered him and knew he remembered her from the way he pointedly avoided her gaze. They had learned Diplomacy in similar classes, back when surviving was a little easier. These stopped before Jessica was ten. She had never learned Hebrew with the other children in the Upper Keep. She thought that they would have refused to teach her, seeing her Venetian mother's features colouring her pointed nose and chin, her red hair. But her knowledge of Diplomacy allowed her to be welcomed into other classes in the Upper Keep with Talia, whose family had for generations studied the works of the ancient Bard.

Talia claimed that she came from a long line of players who not only remembered and recited but performed for admiring crowds. Jessica had been amazed to discover there was a good kind of attention, a way to be seen as different and still be wanted. The other children memorized phonetically, but Jessica memorized with meaning and understanding until she knew every word of each play. She thought that excelling would be seen as impressive, but memorizing the entire Complete Works marked her as even more different. A kind of freak. The people of the Upper Keep already knew the stories, if not word for word like Jessica, and did not appreciate the little redhead girl who paced the balconies chanting to herself. But the Venetians on the Main did not know the stories and would listen to her performing like it was something special.

It was hard to imagine the shouting and bickering Venetians as the adoring and complacent audience from Talia's tales. Ecrin and Zehra, twin skeletons whose features were diminished by hunger, argued over a black dress in a robe-like cut, how it came out of the boxes from Fuji. Whichever woman won would refashion it into a knee-length phiran for easier movement up and down the harbour and tower steps. Grigory was drinking with a group of men whose bodies showed their age, well into their thirties. One man's face was speckled with sickening moles, not the dappled brown of Jessica's freckles, but wound-like growths that faded between black and yellow. Another man's foot seemed too large for his body, wrapped in a bandage soaked in whatever festered on the skin beneath. Grigory caught her eye and gave a cruel smile. He had lost a few more teeth since the last time she ventured into Venice Main. Her own sore tooth ached. They were all in a state of decay.

Jessica ducked behind a mess of half-fallen pillars. Hidden behind these was one of K2's many caves that provided unstable dwellings for Bota's gang or adventurous Feral, or anyone with something to hide who was not afraid to lose their secret in the next cave-in. The upside-down V of the broken stone that had once supported a balcony offered a pocket of privacy, out of Grigory's sight, and was inhabited only by a few Feral who shared an algae block.

Jessica's mouth watered. Everyone up here had food, and green-stained fingers and teeth. But it would all be gone in a few days, at most, and then another riot, until the next month's shipment came. If it came. There would be no more shipments if that distant, merciful empress who opened her heart to feed the world were to discover that she had been repaid with murder and theft. There would only be consequences.

A hand pressed on Jessica's calf. A girl, staring up with teary black eyes.

"Nazli," she said, "what do you need?"

The girl did not answer. The Feral did not speak. They were children who had gone mad in their infancy or early childhood, missing first steps in favour of crawling in anxious skitters. Hissing and howling, or senseless chatter, instead of using words.

Nazli's hand did not move from her leg. Perhaps she just wanted the touch. She put her own hand over Nazli's.

"Nazli, have you seen Andrusha?"

Soon the girl would stop responding to 'Nazli,' but Jessica tried to remember and speak the names of each of the Feral. Maybe if she kept treating them like humans, they would come back.

"I'm looking for Andrusha," she said. "Or Borya?"

Nazli took her hand off Jessica's leg and tugged at her sack. The other two Feral looked up at her, hands green and empty. Jessica opened her sack and pulled out a small pickle jar. Nazli grabbed it and pointed at the Broken Tower.

"Thank you—"

The children raced away. Jessica closed her sack and stepped out onto the ramparts. Another hand grabbed her arm, turning her in a half-circle.

"What you got in that bag?" Zehra growled with a chip-toothed snarl. She was tall, using all her height to look down at Jessica. "You got food?"

Ecrin kept her distance, easing behind Jessica, ready to stop her if she ran. But Jessica would not run. She could certainly scramble up the side of the mountain (*K2*, her father told her that was its name, though Talia said it was *The Savage Mountain*) to the balconies that framed the higher caves. But running made it look like you had reason to run and encouraged others to chase you.

A crowd was gathering around them. Grigory slipped through and caught her eye again with a lopsided smile. She knew he meant to intimidate her, but his body was dying and his mind fading. He always struck Jessica as a fool. The formidable Zehra was a far more pressing issue.

"We all got food," said Jessica. She gestured to Zehra's stained fingertips. "Maybe *I* should ask for a handout."

"You can ask but I'm not giving," laughed Zehra.

"Same goes for me." Jessica wrenched her arm free from Zehra's grasp and kept her face calm.

"I'm not asking for a handout," said Zehra. "I'm curious. What you got in that sack?"

"She keeps songs in there!" Grigory swaggered out from the crowd. "She's a song merchant! Trades in silly tunes and stories. Caws like a gull until we pay her to shut up."

He was mocking her, but Jessica felt a shift in the crowd. If he meant to turn the group against her, he had chosen a terrible tactic.

"Does that mean if I start cawing that you'll pay me?" Jessica asked, and before Grigory could respond or Zehra protest, she hopped up onto the wide stone railing at the edge of the ramparts. Someone clapped. Already worth it, despite the terrifying drop behind her to the waters of the harbour below. Jessica sang a happy song that took something as terrifying as a storm and made it into a joke.

> "When that I was and a little tiny boy,
> With hey, ho, the wind and the rain,
> A foolish thing was but a toy,
> For the rain it raineth every day."

Her voice slipped through and eased the tension, a communal release of breath carrying the crowd's problems away on the wind. Did they notice how they rocked in rhythm or smiled? A few sat down to listen. Did they know why Jessica's offerings seemed as enticing as the algae blocks, garments, and other tangible goods of the market? Most of her audience seemed to be barely paying attention, but Jessica saw the pleasant shift like a bubble of safety in the middle of a storm.

The short peace was broken with a cry as Roman's gang bounded up the steps. Bota's gang of children, who had been watching Jessica from the higher caves and balconies, answered with a matching cry and rushed down to meet them. Venetians swore and shouted as they were pushed by the children who fought to tear the trash off each other. Jessica jumped off the wide railing and wove her way through the chaos to the Broken Tower. Nobody was listening now. It stung as sharply as the unfinished song caught in her throat. But it was a good thing that they did not care where she was going or notice where she had been.

It meant that nobody in Venice knew that she had started the riot.

## Chapter 2 (Cem)

Cem howled as Roman's and Bota's gangs met in a violent clash.

A fist struck his temple, hard enough to make his head ring wonderfully. Fingers grasped at his cropped black hair and his teeth clamped down on an unfamiliar wrist until he was released. A foot stomped on his, nails scratched his shoulder, hands pinched at his flesh, but even in the melee it was easy to lash out only at members of Bota's gang and not his own. Roman's gang dressed in plastic that they gathered themselves ("Honestly," Roman would say, and Cem would nod like he understood) with occasional scraps of clothing snatched from their rivals. Bota's gang wore stolen garments; oversized tunics hanging off one shoulder, skirts rolled up in a thick bunch at the waist, torn dresses pinned together with slivers of dangerous mussel shells. Even their hair looked thieved: hastily assembled with half-shaved heads and fraying braids. Cem thought the other gang looked ugly, an image of cultivated cruelty.

He reached out and was pleased to feel a scarf come loose in his grasp. A fist glanced off his shoulder and he leapt away to the shadows where the ramparts met the mountain. He could see Bota clearly in the crowd; her wide childlike face masking her savagery. A skeleton of a woman grabbed her sack close to her, betraying the location of her prize. The unnaturally golden-haired Nikita, Bota's Favourite, dashed close and grabbed the woman's sack, before disappearing back into the cover of the fight.

Another woman hugged a little girl close as the gangs ran past. Cem felt a twinge of pity. Adults whispered guiltily that the children in the gangs had been abandoned, as if any parent would have been better than Roman or Bota. That small shivering girl only had one person to take care of her, not the safety net of a whole gang.

Sedef, one of Cem's closest friends, found him through the crowd. She did not speak much, but not like the Feral. She was just shy, and when she did speak, it meant she had something important to say.

"They're grabbing blocks," Sedef whispered. "People still have algae blocks."

Cem's mouth watered. Sedef wiped her own drool away with a stained sleeve, leaving a streak of green across her lips. Cem knew that he should run back into the fray, target the adults, but he did not move. He scanned the crowd, stomach twisting in more than hunger, until he saw Farooq by the rampart's stone railing.

Farooq was not taller than the other boys, his teeth as discoloured as anyone's, his hair just as wild, but he stood like he had a right to stand tall. He was peeling off a heavily torn black plastic sheet, a cloak against rainstorms and a blanket in the night, and Cem saw the sweat trickle down his back. Farooq caught him watching and smiled as he stretched. Cem blushed and looked away. Maybe he only thought Farooq was striking because he looked to find him. Maybe he only thought Farooq's skin was not marred because he knew how soft it felt under his hands. Only Sedef, who would never tell or tease, knew that Cem and Farooq were weak for each other. Wasn't smart to be weak for another gang member. Any one of them could die in the next fight or storm. It would be better if Cem was not so obvious, but still he watched Farooq.

Sedef tugged gently at Cem's wrist. Cem turned to see Roman half-crawling up a tipped pillar, making his way up to the higher caves of K2, hidden behind the imposing wooden towers. The heavy doors of the towers were locked to the gangs until they were old enough to be willing to trade only for themselves and not steal for a group, but the caves were better anyway, full of surprises instead of adults. When Roman saw Cem and Sedef looking at him, he jerked his head, a small movement only for them, inviting them to follow. Cem did not want to leave Farooq unwatched, unprotected, but his heart swelled at being singled out by Roman. So he and Sedef made their way up the pillar behind him, copying his swaying steps over a thin rope bridge to a higher balcony in front of a half-collapsed cave, and following higher still.

Cem tied his new scarf around his wrist, freeing his hands for balance. His breathing calmed despite the increased height. He could not worry while he followed Roman, who leapt over cracks that dropped right down to the ocean without fear of the water below. Roman had pulled eels off children's bodies while they still flailed in the water.

Attacked adults twice his size when they had struck the children. Not the same as being weak for one person: it was being strong for many people. It was impossible to care that much and still stand at the edge of the water like he was stronger than the waves and monsters. But Roman did it.

Roman stopped at the entrance to a cave on a balcony that had lost its railing long ago.

"Wait here a moment," he said. "I want to make sure no one followed us."

Cem had never climbed this high before. He saw the pointed tops of some of the shorter towers below, nestling between the dark walls of the ones that continued to grow upwards. The Broken Tower and the Dark Tower stood proud far to his left. Past the ramparts, Cem could even see the dip of their sleeping space at the base of the harbour boulders, and beyond that, the Upper Keep rose from the waves. The head-like homes, balancing on their neck-like legs, glowed in a variety of soft pastels. They were made from a stone mixture called concrete that looked sturdier than the towers on the Main, but, after storms, great hunks of cracked-loose pieces would fall to the boulders. Farooq told Cem that the Jews who lived there stayed separate to stay safe, but according to the teenagers who outgrew the gangs, danger could still find its way up if it wanted to. Death could reach into the base of any hole or reach any height. Cem thought that was why the Upper Keep seemed to be overrun with ghosts, wandering the raised balconies in mournful black dresses. The only person from the Upper Keep that Cem was sure still lived and breathed was Jessica, though it would have been much better for all of them if she too was a ghost.

"I think we're alone," said Roman. "Come on."

Cem and Sedef followed him inside. Most of the lower caves were filled with fallen rocks, collapsed in on themselves from failing to hold the weight of the mountain above. The colourful tiles that decorated this floor were not nearly as worn or cracked as the tiles on the steps up from the harbour, but the delicate designs made Cem more wary. When something was destroyed, it could not get worse. Bota's gang purposefully made a mess of the caves they claimed as their home so none of the adults would want to take them. When something was pretty or you showed how much you liked it, it could be taken from you. So Cem pretended not to be impressed by the high arched ceiling above them or the swirls of colour under their feet.

Roman crouched by a small pile of rocks. He smiled and lifted a flat rock at the top of the pile.

"Algae blocks!" Cem cried out, and jerked his head towards the entrance, terrified someone had heard him. But Roman was right; no one had followed. Cem reached out, his stomach tight with hunger, but Roman shook his head.

"These aren't for now," he Roman. "There's still food to take below. Don't tell anyone about this unless you really trust them."

Cem blushed, already anxious to tell Farooq.

"Why don't we just eat it now?" he asked.

"We'll still be hungry tomorrow," said Roman. "And tomorrow, there might not be anything left to find or take. There might not be any new blocks for a while. If we keep these here, we won't have to worry about the next shipment."

Sedef shifted, biting the flaking skin on her lips. They were all worried about the next shipment, and if there would even be a next shipment, after the riot. Cem could still picture that first sailor floundering in the water as the eels feasted on him. The other Venetians fell on the remaining sailors with teeth and fists. Farooq said one of them was torn to pieces before being tossed to the eels. On top of the deaths, the Venetians looted the blocks from their ships. They did not know if those had been meant for other people, on other mountains. They did not know how the Fujian empress would punish them when she found out what they had done.

"What makes you think we won't come back and eat them?" Cem asked and Sedef hit his shoulder. "We won't! But why did you tell us?"

"I need someone to know this is here," said Roman. "Just in case."

*In case of what?* Sedef looked up at Cem, the unsaid question wrinkling her brow, and Cem shrugged, equally confused. "But why did you tell *us*?" Cem asked.

"You take care of each other," said Roman. "Not everyone takes care of each other."

"You take care of all of us," said Sedef.

Roman smiled at her and she hid her face in Cem's side.

"Will you help me take care of everyone?" Roman asked.

Cem and Sedef nodded. Sedef slipped her hand into a pocket that she had tied into the many folds of her loose black plastic skirt. She pulled out a piece of an algae block, no bigger than her palm, and gave it to Roman. He placed it with the other blocks and covered the treasure. He led them back to the balcony, closer to the edge than Cem thought was safe, and pointed to his feet.

"Do you see how the tiles continue out of the cave?" Roman said. "They curve underneath this rock too. You can see them shine if you're climbing from below. You have to climb a few levels up before you can tell, but then it's obvious."

They followed Roman back down the broken rocks, pausing to crane their necks upwards to see if they could find the cave again. Roman was right; the tiles made it easy to see, if you knew what you were looking for. When they reached the ramparts, Roman broke off from them without a goodbye to break up a fight between two of their gang members. Cem and Sedef pressed into the shadows against the mountain, not looking up, not betraying the location of their secret to anyone. Sedef's face was now smudged with mud as well as green algae; brown and grey dust streaked her hair.

Cem realized he could see the entire top of her head if he stood up straight. He was taller; going to be a grown-up soon. Farooq, too, was taller than Roman now, taller even than Jessica. Soon they would be too big for the gang.

Cem spat on the tiles at his feet.

Farooq caught Cem's attention with a wave and pushed through the crowd to them. "Jessica went into the Broken Tower," said Farooq.

"Why do we care where she goes?" Cem asked. His voice was steady, but his skin flushed with Farooq so close.

"She had her sack with her," said Farooq. "It's gotta be pickles."

Sedef looked up at Cem with glittering, hungry eyes. His stomach too leapt at the thought of something more than the mush of an algae block, pickles that crunched between his teeth and burnt with sharp pleasure on his tongue, but he did not want to fuel her hope. "Could be anything in that sack," he said.

Farooq flung an arm over Cem's shoulder. "Can't hurt to follow."

Cem rolled his eyes but leaned into the embrace before pushing the boy away. Like they were playing. Like he did not care at all. "Come on, then," Cem said. He grabbed Sedef's hand and pulled her into the crowd. Farooq followed close behind. So close, Cem did not realize that the path was not clear. He walked straight into Grigory.

Cem hated Grigory. The adults tolerated him, thought he was nothing more than a nuisance in his decaying state. But the gang members and the Feral were even weaker than him, and their pain made him feel strong. Whenever the other Venetians were not looking, he would hurt the children in small ways. A careless trip, a too-hard push, a kick so swift he was gone before you could cry out. He was a monster, worse than the ghost, because he was solid. For a moment, Cem's vision was obscured by Grigory's loose cloak, and he was overwhelmed by that scent of something rotting, like the flesh of mussels left out in the sun by Feral who had forgotten why they'd cracked the shells open. Cem gagged as Grigory laughed and grabbed his shoulder.

"Looking for food?" Grigory hissed through mangled black and yellow teeth. "Or have you found it already? Going to stash it away somewhere? Might as well just give it to me, save yourself the trouble and disappointment."

Cem thrashed in Grigory's grip. He was not strong enough on his own to free himself. But he was not on his own.

Grigory cried out as Sedef's teeth clamped over his forearm. Farooq jumped on the man's back and wrapped an arm tight around Grigory's throat. Grigory released Cem, and Cem spat in his face as the man fell back, dazed.

The children ran the rest of the way to the Broken Tower, laughing as they pushed through the groups. Cem's arm stung, Sedef's face was freckled with Grigory's blood, and Farooq looked like Farooq, so everything was going well. The sun was too hot, yes, but Cem had a scarf now, and he could cover his head. His stomach still ached for food, but they were going to get it. He was scared all the time, but right now he was laughing, and there were others laughing with him.

He knew that they spat when they saw the ghosts, that they told stories of the world before the Flood when there were more mountains and less water, more animals but fewer monsters, more people but less death. It was supposed to be a better world, something to miss and mourn, to wish for as everyone cursed the present. But surrounded by his gang, Cem thought this was the best time to be alive, and that this was the best world to live in.

## Chapter 3 (Shinobu)

"What are you thinking about?" asked Ama.

The empress's question broke Shinobu from her reverie, far away from the work at hand. She sat outside the Greenhouse, the waves lapping at the edge of the outdoor path, a sound like the steady turning of the pages of an endless book. The pink of Ama's wind-board, fitted with its matching neon mast, boom, and sail had become a pleasant, hypnotic blur at the corner of Shinobu's eye as the empress weaved figure eights, so close to the path that the fabric of the sail often scraped against the bleached concrete.

"Shinobu?"

The young woman's voice snapped the scribe back into focus, and Shinobu let reality settle like the weight of the paper on her lap, the pen in her hand, the inkpot balanced expertly on one knee. She went back to copying. This was new paper, not pulpy like the record that rested on her opposite knee. It was more resistant to weathering, but not immune. The soft spray would warp these pages too, and someday she would be copying the first two hundred pages of *Rebecca* again.

"Don't ignore me!" said Ama.

The empress paused the steady motion of her wind-board with an expert manipulation of the rig so that she was hovering on the water right before the scribe. Shinobu was tempted to stay silent just to keep her still. "I was thinking about *Rebecca*," she said, a half-lie.

There was a mystery in Manderley, something that unsettled the new Mrs. de Winter, but Shinobu did not have enough information to identify the mystery, let alone solve it. But it was not the absent mystery in *Rebecca* that pulled her gaze anxiously back to the horizon. Something was coming.

Ama let the wind turn her sail once more. "What ending have you conjured up today?"

Shinobu resisted the urge to tell Ama to stop tilting so much in her turns. "I was thinking, perhaps the new Mrs. de Winter grows tired of her decadent transformation," she said. "She leaves the mansion, and on the path away from Manderley meets someone very old. Then she meets someone very ill. Then she meets—"

"That's the Gautama Buddha," Ama interrupted.

"Well then, what do you think happens?"

"I think she is tempted away from her home by a prince who brings her fragrant flowers to smoke and ease her pain—"

"She's not in pain," said Shinobu. "And Rebecca would not have met anyone from Kilimanjaro."

"A prince who brings her electric gadgets that promise light in darkness and energy to propel ships right out of the sea into the sky—"

"Les Alpes was a very different place when *Rebecca* was written."

"A prince who wants to take her to his kingdom where there are no responsibilities, and everyone plays war games for fun—"

"The games at High Rock Ridge aren't so fun in person."

"You wouldn't know," said Ama. "You've never been." She hooked her feet into a strap that ran the length of the baseboard as she caught the breeze and leaned back towards the waves.

"Could you stop doing that?" asked Shinobu, trying to sound aloof.

Ama's body was almost horizontal, mere centimetres above the surface. If she had been wearing one of her longer wigs instead of the pale pink bob that adorned her like a halo, the synthetic strands would have broken the surface.

Even though it was stressful making sure the empress did not hurt herself, Shinobu enjoyed watching Ama, keeping her happy, trying to curb her more extravagant whims. She could not stop the empress from getting a new piercing every few months but had talked her out of exploring the art of tattoos. She could not stop Ama from trying to save any creature she found pitiful but was able to stop the childhood habit of demanding the destruction of any creature she found distasteful. This young woman, full of childish impulses and prone to indulging in fictional fantasies, was an empress who could make monuments rise from the ocean at her demand and as easily send them sinking once more.

Ama was twenty-five, and Shinobu was only five years older, but Ama's lack of maturity made the scribe feel more like a guardian than a friend and confidant. Sometimes Shinobu forgot Ama was no longer the little girl sitting up in bed, begging the scribe for a bedtime story. Shinobu would tell her tales of monsters that lived under the waves. The empress would ease off into sleep while Shinobu described the gentle *shush-shush* of the sting-waves, those mile-long masses of bulbous electric-tentacled creatures that merged together after they spawned.

Ama smiled from her precarious position skimming the water. The gold and silver piercings that curved up her eyebrow and curled out of her lower lip glittered in the sunlight. Shinobu, looking up, saw the sun breaking through the constant cover of clouds.

"Only you could glare at the sun," sighed Ama, pulling herself upright.

"It might affect the new paper. I should probably go inside."

"Can't you just enjoy being outside?"

The water was well above its usual surface marker on the poles that supported the pathway where she sat. Probably because of the recent storm, but maybe it was just rising. The vines inside the Greenhouse were doing better now, but the ones covering the outside of the buildings of Fuji looked wilted, darker. Mizutsuki, the head Greenhouse technician, insisted there was something wrong. The newly installed solar lights were working perfectly, but were one more gift from Les Alpes that Fuji had neither asked for nor repaid. The blackouts were becoming more frequent, despite Mizutsuki and engineer Etsuna's combined efforts to increase Greenhouse output, and despite the gathering ships' increasingly dangerous ventures further across the ocean to glean more plastic to fuel the Station.

"No," said Shinobu. "I don't think I can enjoy it."

"Did you see Yuki's wig?" asked Ama, and Shinobu did not think the empress even heard her response. "I went to the hospital to see if Shinku had her baby yet, but it was another false labour, but then I was looking at Yuki's wig—"

Shinobu copied the words from the soft fragile parchment to the new one that lay taut with false promises and let Ama's chatter wash over her like a tide. The empress spoke like a child, but even the most mature Fujians fell into this open manner with Shinobu. She was easy to talk to, friendly, if unusual, though she tried to hide her asymmetry with a clever head-tilt and half-smirk. Her left eye slipped lower than the right, like she was always looking towards something out of the corner of her eye. Her lip was fuller on the left side, giving her a permanent one-sided frown.

Ama assured Shinobu that the asymmetry was not as noticeable as the scribe feared, but it had been noticeable enough for everyone in Fuji to have assumed that she was a Dreamer. Shinobu worked hard to disprove this, eventually taking the position of head scribe of Fuji, and more recently, the role of advisor to most of Fuji's residents. Though she wished it had been because of her accomplishments, she had come to accept that people enjoyed talking to her *because* she looked like a Dreamer. She looked safe. Like she would hold information, but not manipulate it.

"I might just tell Yuki she can have any of my wigs that I'm done with," said Ama, back to tracing her figure eights. "It would save her the trouble of stealing them."

"I don't think you need to do that," said Shinobu.

Ama shrugged, the idea already slipping away.

As the second nurse, Yuki did not have much power, and knew it. That resentment could have caused tension between her and the head nurse, Kazuku, but Yuki found her own power in innocent theft. She did not know that she only managed to take the wigs that Shinobu purposefully misplaced, ones that the scribe knew Ama no longer enjoyed. And Ama did not need to know that Yuki lived under the false impression of having power over a person so much more powerful than she would ever be.

"Shinobu, what is that?"

Shinobu looked up. "What are you pointing at?"

"That thing in the water…"

Ama's voice was soft, and Shinobu had to hide her surprise when the empress hopped off the board to stand next to the scribe, dragging the sail up with her. Shinobu stood up to better see the water, but anything more than a few metres away from her was a vague blur.

"I don't see anything," said Shinobu, frustrated, swearing to keep her glasses secured in her sleeve from now on. "I can't see that far away."

"It's not far away," said Ama.

"What?"

"It's… what is that? Shinobu?"

Shinobu peered at the buildings that thrust out of the ocean, shining white beneath dangling vines. Shinobu imagined them as planets orbiting the star that was Fuji. Just as the Coil, the main residence on Fuji, wound up the mountain, the buildings that grew up from the Flood coiled outward from it.

The buildings closest to the Coil were tall and connected to each other with floating bridges. They stood in towering contrast to the lowest buildings far from the mountain, with their dark windows peeking through vines like bashful eyes: the Sailing Centre where children once trained to be sailors or skimmers and runners, the Station where the skimmers and runners who manned the gathering ships brought their haul of ocean debris to convert to energy (as useful as the Greenhouse, but the noxious smell of burning plastic meant no one visited), and the squat building straight ahead that used to house Etsuna's vegetation experiments before he invented the sōrui-jin, the engines that produced algae blocks, and moved his lab into the Algae Plant.

But that last building...

She could not remember. But Shinobu knew every building, the history of every building. She had recorded and re-recorded the maps of Fuji before mastering letters. This structure should not have been there. She should not have been able to see the vines on it this clearly, which meant they were too wide to be vines, and they moved, not in a breeze, but erratically, wildly. And she should not have been able to see the building this clearly, see its rough edges that did not match the clean lines of Fuji. This thing was not in line with the other buildings, that was an illusion of depth. Shinobu's eyes had convinced her that it was as far away as the other structures, because it was very big, but it was not far away. It was close.

And then it sank down, slowly, and was gone.

"You must have seen it!" said Ama. "What was it?"

Shinobu continued to stare at the place where it had disappeared into the water.

"I'm not sure." Her voice did not shake. She would not be scared when Ama needed her to be calm. "Perhaps we should go into the Vaults and check the records of sea creatures."

Ama was already starting to walk around the path to the door. Shinobu gathered up her supplies. She thought she must have spilled her ink, but the pot stood upright next to the pages, unconsciously set down safely even as Shinobu's attention was elsewhere.

"It didn't look like a giant squid, though those wiggling things could have been tentacles," Ama said. "Too many tentacles, but wasn't that part of the legend of the kraken? Its body didn't look like a squid's, though. Maybe a giant serpent…"

Shinobu corked the ink bottle and slipped it into her sleeve. The *Rebecca* record was less safely placed than the ink, set down on the ocean-sprayed path in her distraction. It had reacted poorly to the exposure to moisture. She could see her fingertips through the fading paper. Shinobu felt sick at the thought that a few more words might be lost in this next record.

A monster had risen from the waves, an answer to a question she would not have thought to ask. But even as she hurried to join Ama with long sweeping steps, her eyes were drawn back to the horizon. Something else was coming. She could not imagine what she expected to see, but it distracted her more than the appearance of a monster, and she worried that meant it was worse.

## Chapter 4 (Jessica)

The walkway leading to the Broken Tower extended high above the ocean, a fragile ribbon weaving outward from K2. Jessica was alone on the path. The rest of Venice packed together on the ramparts, close to the apparent solidity of the mountain, but Jessica knew that mountains could fall as easily as bridges.

She had never seen the Everest Crater, but the sailors said the stories were true. It was a famous peak before the Flood, attracting survivors from across the globe. Everest had been built up and dug into, deeper and deeper, until the mountain collapsed from the inside out. The survivors spread out, many to K2, and once again dug into the fragile mountain. Here, however, the living space provided by the disaster-resistant architecture of the region meant the immigrants were less dependent on the caves, which did not hold up as well in the storms and earthquakes. The lower cave system had already collapsed. Jessica was sure the upper caves would follow.

She entered the tower through a jagged arch that gave the building its title, though the entrance was clearly an aesthetic choice. A matching arch on the opposite side of the tower allowed the walkway to extend further, but Jessica abandoned the central path to take an angular spiralling staircase that hugged the inner walls. As she climbed, intermittent zoon dubs with partially ripped frames

– more likely caused by vandalism than storms – yawned and dripped condensation like open mouths, offering a view of the distant, abandoned Dark Tower.

This loomed on the far side of a wide gap where the walkway from the ramparts had collapsed. There was no way to breach the gap and no way to reach the base of the tower. The water was infested with sting-waves, whose burning tentacles could scar the sides of ships. Sometimes Jessica thought she could see people inside, shadowy figures only visible at sunset, their outlines revealed by the perfect angle of the dying light. Jessica thought they might be ghosts. Macbeth's spectral banquet. Hamlet's vengeful king. Realizing she was leaning away from the Dark Tower, Jessica pulled upright and continued her climb.

At first, the only sounds were the caws of disturbed gulls, but further up these were joined by human chatter. The steps ended beneath a landing with a small square opening. Jessica gripped the edge of the hole and hoisted herself through. Her sack flopped against the floor, but nothing cracked. As she scrambled up, Jessica joined in with the group's laughter at her clumsy arrival, playing at ease despite facing a larger crowd than she anticipated. Three, no, four people. Too many if this went wrong.

"I wondered when you'd come to trade," said Andrusha.

He lounged on the sill of a wide window that rose to twice his height, one of four windows that exposed the top of the Broken Tower to the open air. He did not seem worried about falling. He was a small man, but confidence made him stand out in a crowd, as well as his hair, which was as red as Jessica's though as straight as hers was curly. He kept his hair trimmed short, from the top of his head to the tip of his pointed beard. That mutation marked someone in his lineage as an immigrant from the north or west, like Jessica's mother's ancestors. His difference could have made him a target, if he had not adopted the role of hero.

Not long after Jessica's mother died, Andrusha sent a letter to the empress, begging for help. The sailors had come at first looking for art, some tangible piece of the past to preserve, though they found nothing but the worn mosaics. When they returned with dresses, sake, and vinegar to trade for masses of plastic trash (the Venetians still had no idea why they hoarded it) as well as amusing oddities like pickles from the Upper Keep, Andrusha presented them with his request scrawled in black ink on a sheet of plastic: *Please send us food, or we are going to die.* No one expected the empress to listen, but she did. The algae shipments were enough for a while. Then the population expanded. Andrusha had been sending letters for the past ten years explaining the suffering of the Venetians; families abandoning children they could not feed, the rise of the gangs, and the transformation of the Feral. But the amount of food in each shipment stayed the same. The Venetians admired Andrusha for continuing to write. Continuing to hope.

"There's not much to trade for anymore," said Borya. They leaned beside another window, not as reckless as Andrusha. "You should have come earlier."

"I don't need much," said Jessica. "Just algae blocks."

"You came all alone for something that basic?"

Andrusha slid down from his sill and wrapped his arms around Borya's waist.

Borya resided comfortably at the intersection of identity, not something between man and woman but someone entirely different. Their skin was an even golden tint, their arms smooth and hairless, their straight black hair did not tangle.

"Survival isn't basic," said Jessica, and the group spat in sympathy. Then she saw Luka at the far side of the room, half-hiding in the shadows. She swallowed a gasp. Andrusha and Borya did not notice, but Luka did. He stared at the ground, feigning lack of interest.

*Not feigning*, Jessica reminded herself. *Just uninterested.*

She looked past him, past the mocking expressions of Andrusha and Borya, to the fourth person in the room, and had to stop herself from recoiling. It was one of the Fujian sailors. Jessica thought he was hugging himself, until she saw the ropes. His arms were crossed tight against his chest, knees tied against his torso, ankle strapped to ankle. His black hair hung in a tangled mess over his face. He was trembling, but he seemed, for the moment, unharmed.

"Who is that?" she asked.

Her voice wavered. In fact, she knew this sailor, though he had never spoken to her. He preferred to let the others conduct business while he readied the ships to leave. He could have died because of her, and she did not even know his name.

Jessica clenched her hands into fists. She was not sure if she was more worried about what these Venetians planned to do to their captive or what he might have told them about her role in the riot.

"He's a survivor of the… last shipment," said Andrusha.

"Are you alright?" she asked the sailor. She spoke in Diplomacy: not only the language of Shakespeare's plays, but also the international language of trade. The sailor replied quickly in a language Jessica did not understand. He realized she was not following and abruptly fell silent. His eyes seemed to be drawn somewhere past her shoulder, his expression open and confused, but not nearly as frightened as he should have been. Nothing about him seemed Feral, but Jessica sensed a strange similarity between this man and Nazli. Perhaps he did not realize the danger he was in. Perhaps the part of him she saw mirrored in the wild children protected him from the terror, both within this room and out in the world, in the Flood.

"Doesn't know Diplomacy," said Borya as Jessica backed away from the sailor, pushing down her empathy and guilt. "You think we didn't try that already? Think we're stupid?"

"I'm not here to convince you otherwise," said Jessica, switching back to Venetian. Luka's cough might have covered a laugh. "I'm here for algae blocks."

She pulled her sack open and revealed the three jars of pickles. Borya's dark eyes glinted. These people were used to Jessica's songs, but she rarely traded food, saving the pickles for more fruitful exchanges with the Fujians.

"Three algae blocks for the three jars," said Andrusha.

It was so much less than the jars were worth. Algae blocks were merely sustenance, but her aching teeth would not let her eat anything harder than the gelatinous blocks.

"Don't be greedy, Andrusha," said Luka, reaching into a sack by his feet. "We've all got a spare algae block. One jar for each of us. One algae block each for her."

Jessica reached into her bag and tossed one of the jars to Luka. He caught it with one hand; she grabbed the algae block he lobbed to her. She repeated the trade with Borya before tossing the last jar to Andrusha. He caught it easily while Jessica waited, hands open in front of her.

"Are you confused about what constitutes a trade?" she asked.

If Andrusha did not hand over an algae block, there was little she could do. Borya and Luka would not come to her defence. But Andrusha did not seem to be dismissing her. He was thinking.

"What do you think we should do about him?" asked Andrusha, nodding to the sailor.

"What?" she asked.

The sailor was mumbling to himself, the same phrase over and over. It reminded her of the prayers some of the older generation repeated in the Upper Keep. And, like their prayers, seemed to be keeping the sailor calm.

"He survived the riot," said Andrusha. "We decided to hide him up here, where he would be safe."

From the way Borya rolled their eyes, Jessica knew it was more Andrusha's decision than a *we* kind of decision.

"He's been here for three days," grumbled Borya.

"It seemed like a good idea at the time." Andrusha smiled at Jessica but shifted his weight with obvious unease. "I don't know what to do with him. What do you think we should do?"

Jessica knew Andrusha wanted her to say they should kill the sailor. Perhaps he thought if the idea came from her lips, it would assuage his guilt. If none of the Fujians survived the riot to report it to the empress, the Venetians could pretend they had no idea what happened to the sailors. The sea was a dangerous place. Andrusha clearly regretted his predicament, Borya was unhappy at the sailor's continued presence, and Luka would support the most popular decision no matter how he felt. Andrusha was setting Jessica up for blame if the decision became less popular but was also unwittingly offering her an opportunity to remove a potential witness to Hirokai's death.

"It's obvious," said Jessica, then stopped.

"Obvious?" prompted Andrusha.

Jessica knelt, mesmerized by the sailor's feet. The Fujians always wore shoes, but this sailor was barefoot, probably robbed during the riot. The bindings around his ankles forced his feet to point up, and she could see the skin of his soles: smooth, plump, unbroken. Her own feet were peeling, bleeding, but his were perfect. She could hardly imagine a world where people did not have a constant list of problems adding up in their head, but it clearly existed. Fuji.

Hirokai had refused to take her with him, but this sailor would have no choice.

"You have to keep him alive," said Jessica.

"That's not the answer I expected," said Andrusha, suddenly still.

Jessica stood up and slipped her shoulders back, a practiced pose taught by Talia to help their voices carry. Luka smirked. He knew when she was preparing to perform. He used to watch her every morning on the Main.

"You're in such deep shit," she said.

Only Luka laughed.

"I think we're all in deep shit," said Andrusha.

"Oh, yes, of course." Jessica secured her bag to her shoulder, acting out the process of departure. "But you carry a kind of influence. You convinced an empress to help a city of strangers! From an outsider's point of view—"

"Like yours?" asked Borya with a sneer.

"I suppose I'd know an outsider's perspective better than you," Jessica said, shrugging off the insult. "And an outsider would think that any actions taken by the Venetians would have been prompted by their leader."

"I'm not really a leader," Andrusha protested. "And people die every day."

"I don't think they do in Fuji," said Jessica.

Luka was staring at her, a slight frown curving his full lips. She kept her face blank. He said, "You think they're going to blame him for the riot."

"That's one story," said Jessica. "The man who could have swayed the crowd but stood back and let it happen. Or even the man who encouraged them—"

"I hope there's another story," interrupted Andrusha.

"You mean the story of the hero who faced down a mob to save one man?" proposed Jessica. "That's very admirable. Worthy of a reward."

"The rest of us will still suffer," said Borya. "Maybe the empress will reward Andrusha, but she'll have as much reason to punish everyone else."

"I'm sure such a noble individual would speak on behalf of his people," Jessica said, innocently. "Make some requests she'd be happy to meet. More food, perhaps. As long as we move first."

"And if we wait?" asked Luka. Light filtering through the windows reflected off his black eyes. Jessica wanted to believe those eyes were kind, but that was more memory than present reality.

"They probably already know something's wrong," said Jessica. "I'm sure they've already started plotting their own account of what they think happened. The longer we wait, the more their story will seem true."

Andrusha tossed Jessica the last algae block.

"What are you saying?" asked Borya.

"We need to go to Fuji," said Jessica.

There was a whispering, and then *Hush!* from beneath the landing. Luka ran to the opening in the floor and pulled up a boy, one of Roman's gang. Jessica recognized him, Cem, she thought that was his name. He would act like he did not like her songs, and yet always showed up for her performances. Another boy popped out and grabbed Cem's arm, and a very small girl crawled up after him, cautiously.

"What are you doing?" growled Luka.

"We were following her," Cem said, jutting his chin at Jessica.

"To jump her?" Luka asked.

"She had stuff to trade," the other boy insisted.

"I've made my trade," said Jessica. "You're too late."

The children looked disappointed.

"I might need something," said Andrusha.

Luka released Cem. The group scrambled towards Andrusha as he reached into his bag. Jessica did not think he would give out the pickles before receiving his own due, though the children looked hopeful. Their faces dropped when he turned back with a handful of sticks. The way they grew out from his fist, it was impossible to tell which were long, and which was the short one. The gang knew the game and gathered around.

"Who wants to go first?"

Before Andrusha could finish his sentence, each child had grabbed the stick nearest them, trusting fate over their own unlucky decisions. Cem held the short stick.

"I'll stay here and guard," said Borya, but the way the blood drained from Borya's face betrayed how they had a different reason for staying behind. A few years after the first shipments, the Fujians had tried to teach the more adventurous Venetians how to sail. Borya had learned how to manoeuvre their ship with the ease of a soaring gull, until the day a wave toppled them over. They were caught under their own sail for several minutes before anyone managed to pull them onto the rocks. There were few eels out that day, but the ocean did not need eels to hurt. One of the sailors pumped at Borya's chest, blew into their mouth, until they woke with a rush of water from their lips. Andrusha had screamed at the sailors and told every Venetian that the Fujians did not value the lives of foreigners, that this "training" was a deadly game, until no one would take any more lessons. Jessica had not seen Borya near the water since that day.

Andrusha guided the children down the tower. Jessica joined them, desperate for a moment alone to convince him of her plan, but Luka was too close behind. They descended past the opening to the ramparts, down the tower to the water below. The small trefoil archway at the base dropped them off on a cluster of boulders. Dark waves lapped at the rocks, warning of deep waters and the monsters they held.

Though that was the point: Finding the monsters.

"You can run home now," whispered Luka. He gave her a shove that was too hard to be teasing. He always acted like this when there were more than a few Venetians around, and she did not know if he was performing for them, or her, or himself. It annoyed her as much as it hurt, this game he made her play with rules he never explained.

"I'm not done negotiating," she said with a glare.

His silence was an infuriating rebuttal.

"One pickle for each eel I get," said Andrusha.

Cem nodded and rolled up his sheer plastic sleeve. He knelt on the rocks and plunged his arm into the water.

The splash from his arm breaking the surface had not even struck against the boulder before he twitched in pain. His friend held onto his shoulders as his arm jerked back and forth. Cem pressed his lips together, thin tears trailing through the scum on his cheeks. His back shuddered, and Jessica took a step forward, unsure if he would faint, wanting to stop his fall, but too scared to move any closer to the frenzy in the water. Finally, with a deep gasp, the boy pulled up his arm.

It was covered in writhing eels, their circular mouths suctioned tight to his skin. They seemed distressed at the sudden change in scenery, but too hungry to let go. A large one – nearly the same size as the boy's arm – fell, leaving a bruised and bleeding weal behind. Jessica glimpsed the circular rows of sharp teeth before the eel disappeared beneath the waves once more. The rest of the eels hung fast, and the children pried them loose, pinching gently at the skin around their mouths, forcing the teeth free from their hold. Each child held a jagged mussel cut – a crude knife made from a mussel's sharp shell – and once an eel was fully detached, they sliced off its head.

The children lined the severed creatures against a semi-flat boulder. Andrusha unscrewed the jar in his bag and handed Cem, whose skin had taken on a similar greyish colour to the eels, eight pickles.

"There were nine eels," said the other boy, holding up Cem's arm, showing off the nine bruised and bloody welts. "See?"

"One broke free," said Andrusha. "I said a pickle for each eel I get."

As they haggled, Jessica felt the weight of Luka's hand on her shoulder and jolted at its surprising gentleness.

"Andrusha's not going to let you come with us," he said to her.

"Why do you think you're going?" she asked.

Luka smiled. There were few things in the world as beautiful as his black eyes, thick black hair, golden brown skin so smooth beneath a few pink scars. People liked beautiful things in a world so full of ugliness and pain. If Andrusha brought Luka, he would be assured that there would be something about their arrival that the empress would like.

"Why do you want to go?" asked Luka.

"Someone has to speak on behalf of the Upper Keep," she lied. "And I don't trust you or Andrusha to speak for them. They didn't take part in the riot, and they shouldn't be punished with the rest of Venice."

"You're lying," said Luka. "You don't feel the way you should about the Jews."

"What are you talking—"

"You should say, '*We* did not take part in the riots. *We* shouldn't be punished.' Not *they*. Not *them*."

Jessica almost protested but then remembered that she had told him about her struggles to belong to two worlds that did not want her, back when they were children.

When they were friends. Luka and Jessica would meet every day, playing in the shadows of the Upper Keep, running up and down the towers of K2. They shared the books the Fujian sailors brought, making up stories about the fantastic creatures illustrated within: *parrots*, colourful as tiles and constantly chatting; *dogs*, friendly with humans or snarling at each other; *rats*, keeping council in huddled groups under floorboards, clever enough to stay out of the way. But something shifted in Luka. He was still there when she needed help: to fix the crack that nearly split her home in half during the massive earthquake last year; to recover the shipment of dresses Jessica had traded for that had been snatched by Bota's gang; to find her an isolated cave to sleep in during that month when her father had reacted to every movement she made with violence. But Jessica thought he liked being needed more than he liked her.

"Come on, Jess," said Luka, quieter now. "Why do you need to go?"

Andrusha had already disappeared back into the Broken Tower. The little girl had run off, but the two boys lay on the rocks. Cem was half-conscious; the other boy let him rest against his chest and placed his hands over the wounds that still bled. Cem would be okay. He would be ready to fish again after he had had time to heal. And this boy who cared so much could not care forever. One day, Cem would be lying on the boulder alone.

"I can't stay here anymore," she whispered. "I don't want to. I need to get out of here."

She turned to Luka, expecting him to turn away, but he was looking back. For a moment, she thought he was going to say *no*. That he would convince Andrusha to leave her behind, just because he could. Another move in his game. He was the player, and she was a piece.

"I need your help," said Jessica.

The gleam of joy in Luka's eyes shifted, softening. He looked at the boys on the rocks, and then over his shoulder at the Upper Keep. He was still looking at the Upper Keep when he finally spoke.

"Then I'm going to get you out."

## Chapter 5 (Shinobu)

Ama brought her wind-board through the archway into the Greenhouse but quickly abandoned it on the path running along the internal waterway. She did not notice Shinobu lift the vines that hung over the entrance like a delicate curtain so she could pass through without becoming tangled. She did not notice Shinobu, with a small flick of her long sleeve, catch the attention of Mizutsuki, instructing the woman to tie the board in the waterway. Ama moved without obstacle because Shinobu ensured obstacles were removed.

Mizutsuki bowed to Ama, who was now waiting in the lift, tapping her foot impatiently. Shinobu tucked her chin to hide her smile, not able to remember the last time she had bowed to the empress.

"Shinobu," Ama chided, and Shinobu picked up her gliding pace. The lift door closed behind them, carrying them up to the top floor. Ama tried to straighten her wig, but the bangs were still crooked, tilting down to brush the row of piercings adorning her eyebrow.

"What do you think that creature was, if you had to guess?" Ama asked.

"It could have been a sturgeon," Shinobu said.

"A fish? A *fish*? It was huge! It's not just a fish."

The lift opened and Shinobu followed Ama out into the cafeteria. Etsuna and Yana, one of the plastic runners, were sitting at the far table, bowls of green noodles in a deep brown broth abandoned in front of them as they whispered in a heated conversation. When they saw Ama, they both ceased speaking and began to rise, but Shinobu nodded for them to sit back down. They still gave small bows from their seats as Ama passed.

"How can you think it was a fish?"

Shinobu followed the empress out the glass door that automatically slid open in front of them and stayed a few paces behind her as they crossed the covered bridge to the Vaults. Each circular window offered an isolated view to the horizon.

"It could have been Gojira," said Ama.

"I highly doubt it was Gojira."

They reached the end of the bridge. Another door slid open, releasing a blast of cool air.

"*Ai*," shivered Ama. "I don't know how you handle this cold all the time."

Shinobu relaxed in the breeze. She much preferred the cool atmosphere of the Vaults to the wild humidity outside.

They entered the dark room, and the neon green glow of the fluorescent lights rose on the metal path by their feet, guiding them forwards. Shinobu could have manoeuvred through the Vaults with her eyes closed, the shelves waiting in a peaceful silence broken only by the gentle hum of the lift. Ama clutched the railing and peered over the edge at the fifteen-floor drop. There were no solid walls to protect them, but the railing was supported by crisscrossing metal bars too tightly woven to allow even someone as petite as Ama to slip through. They walked towards the lift in the middle of the great rectangular building, a small cube supported by a metal frame that blended into the muted darkness. A curving staircase wound around the lift shaft. Shinobu preferred the stairs, but she did not propose that route now.

"You know I'm not afraid of heights," said Ama and Shinobu nodded at the lie. "The lift is easier."

More lights illuminated walkways extending to the left and right (a fourth walkway hidden behind the lift), leading to the Vaults that lined the inside of the building. But even when the Vaults were hidden in darkness, Shinobu did not have to see them to *see* them, shelves and cabinets, each file in its perfect place, images behind cold glass, locked boxes that hissed a freezing steam when they released their treasures.

When the lift arrived, Ama and Shinobu squeezed inside, and Shinobu pressed the button for the eighth floor.

"That's not Mythology," protested Ama.

"I need to return *Rebecca*."

They descended in silence, uncomfortably close, until the door opened once more.

"I'll wait for you," said Ama. "So be quick!"

Shinobu nodded, but a growing calm stopped her from really rushing. Light flooded the path as she glided forward with wide steps, the swish of her skirt offending her own ears in what should have been hallowed silence. Mythology, theology, and philosophy were Shinobu's archival specialty, and she considered the Vaults her own personal temple, a place of spiritual clarity.

*Rebecca* had become her responsibility when she was only eight. The limited fragment was both short and possessed a narrative, which made it ideal for a young Dreamer who did not baulk at the darkness of the Vaults. Her ease with transcription convinced the Fujians that she was not a Dreamer. *Rebecca* was the only narrative she was ever instructed to copy. Though she enjoyed stories that did not carry the weight of religion and could now assign herself whatever she pleased, she avoided other fragments of literature. Narratives were gifts for Dreamers who needed help focusing on their work, and she did not want to give anyone the idea that she needed that kind of help.

All the floors in the Vaults had four walkways extending from the lift, mirroring the design of the top floor. Shinobu followed the western walkway to their collection of Diplomatic literature. She was surprised to see the southwest corner already illuminated, and a figure hunched over a desk. Shinobu diverted from her path, and Makoto looked up from his work and smiled.

"What are you recording today, Makoto?" Shinobu asked.

"The *Mercy* verse," slurred Makoto. His asymmetrical features were splayed across his wide face in a way that a head tilt could never hope to hide. The other scribes praised his kindness, but Shinobu did not think it a success to be kind when your mind was incapable of the manipulations needed to be cruel. He had ink on his sleeve. A mess, and a waste.

"The words are beautiful…" Makoto looked up, wistful, as if he could see the calligraphy above Shinobu's head. "What are you recording?"

"I'm returning *Rebecca*," said Shinobu.

"You took it outside?" asked Makoto. "Won't the water hurt the paper?"

No one else questioned her decision. Caught by the one person who was not trying to catch her; exposed by someone who could not understand.

*Yes, it will hurt the paper. It might be ruined. But it does not matter. Because Ama was the last child to be born who was not a Dreamer, and that was twenty-five years ago, and now the children are so much worse. And children are going insane all over the world, if they do not die first, like Venice's starving population, reaching out to Shinobu with hopeless letters and a pain no one could make disappear, so she had hidden it from the empress, who would not be able to handle the hopelessness. Why would a lost story matter if there is no one left to read it?*

"How would you like to copy *Rebecca* when I'm done with this recording?" asked Shinobu, locking away the despair.

"Oh, I'd love that!" Makoto laughed, and Shinobu hurried away, her footsteps echoing hollowly against the metallic floor.

On the outer end of the row of metal shelves was a drawer marked *M*, for *Maurier, Daphne du Maurier*. Shinobu pressed against the drawer, and as she released her hand, the lock within released with a cold hiss of steam. The drawer stretched outwards. She placed the original paper inside first, now even more crumpled and torn, then set the new and incomplete recording next to it. The new pages would be easier for Makoto. Harder to tear.

She stopped for a moment at a single drawer opposite du Maurier's. This contained works recorded under a single name: *Shakespeare*. A poet, the greatest poet according to other historical texts, with the loveliest plays that sustained through generations of turmoil and change. They did not make it through the Flood. Just the memory, fragments like the *Mercy* verse that hinted at something greater.

Sometimes Shinobu told herself that the plays could not be as good as the scholars claimed, that they were not worth the endless essays in which ancient historians fought over themes, accuracies, and whether live bears were used onstage to encourage the actors to exit. But everyone knew that they must have been great. Even now, everyone at least knew Shakespeare's name, if not a small passage from his works. Another mystery, a bigger hole in the preservation of literature than the lost ending to *Rebecca*, and too devastating a loss to think about for long.

Shinobu walked back. Makoto had returned to his work, and the only sounds in the Vaults were the steady scratch of his pen and the gentle swish of Shinobu's steps as she returned to the lift.

"That took you awhile," said Ama. Shinobu looked down at her spotless sleeves.

After a brief, smooth descent, the lift opened again on the third floor, and Ama rushed out onto the walkway. Shinobu followed, also eager to be back home in the Mythology Vaults.

Ama ignored the large stacks of theology and turned into the fifth row. Shinobu trailed her past the Ghosts, the Monsters of Evil, and the Monsters of Good. A large print displayed in glass between the Monsters of Good and Evil showed a pair of figures locked in an embrace as they fell from some unimaginable height above to an unknown depth below, one dressed in a white robe, the other dressed in red with horns protruding from his head. Despite the protective casing, she could see the edges were fraying. If she waited until it was rotting before she assigned a scribe to copy it, there might be no scribes left to do the work.

"Shinobu, come here!"

Ama was already at the Sea Monsters vault and had opened multiple drawers to pull out her favourite stories. Shinobu glided over, closing the drawers that the empress had left open.

Above the Sea Monsters Vault hung the remnants of a map. The Head Scribe before Shinobu said an emperor who reigned in the first few years of the Flood decided to flood in turn this artistic depiction of the world with black ink. The black stains were broken by swathes of land and tips of mountains representing Fuji, Les Alpes, Kilimanjaro, High Rock Ridge, and the Andes, as well as a few other pockets that escaped the ink-spill destruction: the small pieces of the surviving world. In those clear pockets, Shinobu could see partial sketches of monsters drawn long ago, that apparently only existed in imagination. Shinobu liked to think that the other monsters caught under the black ink spill of an ancient ruler's tantrum had fled into the vaults below, where the scribe could keep them safe.

When Shinobu was younger, she asked Ama if her parents had told her anything about that emperor. The empress's parents had died when she was five, but must have begun instructing her about her history, her legacy. Ama nodded but refused to tell Shinobu anything about him. She asked the scribe why she wanted to talk about someone who was only famous for destroying something beautiful. She wanted scribes to ask questions about her, someday, for doing something good, for being the best empress.

Shinobu told her that people rarely talked about you if you did your job well. She had not expected that little girl to one day enact the Mercy Experiment. The empress was now sure to be remembered, for as long as there were people to remember.

"It could have been a dragon," said Ama, her fingers tracing the ink-drawing of a sea-dragon that accompanied an explanatory text.

The ink-drawing was Shinobu's. The copy she worked from had been terribly worn. She could have recorded simply the faded design, the idea of a gaping mouth and wild eyes, the half-formed mane that flowed back from its head, the single pencil arc to indicate an arching back. But she had other copies of dragon sketches, lucky Chinese dragons and greedy English dragons, so she embellished a little, adding blues and greens for its body, and gold-yellow eyes. She made that artistic decision ten years ago. She was not so free with interpretation these days.

"I don't mean like a *dragon* dragon," said Ama. "I mean like a giant squid for the kraken, or eels for sea serpents—"

"I know what you mean," said Shinobu. "We have not yet found anything resembling a dragon, and it makes sense that there's truth to the myth."

"Those lines coming out of the mane," said Ama as Shinobu sat next to her, folding her legs under her skirt and smoothing the crinkled front of her blouse. "Those could be those tentacle things."

"They could be," agreed Shinobu. She had added the lines with the rest of her creative flourishes.

"It looks large," said Ama.

"Other dragons were large," said Shinobu. "The size of a castle."

"Why don't we have castles?" asked Ama.

"They were drowned in the Flood."

"I mean, why didn't we build *more?*"

"We have better structures now," said Shinobu. "Smarter architects and engineers."

Ama gasped, pressing her hand over her heart.

"What's wrong?" asked Shinobu.

"Did you just compliment Etsuna?" Ama asked, offering another melodramatic gasp. "What will we do if he finds out?"

"He won't find out," said Shinobu, smiling.

"Of course," said Ama. "It would not do for people to know that you are pleased with their work."

"You don't get a prize for—"

"Doing your job, I know," said Ama. She opened the drawer behind her, getting up on her knees to tuck the copy of the dragon back in its place. "Do you think you'll make a record about the monster we saw today?"

"No," said Shinobu.

She never made new records. It was one thing to protect the records of the past to honour those who worked so hard to preserve them. It was another to pretend there would be anyone to care about what she wrote.

Shinobu watched Ama rifle through the materials. The brush of paper against metal made her cringe. It took her a moment to realize why.

"That drawer is too empty," she said, getting to her feet, trying not to push Ama out of the way as she made her own exploration. "Why are there pieces missing?"

"I think the sailors took them," said Ama.

"*Took* them?" asked Shinobu, horror sending shivers down her back.

"They bring them back."

"You knew about this?"

"Yes, they asked me." Ama stood, making herself as tall as she could be, which was not very tall at all.

Of course, they asked Ama and not Shinobu. They knew Shinobu would say *no*. They knew if the empress said *yes*, Shinobu would not be able to say *no*.

"Don't blame the sailors," sighed Ama. "It's a long journey to dismal places with nothing beautiful to keep them entertained."

"And by *entertained* you mean?"

"Well, Hirokai asked to borrow *Tako to ama*."

"*Ai*," groaned Shinobu.

"I didn't think you would miss that amorous octopus so much," smirked Ama.

"If he doesn't bring it back—"

"They bring almost everything back," said Ama.

"*Almost*? What did they lose?"

"Not *lose*. Sometimes they gifted—"

"Ama!"

"It's good for international relations," said the empress, with the fake smile she offered to visiting representatives. "We are generous with both food and culture. We are not here only to sustain, but to educate."

"With erotic prints."

Ama's smile grew more sincere.

"The best kind of education," she said. Shinobu's hand tightened on the drawer, and Ama's smile dropped. "That was a joke."

Shinobu did not look up from the drawer where the missing records were as clear in her memory as the pieces coming together to form an answer to a question that she now understood.

"Shinobu?"

The sailors were not back yet. They had not returned the records they borrowed because they had not yet returned to Fuji. It had been too long. She was looking for their ships on the horizon, and there were no ships.

"Shinobu, stop it."

What if the ships had been wrecked halfway through their journey, before reaching the riotous savages of the High Rock Ridge, maybe before reaching the shores of Kilimanjaro, insulting the already suspicious populace? Or what if they had been wrecked before reaching even their first stop, leaving K2 hungry and expectant and betrayed?

"Shinobu, tell me—"

"Why haven't the ships returned?" asked Shinobu. Ama stiffened next to her, like those terrified bright-red squids that sometimes caught in the skimmers' nets and froze in fear.

"It hasn't been so long," said Ama, but her voice shook.

Shinobu wrenched her hand from the drawer and unconsciously shut it, instinct protecting the records even as her mind had already left the Vaults. Ama raced after her as the scribe retraced her steps, through the Cafeteria, out of the Greenhouse, until they could see the horizon once more.

"Can you see the ship?" Ama asked, clapping her hands.

Shinobu still did not have her glasses, and the distant vessel was a blur, yet she saw it more clearly than Ama did in the empress's initial excitement. It was not the deep green of their own merchant ships. Shinobu felt Ama's joy dissipate as she took in the low hull, the only visible part of the sub-hybrid ship, a petal-purple monstrosity interwoven with ropes of gold.

"It's from Kilimanjaro," said Ama.

"I know," said Shinobu, but the empress had already turned away.

Ama needed to transform, and her transformation took much more work than a head-tilt. Shinobu did not follow her. She kept her eye on the ship as it grew larger, though it remained just as blurry. She probably had time to run for her glasses before it arrived, but she did not like the idea of wearing her weakness on her face.

A pink sail flew past and Shinobu jumped back. Ama had grabbed her wind-board from the waterway and was rushing over the Flood away from the incoming visitors.

"You can't sail the entire time that they're here!" shouted Shinobu.

Ama did not respond, but she leaned back, far back, her body almost brushing the water, and that was answer enough.

## Chapter 6 (Cem)

Cem ran his hand up and down his sore arm. Deep bruises blossomed around the dried scabs where the eels' teeth had been torn free. At least they would fade.

Closing his eyes, he listened to the steady *crunch-crunch* as Sedef ate the last pickle. By the water, Roman was whispering something to Roksana, the rise and fall of his low voice like waves. Roman pretended not to have a Favourite but everyone knew it was Roksana, the girl with wiry muscles and long black dreadlocks woven through with colourful tiles. These soft sounds of an ending day would have been soothing, were it not for the harsh *shh-shh* of Shen sharpening his mussel cut on the edge of one of the harbour boulders. The other children kept their distance from Shen. It was an unspoken agreement that he was going crazy, but since he was too old to go Feral, he was still recognized as a member of the gang.

"The Jew-girl's back," whispered Farooq, quiet lips close to Cem's ear. Cem watched, distracted, as Jessica weaved between the clusters of sleepy children on the rocks. She pounded on the leg of Cem's house with her mussel cut, and the clanging reverberated round Cem's skull. Someone in the Upper Keep lowered a rope ladder down to Jessica, stopping the noise.

Sedef tugged Cem's arm, right on the bruises, but he looked where she was pointing, away from the Upper Keep, back to the harbour. One solitary child stood out, crouched on a boulder not far from the steps to the ramparts. The red sunset lit the boy's face, cut with pink scars that were less shocking than his half-shaved head and torn-fabric tunic.

"Ghanim," Cem whispered. A boy from Bota's gang.

Ghanim looked confused, like he did not know what had brought him from the safety of the ramparts where his compatriots would be settling down amid the rubble of their caves. Roman's gang shifted from confusion to delight. Their brief scrap this morning had been fun but was nothing like a real fight.

The children used to fight all the time, sometimes with fatal consequences that made them feel like their actions mattered. But Roman and Bota decided too many of the children were dying, and they made rules. A fight could only happen for a reason and must be fair. Ghanim's unannounced arrival was reason enough. Roman's gang spread out, forming an arc around the boy, who seemed unaware of the danger. Roman would pick someone as small as Ghanim, but also as vicious as a boy who scarred his own face and arms with mussel cuts. They would be smaller than Cem, and that was the reason, he told himself, why he was scrambling away, deeper into the shadows. Nothing to do with the image of a sailor in the water, his body covered in hungry eels, a cloud of blood growing around them.

A sudden hollering meant the fight had begun, but Cem did not turn to see who was risking their life against Ghanim's. He pressed his hand against the house leg riddled with small chips made by Jessica's mussel cut from years of demanding to be let back into the Upper Keep. The sounds of the fight grew fainter with each step he took from leg to leg, from shadow to shadow. The darkness was broken by slashes of red light where balconies and rope bridges separated the houses above, a dimming glow that was slowly turning purple. Cem stopped in a shaft of light and craned his neck back, looking towards Upper Keep.

One of the ghosts was peering down at him.

For a moment, Cem considered running back to the group, but a strange sound stopped him; short mournful cries, one after the other in a rhythm that reminded Cem of Jessica's songs. It came in bursts, then paused, then began again. It sounded familiar, like the thump of Jessica's mussel cut. The ghost above must be banging on the leg or the balcony to make these hollow beats.

Cem once again felt the urge to run back to his gang, maybe find Farooq and ask what to do when a ghost tried to talk to you. Ghosts belonged in the past, a time of bloodshed and death and rising waters. But this ghost did not seem like it wanted to hurt him. The banging even sounded like a one-sided conversation. Maybe it was lonely. Cem grabbed his mussel cut and answered with his own short rhythm.

When he looked up again, the ghost was gone.

It was darker now, and dangerous to be this far from the gang. Cem knew he should go back, but the echoing rhythm came again, this time a few houses down, deeper into the shadows. It would be foolish to go further, but the rhythm was inviting him to… *play*? Cem remembered playing when he was small. Games of skipping rocks or scratching boards into the tiles to move coloured chips in organized competition, or slapping beats in a circle to make music beneath Jessica's songs. The sound of the rhythm repeated several legs away, and Cem followed, banging the rhythm back from the base. There was a pause, and then the rhythm repeated, even further away, pulling Cem into the shadows, and he laughed as he followed. The light guiding his path was now a deepening blue that warned of imminent nightfall.

The rhythm stopped, not suddenly, but Cem realized he was banging, and waiting, and banging again, with no response. His ghost had ended the game. Cem let the final echoes of his own beat waver into silence. In the dark, he heard shuffling. He felt eyes watching him, not from above, but all around. He was surrounded by a mass of bodies colliding into each other, hissing in distress as they pulled apart. The hissing told him what he had discovered in the dark: Feral.

Cem had never known that there were this many Feral children. He recognized faces, children from their own gang who they had assumed were dead; children from Bota's gang whom they had never really thought about; children who had aged out of the gangs. You were only supposed to go Feral when you were very young. But Cem could see Nazli, who had once been able to talk, and had almost joined Bota's gang. Nazli stared at him with blank confusion. Like Ghanim.

Now Cem understood. Ghanim was Feral. If Roman had known, he would have never allowed the fight to take place. The Feral could not defend themselves properly. They could not understand rules. Cem turned to go back and stop the fight from happening, but the shuffling and hissing were behind him now. Why had the ghost brought him here? Was it trying to kill him? Was being dead so lonely it needed a friend?

The Feral were known for attacking on sight, unable to think through consequences, and there were so many Feral here now. Even so, Cem was not thinking about how to fight his way out. Instead, he was thinking about how much food they must need. In the dark, each individual Feral looked like a collection of sharp lines, concave and wasting away. Cem thought about Roman's small stash of algae blocks. It wasn't enough even for all of Roman's gang, but Cem was overwhelmed with the need to help, and the knowledge that he could not do anything for this mass of children, all blank stares and snapping teeth.

The Feral did not attack. Instead, they watched him warily, inching closer, but without the warning hiss. Cem moved over the rocks, dark and unfamiliar this far from the harbour. The Feral did not follow. Cem looked up to see if his ghost might help him back to his gang, but the balconies were empty. Cem hummed softly to himself to keep his panic at bay, only stopping when he realized it was Jessica's song about the wind and the rain.

Eventually, the house legs thinned out, and Cem knew he was closer to the harbour. He heard whispers and looked up to see a solitary figure with bright red hair sitting on one of the high balconies, legs dangling over the edge. Cem picked up his pace until a small hand slipped into his with a comforting squeeze and a sure arm swung over his shoulder: Sedef and Farooq, safety, home.

"Is it over?" Cem asked. "Who won?"

"Shen," said Farooq.

Cem shuddered. "Ghanim?"

"Dead," said Farooq, without elaboration, which meant it had been worse than usual. Ghanim's body would be gone already, fed to the eels.

Cem unwrapped himself from Farooq and felt his way out into the darkness. He needed to tell Roman what he had found. Maybe Roman could figure out what to do about all those Feral.

Cem felt gingerly for the solid boulders, careful to avoid the gaps of dangerous water between them. He was so intent on not slipping that he did not hear that *shh-shh* of Shen sharpening his mussel cut until he was almost on top of the boy. Shen lunged at him, but he did not slice. He brought his face close to Cem's and *hissed*.

And Cem hissed back.

He clamped his mouth shut and stumbled backwards. He had no idea where that sound had come from. He had no idea he could make that sound. Dashing over the boulders, he sang Jessica's song to himself. The words formed easily in his mouth:

> *"When that I was and a little tiny boy,*
> *With hey, ho, the wind and the rain,*
> *A foolish thing was but a toy,*
> *For the rain it raineth every day."*

He could still speak! He could think… for now. How long had it taken for Nazli to go silent and Ghanim to fade?

Poor Ghanim, lost and confused, stumbling along the boulders. Perhaps the boy had known where the Feral slept, or some animal part of him had clicked when he went fully Feral and he knew instinctively where to go. Or maybe the Feral needed help to find their way after they turned… Cem thought about that ghost leading him deeper into the darkness, not towards a trap or death. The Feral never attacked one of their own. Cem did not think he looked any different than the other members of his gang. He did not feel any different than he had yesterday. But the ghost must have noticed something changed.

Behind each word of the song, Cem now heard a hiss in the back of his brain. He sat on one of the boulders, tired and frightened.

Farooq and Sedef found him again. They must have been worried. Cem never wandered too far away from the group, and never alone.

"Are you okay?" whispered Farooq.

Children and adults avoided the Feral. Cem had never thought how lonely it must be until this moment, with Sedef and Farooq so close. He could not imagine sleeping without the comforting warmth of their bodies. He could not bear to think of his friends terrified of him.

"No," Cem whispered back.

Sedef curled up and lay her head in his lap. Farooq lay next to him, arms around his shoulder and waist, head on Cem's chest. Their breathing slowed as they slipped into sleep. Cem hugged them tight to him.

He thought about the riot. Easy to blame everything – the lack of food, the turn to Feral in children too old to change – on one clear moment, one person. He did not think anyone else had seen Jessica push that sailor into the water. They only saw the splash and followed her example. But Cem knew it was all Jessica's fault.

## Chapter 7 (Jessica)

Jessica did not see who dropped the ladder to the Upper Keep for her. No one wanted to be caught helping her. She tried to hate them, every last one of them, everyone in the Upper Keep who did no more than tolerate her or helped her just enough but no more. But it was hard to hate without a clear target in mind.

Climbing the kelp ladder rubbed loose the skin on her palms and between her fingers and, at the top, she sat peeling the skin and letting her hate simmer down. The night breeze cooled the air and eased the humidity. Jessica murmured a melancholy tune, and her spirit rose with the familiar words.

> *"And will he not come again?*
> *And will he not come again?*
> *No, no, he is dead,*
> *Go to thy deathbed.*
> *He never will come again."*

"Jessica?" called Abraham. He sounded strained.

The wind blew Jessica's curls across her face, whispering of witches and premonitions. She clenched her teeth against the words of the song in case some playful emperor in the sky took them as a suggestion. She crawled in through the window, landing hard on her ankle, but did not let this slow her down. She dropped her sack and ran to Abraham's side.

"What is it, Father?" she asked.

The lamp in the corner was lit, and the little flame wavered across Abraham's face. He was exactly where she had left him that morning, sitting in the great chair she fashioned months ago from seaweed-stuffed plastic. The interior was rotting, but Abraham did not seem to mind the smell.

"I… I can't," he said. "I can't get up. I need to use the pot."

Jessica squeezed behind the thin space where the chair leaned close to the wall. She reached her arms around his back, hooked under his arms, and lifted him, easily. He was too light.

"I brought algae blocks," she said.

He took stiff steps towards the pot in the corner. She looked away at the darkening view of the horizon as he aimed and missed. She wondered about everything she could not see. Everything that she *would* see, soon, tomorrow. Her father returned to the chair without her assistance. He would be fine without her.

Abraham eased back into his chair. "You're only quiet when you want something."

"How are you feeling?" she asked.

"My back's sore," he said.

That was not what she meant. Sometimes he was easy-going because he had gone to a better past, before her mother died. Sometimes he was soft when he thought Jessica was her mother. Sometimes he turned mean.

"Do you know who I am?" she asked.

"Jessica, how could you be anyone else?" He gestured at her halo of hair. "Dasha did not sing. What were you singing?"

Jessica sat by his feet. A child's place, the crossed-leg student. But she *was* still Abraham's child, no matter how long she lived.

"Ophelia," she said.

"The flowers."

"Yes."

"Sing it again," said Abraham, closing his eyes. "I haven't heard it in a while."

Jessica sang again. This song would never get her any food or friendship. No one on Venice Main wanted to hear the sad stories. It made them feel worse. But it made her feel better, with its mournful ache and easing sigh. It broke down the mask smoothed over her face and the stone wall built around her chest. It made her feel heard, even if her father looked like he had fallen asleep.

> *"His beard was as white as snow.*
> *All flaxen was his poll.*
> *He is gone, he is gone.*

*And we cast away moan.*
*God ha' mercy on his soul."*

Jessica listened for snoring, but Abraham was not sleeping. She looked out the window again. Even harder now to make out the line between the deepening purple sky and the blue-black ocean. She grasped her star pendant between her fingers and ran it back and forth on the chain.

"You didn't leave soon enough," said Abraham. His eyes were open, and he did not look calm anymore. He looked angry. He must have known already, before she came in. But how? Jessica pushed away but wasn't fast enough. He kicked out, hitting her shoulder. He was too weak for it to hurt, but she scrambled away, fuming. She was not a child.

"You can't treat me like this!"

Her shoulder stung, but it was no worse than getting jostled on the ramparts. Nothing like how he used to hurt her, in the years after her mother's death.

"You should have run away long ago," said Abraham. "Do you stay because no one else wants you?"

"It's your fault!" she shot back.

The children in Venice believed that anyone with white in their hair was a ghost from before the Flood, personally responsible for the destruction of the world. Jessica knew that the world had been flooded longer than Abraham had been alive, longer than his father had been alive. He was not responsible for the world's pain, but he was at least partly responsible for hers.

"Blame me for everything," said Abraham.

"You're a horrible old man," Jessica said. "I'm going to leave you and I'm not even going to think of you—"

"It's too late."

"It's not too late!"

She rushed towards him and gripped his arms to stop him raising his hand. She could not remember the first time she had hit back. She thought it would mean he would never hit her again; she was shocked when she learned she was wrong. He never seemed to mind, after their fights were over. She thought it made him proud to know she could give back as much hurt as she took. It made him feel better to know that the first time someone on the ramparts had struck her, she had not hesitated to strike back, harder.

"You were always too weak for this place," said Abraham. His eyes were unfocused, and his breath reeked of mould. She wrinkled her nose but did not turn away from the smell. She would not be weak for him.

"I'm going somewhere better," she said.

"There is no place *better*," said Abraham. "Every place has its own problems. Every place is looking for someone to blame. If you go elsewhere, they'll blame you. They won't stop to consider if you're Jewish enough. Once they realize hating Jews is an option, they'll hate you."

"You're wrong," said Jessica. "It'll be better after I go."

"You're already gone."

"What?"

"You're already gone, Dasha," he said.

Jessica's anger flooded away, replaced with a deeper pain. "I'm not Dasha," she said, releasing his arms. "She's dead."

"You still wear the necklace I gave you…"

He frowned, like he knew something was wrong, that this woman who wore his necklace was not his wife. But then he turned away from the truth he did not want to see.

Jessica grasped the pendant between her fingertips. Her mother's necklace. A Jewish necklace for the woman who never tried to be Jewish. Jessica never had the chance to ask her mother why she did not convert; why she had married Abraham in the first place, when she had no desire to be part of the Upper Keep.

Not that this had saved her. Dasha had died with the Jewish women of the Upper Keep in the massacre. When Abraham put the chain around Jessica's neck, it had been sticky with blood; the star had stained her fingertips red. It took a decade of rain and wind to turn the necklace silver again.

Jessica missed her mother. She missed her smooth hands braiding and unbraiding her curls. She missed resting her chin on her mother's soft thigh. She missed how Dasha could quiet Abraham's moods. She missed being a family of three. She knew that her mother was just as responsible as her father for making her half-and-half, two mismatched wholes that made one whole *other*. But her mother was not here, and Jessica could not bring herself to blame her.

"I'm leaving," she said.

"Leaving me to die. Good. I always knew you would." Abraham did not look so lost now. "I always knew you would run away someday. Figure out how to survive without me. That's the important thing, right? Surviving. I hope you never come back!"

"Shut up," Jessica said, quietly. She turned towards the window. The breeze did nothing to soothe her.

Eventually, she heard a sputter of snores. Abraham had fallen asleep. A lump stuck in her throat that she could not swallow down. Instead, she sighed it out.

> *"And will he not come again?*
> *And will he not come again?*
> *No, no, he is dead,*
> *Go to thy deathbed.*
> *He never will come again."*

Abraham's snores continued after the final shaky note. She brushed the last tears from her cheeks and tucked her curls over her ears. They immediately popped back out.

Jessica slipped out of the window and went along the balcony to a rope bridge leading over to the balcony of a neighbouring house. Within, a woman was faintly singing a prayer. Jessica moved on, crossing another rope bridge to a third house, then a fourth. Light rain began to fall. The houses clustered together here, and the curtains were drawn, protecting the inhabitants from the weather. There was no more singing. They were probably sitting down to dinner. No one would appreciate an interruption at this time of night, but Jessica still knocked next to the window.

The curtain parted enough for Jessica to see one dark brown eye, and then the curtain swept open. Abby's body blocked any view further inside, her large belly as effective a barrier as the curtain. From outside the house, Jessica could not see Abby's one twisted leg, but she imagined it made standing up while so pregnant even more difficult. Abby was due, for at least a week now, and Jessica cursed that she was dealing with a heavily pregnant woman who had better reasons than hunger to be in a bad mood.

"Did someone die?" Abby asked.

"My father needs help." Vague enough for Abby to keep the curtain open.

"Is he sick?" she asked.

"Who is it?" Abby's husband Daniel called from deeper within the house.

"He's not sick," said Jessica. "He's just going to be on his own for a while."

Abby pursed her lips, making Jessica feel like a child. Abby was only a few years older but was mature in a way Jessica was not. Maybe it had something to do with being a mother. Abby already had two children.

"Are you running off to Venice Main again with that boy?" Abby said.

"I'm going to Fuji," said Jessica.

Abby's eyes widened.

"I don't know how long I'll be gone."

"Nobody goes to Fuji," Abby protested. "Nobody goes any-where. How will you even get there? Why would you go? What about the riot? If the empress finds out—"

"Andrusha, Luka, and I are going to talk to the empress," said Jessica. "We need more food, and they need my help. I'm the most fluent in Diplomacy."

Luka had used that excuse to convince Andrusha to let her come, though Andrusha was probably as fluent as Jessica.

"I need someone to check in on my father…" She did not say she was not planning to come back. No one would ever commit to taking on Abraham.

"I have my own family to take care of," said Abby.

"I understand," Jessica lowered her eyes and tried to look pathetic.

Abby sighed. "I'll have Ruben stop by every couple of days."

Ruben was Abby's eldest. He was only six. But Abby seemed to think he was old enough to be helpful, so Jessica decided to believe her.

"I was hoping for one more favour," said Jessica. "Our jug's empty. I won't have time to refill it before I sail tomorrow."

Abby shuddered and spat at the mention of *sailing*. "I've already wrapped the desalinator," she said, wiping her mouth with the back of her hand. "But wait here."

The curtain closed. Jessica heard angry mutterings inside. It didn't matter if anyone protested: a mother's decision was the final decision.

The curtain opened.

"Take this jug," said Abby, thrusting it into Jessica's hands. She almost buckled under the weight. "We have enough to last us until tomorrow. And Ruben can pick it up when it's empty. And take this."

Several strips of gull jerky tied together with kelp twine. An extra loop in the tie slipped easily over Jessica's hand, resting on her wrist.

"You didn't have to do that," said Jessica. "We have pickles. And I got algae blocks." Another gift she had no intention of paying back.

"The kids were lucky hunters and I'm tired of gull," said Abby. "Besides, we can't survive on the sea's gifts alone."

*The sea's gifts.* The edible algae blocks were a breakthrough, but Jessica would hardly call the wild poisonous algae a gift. The sea gave waves that swallowed boulders and houses and people. It gave eels, their sharp teeth, the tearing and the blood. It gave mussels with sharp edges that sliced through ankles in accidents and through throats when children clashed with children. Those were the sea's gifts.

"You're right, we can't," said Jessica. "We survive despite them."

The curtain opened wider. Omar, Abby's father-in-law, appeared over her shoulder. He was almost as old as Abraham. Wrinkles like threads pulled at the corners of his mouth. His eyes widened, and he placed his fingertips against his lips.

"Jessica! You look just like your mother!"

Jessica blushed, and Abby flushed with her. Then a child started crying from inside the house. Omar rushed away from the window. Jessica shrugged off the apology before Abby could issue it and shuffled towards the rope bridge.

"Be careful," Abby called out. Then the curtain was down, and the world was dark.

Jessica did not have to be careful. She had to be brave. Tomorrow, she would be sailing. A rough wave crashed against the rocks below, and her stomach heaved.

*Sailing.*

Jessica spat over the ledge.

## Chapter 8 (Jessica)

The storm was probably going to kill them, but Jessica was happy.

The slanting wind and rain threatened to capsize the ship even as the sailor struggled to keep them afloat. He forced the ship to weave when the wind wanted it to fall, sliding over the slippery metal deck to untie this rope, pull on that rope, while she, Andrusha, and Luka clung uselessly to the sides. Something had struck them on their journey, something large, and by the time Jessica reached to peer out of one of the small portholes, whatever had attacked them was a rapidly retreating shadow in the water. The single crack in the side of the hull was enough. The brig started to flood, forcing the Venetians to go out into the rain rather than becoming trapped below deck. It was not clear that the sailor would get them through the storm before the ship sunk, but Jessica did not care. She had escaped. She had made the impossible possible. She had left the Upper Keep and Venice Main.

She had abandoned her father.

"How far are we from Fuji?" she yelled over the wind at the sailor. Perhaps it was foolish to distract the one person who could keep them alive, but she did not need an answer. She wanted to think ahead, to where they were going, not dwell on what she had left behind.

The sailor ignored her. Before they left Venice, she had learned his name, Sora, using the same techniques of gestures and kind smiles that worked with children turning Feral. She thought it might create a bond of trust, but he did not often respond to his name. Perhaps he was more like the Feral than she imagined.

The ship turned, sharply. The portside disappeared entirely under the waves, taking Luka with it. Sora pulled at one of the ropes, straining, then righting the ship, and Luka reappeared, gasping for air. A flimsy sea creature had latched its toothless gaping mouth around his foot, a slick sock-turned-monster. Jessica grabbed its tail and tugged it off easily, its bag of skin slick against her palm. Its little black eyes looked at her in bewilderment. She tossed it over the side of the boat.

Luka's eyes were squeezed shut, and he was coughing up water. Did he even know that a little monster had tried to swallow him? Perhaps it would grow and grow until it could swallow ships bigger than this one in a single gulp. Perhaps its father was lurking under the waves, considering how best to exact revenge. A sea monster.

*"It's a mermaid,"* said a memory of her father.

The rock and lurch of the ocean forced bile up Jessica's throat. The first few days at sea had not been this strenuous. They woke in the morning, Sora already at work at one end of the ship, Jessica, Luka, and Andrusha curled up below. Jessica counted the empty beds, one for each sailor that had died in the riot, and breathed out her overwhelming guilt on a shaky breath. The Venetians tried to be helpful but only got in the way. Sora worked until the sky grew dark behind the clouds. Then, they lay in terror while Sora slept, leaving the ship to nature's whims, before exhaustion overtook them.

Jessica wished she knew how to sail.

*"Where would you go?"* her father had asked her, a scant two weeks ago. "Who could you run to?"

It wasn't even a terrible storm, not in the way the Venetians knew storms. If this rough rain had been hitting them on dry land, Jessica would have simply closed the curtain to wait it out. But here, at sea, the rain was terrifying. Here, the cloud-induced darkness and her own shut eyes made time endless, turned days to years.

Jessica bit the inside of her cheek and sucked on the salt from the bleeding cut. *This is what it's like to be an eel*, she thought, and fought the urge to giggle.

*"She's a monster,"* said the memory-voice. She saw her father's face, frowning down at her so clearly that for a moment she was sure she was seeing a ghost. Was she going to be haunted by him for the rest of her life? The image vanished, and Jessica wondered how much salt water you had to swallow before you started hallucinating.

*"Ai!"*

Sora called out. The Venetians snapped to attention, though none of them understood. Sora, leaning against the prow, did not clarify. His entire body was as taut as the air when lightning is about to strike, turning him from something pitiful to something sure and strong. He shouted again, pointing in front of them.

Ahead, Jessica could see… *stars*. It did not make sense, but there they were: right above the water, through the rain, even though it was not yet night, there were stars, a steady string of lights guiding their path.

"We're almost there," said Luka.

To the stars?

Perhaps their ship had turned vertical in one of its more aggressive tilts, and ever since they had been sailing up to the sky and were now so close to the stars that refused to dampen in the rain. They were riding the storm clouds, up, up, up. The rain was even lessening now, like they had passed through part of the atmosphere, the dangerous layer humanity was doomed to inhabit where pain fell upon them and had ascended to a place where hope sailed up in delicate bubbles.

Sora cried out again – in…

Hope. That was it! Sora was hopeful!

Jessica squinted at the lights, letting the rain drip into her eyes. Those were not stars. The colour was wrong. It was not white, nor tinged with yellow, nor even that odd red that some stars became when she peered through Daniel's old glass, the strange standing tube he pointed at the sky to study the heavens. These lights were different. A very pale green, like light just breaking through water. The kind of light that was alive, or could be alive, but did not grow. No, it sustained.

"Jessica, sit down!" shouted Luka.

She did not know when she had risen to her feet, but here she was, standing. Andrusha was glaring at her, and Sora gestured that she should sit down, but she ignored them. She walked to the prow, grasping the edge, pressing her body forward, her head and chest thrust out above the water.

She remembered sitting by her father in their home in the Upper Keep, spreading the picture the sailor had given her on his lap.

"What is she?" Jessica had demanded, pointing to the picture.

The image of a ship, what the sailor said ships used to look like, unwieldy and made of wood. She knew what a ship was but did not know the figure fused to the prow. If it was a woman, she was terribly deformed, and she was too beautiful to be anything so wrong as *deformed*.

"It's a mermaid," her father told her.

"What's a mermaid?"

"A woman who lives in the water."

The woman did not look scary, but Abraham said she lived in the water, and that did explain the eel-tail.

"She's a monster," Jessica decided. She had never seen a monster like that before. Her father's stories did not include beautiful women, just giant beasts waiting beneath the waves for their next meal. They wanted to eat people more than anything else, to punish those who had choked their ocean home with plastic islands and killed off all the nicer fish that once filled the water with jewelled sparkles called *scales*, leaving them with nothing to eat besides the blood-thirsty eels, the sting-waves, the silent mussels, and other more terrible creatures. Perhaps this mermaid was a terrible creature too, blood-thirsty and menacing and powerful.

Jessica wanted to be a monster. She wanted to look that brave, sticking out at the front of a ship.

"She's not real," Abraham said, taking the picture from her.

Jessica was crying. She thought she should be crying for her father, for the man who refused to leave her be as she sailed for freedom, but she was crying for the picture that she never saw again and had forgotten about until this very moment. She wondered if Abraham was safe, if Ruben checked on him, if Abby kept her promise, if he missed her, if he was dying without her to take care of him. But he was not her problem anymore: the man who made her feel more like an outsider than anyone else in the Upper Keep. The first one to explain to her that her mother's refusal to convert left a mark of otherness on her skin, in her blood.

The first one to make her feel like some hybrid between human and monster.

Jessica was not a mermaid. She did not live in these waters. She lived above them, apart from them. It would take a truly terrifying woman to be part of a ship, part of the water and waves, and yet look so serene. Jessica could imagine a woman like that – a woman with her own ship, a part of her body, a part of the ocean, an imaginary monster straddling the space between land and water that she always wanted to believe could exist. But if Sora had not waved her over, Jessica would have never believed that this woman who sailed up to their ship was real.

## Chapter 9 (Cem)

Cem could not find Sedef.

He weaved between the groups under the Upper Keep as Farooq tried to trade for a bite of algae block, smaller bites each day as Roman dipped into his secret stash. He thought of the Feral, whose howls seemed louder each night, and his chest grew tight as he imagined Sedef crawling among them, her whispers turned to hisses. She had still been speaking last night, and the change could not have happened so quickly, or else Cem would already be… He could not think about that.

"Any luck?" asked Farooq. He stepped over two still-sleeping gang members to reach Cem. If it were not for the quick rise and fall of their chests, Cem would have guessed the girls were dead.

"She probably went up to the Main to look for food," said Cem. "Maybe to raid gulls' nests in the Broken Tower."

Farooq nodded, although they both knew that all the nests in the Broken Tower had been emptied out days ago. The gulls had moved. The children could see them circling the top of the Dark Tower and the supported undersides of the homes in the Upper Keep, unreachable.

"Here." Farooq passed a bite of algae block into Cem's hand so smoothly Cem doubted any of the other children had noticed.

"Where did you find this?" asked Cem.

"Roksana."

"Is she dead?"

"No," said Farooq, with a slow drawl that implied, *not yet.* "Her stomach's been hurting. She can't eat."

Cem shivered. Sweat trickled from his shoulder blades to his lower back.

"I'm going to keep looking," he said.

"I'll split mussels," said Farooq.

Farooq's hands were already covered with new, shallow cuts from gathering the sharp mussels. Cem reached out to take Farooq's hand in his own, gently tracing the lines of dried blood on the boy's palm with his thumb, before pulling away.

"Sedef will be hungry," said Farooq. "Come and get me when you find her."

Cem hopped over the boulders, past Roman, sitting with eyes closed but head cocked, listening for danger at the harbour's edge. Cem hurried past where Shen was making deep gouges in one of the rocks heedless of the sun that beat down on his black hair, pausing briefly to snatch an algae-covered kelp rope from two Feral who were chewing at the vegetation. They hissed at its loss. Cem assumed the rope tasted something like an algae block, but every Venetian with the ability to think knew that the algae on its own was poisonous. Whatever magic the empress worked on her blocks made them edible, safe. Those two Feral who skittered away would spend the rest of the day vomiting up the little they had managed to ingest.

Cem's hair was soaked with sweat by the time he made it to the ramparts. He could not see any other children around, not even Bota's gang, who must have been hiding in the shadows of the cave. A small group of adults sat on the ledge above the harbour, laughing too loudly, sharing a bottle of sake. Cem and Farooq had shared a bottle with a few other boys when they were much smaller. He had felt like a happy idiot before he felt sick.

"Care for a taste, boy?" asked one of the men, swaying up to standing. Cem saw Grigory sitting behind him and fought the urge to run. "I'm sure you're looking for something to fill your belly."

"Or are you looking for something else?" asked Grigory. He stood much more surely than his friend. Cem shook his head and tried to slip away, but Grigory caught up to him quickly and slung his arm over Cem's shoulder.

"I don't care about sake," Cem said, resisting the urge to bite.

"But you care about your friends, don't you?" whispered Grigory, breath hot and rank next to the boy's ear.

"Where is she?" demanded Cem.

Grigory walked away. Bitterly, Cem thought he had been teasing him and had abandoned the joke. But when Grigory began climbing a toppled pillar, Cem realized he was meant to follow. The adults lived in the towers. They only went to the caves if they had something to hide.

Cem scrambled up, gagging on the scent of sour rot that wafted towards him with each wave of Grigory's cloak. They went up two levels, hopped over two balconies, and then Grigory led him into a cave with deep cracks cutting through the walls on either side. If the walls collapsed, Cem would have enough time to run out before being crushed...

Not so Sedef and Nazli, sitting in the cave, bound tight with knotted kelp ropes. Cem rushed forward, but Grigory grabbed his arm.

"Not so fast," said Grigory. "If you want to help your friends, bring me algae blocks. One for each of them. I'll wait on the balcony. If you come back with your gang to try to force them free, I'll crush them before you can touch me."

He knocked lightly on the wall of the cave. Cem could hear the stones above groan as they strained to hold their shape. One of the girls whimpered.

"And if you don't come back by the end of the day, I'll crush them anyway" Grigory said. "If I were you, I'd hurry. *Hurry!*"

Cem ran out the of the cave and tripped down the broken pillars and steps of the ramparts, back to the harbour. What should he do? Take Roman's blocks? That would be to act like a hero – but heroes sometimes made mistakes. He knew that from Jessica's stories. People turned on their heroes all the time in that fantastic world of Rome. Like the man with the long funny name who was banished from his friends because things were going wrong and they decided to blame him for it. *There is a world elsewhere…* That was what the man had said to make himself feel better. But there were no other worlds for Cem. There was only the harbour, the Main, Farooq, Sedef, and a hero willing to make a decision that could be a mistake.

"Roman!" Cem shouted.

Several of the children's heads popped up. He couldn't let them know about the bound girls, because then the whole gang would come. They would run up the steps before he could warn them about Grigory's plan to crush them.

"What's wrong?" asked Roman.

"Grigory stole Sedef," whispered Cem. "He has her, and Nazli, tied up in a cave. He said one algae block per girl, and he'd let them go, or else he'll make the cave fall and crush them."

Roman started up the steps to the ramparts, walking without panic but with purpose. Cem skipped to catch up with him. The adults on the ramparts glanced at them briefly before turning their attention back to the horizon, keeping watch for another shipment.

When they reached the depths of Roman's cave, Roman lifted the lid on his small treasure box. Cem's stomach dropped. There were only two blocks left. Roman took them both.

"We only need one," said Cem. "Nazli isn't ours. We need that block." But Roman walked out of the cave.

It was barely anything, a few mouthfuls, but a few mouthfuls they wouldn't have if Roman traded them for someone who wasn't part of their gang. For a Feral! Cem wondered if he could grab the block from Roman. Maybe… He didn't chance it. Instead, he led Roman to Grigory's cave.

"It's just us," Cem said quickly when he saw Grigory's scowl. "We have blocks. We promise."

Grigory nodded to him to enter. Cem ran to the back of the cave to untie Sedef. He couldn't watch the trade, see the last of the algae blocks go. Sedef was weeping. The bindings on her wrists and ankles had left white marks that blossomed purple as the blood rushed back. Cem untied a gag from her mouth. She flung her arms around Cem's shoulders. Her tears mixed with the sweat on his neck. Roman came to crouch next to them, hands empty, and untied Nazli. Nazli did not make any noise as the rope was released from her mouth. But tears were running down her cheeks as she ran out of the cave.

And Cem would have left her there. He held Sedef tight.

"I wasn't going to hurt them," said Grigory. "Not really."

Cem glared up at him. Grigory's lips and matted beard were stained green. One block, half-eaten, was in Grigory's hand, and the other was already gone. Grigory had gobbled through blocks that could have fed the whole gang for days.

"You *did* hurt them," said Roman. His voice was so low and strong that Cem thought he sounded like an adult. How an adult should sound.

"I was hungry," said Grigory, curling in on himself, so old, so small.

"You made Sedef cry," said Cem.

Sedef would not release her arms from around Cem's neck, forcing him to curve one arm under her and one arm around her. He carried her back down to the ramparts, Roman a little ahead. The other adults could hear and see everything, but they did not look at the children and did not ask if Sedef was okay.

When they reached the harbour rocks, Roman returned to his perch by the edge of the water and stared as intently at the horizon as any adult on the Main. Roksana and a few of the smaller gang members hopped up from their resting places to Cem's side. A flurry of soft hands touched Sedef's shoulders.

"What happened?"

"Is she okay?"

"She needs to rest," said Cem. "She's just hungry. Sleep will help."

Roksana nodded, sympathetic, and herded the others back to the shadows. There were few protests. Everyone was hungry. Everyone was tired.

Farooq leaned against one of the house legs, watching Cem approach. Sedef refused to let go, so Cem gave up on releasing her and leaned beside Farooq. Cem waited for Farooq's questions, but none came.

"Grigory stole her," said Cem after the silence became too much to endure. "Nazli, too. Said he would kill them if he didn't get algae blocks."

"Looks like he got the blocks, then," said Farooq, his voice flat.

"Roman took care of it," said Cem.

"I would have given blocks for them, if I had any," said Farooq. "Or, I would have found another way to help Sedef. I told you to tell me when you found her. Why didn't you ask me for help? Why did you leave me behind?"

"I knew Roman had blocks," said Cem, uncertainly. A couple more days when everyone was hungry, Roman might not look like a hero anymore.

"But what if Grigory hurt you?" Farooq's hands were shaking. "What if he killed both of you? I wouldn't have been there to try to stop it! I wouldn't have known what had happened!"

Sedef was not crying anymore. She had turned her head to Farooq. Her arms did not cling as tightly as before.

"Nothing bad happened," said Cem.

The corners of Sedef's mouth were still rubbed red where the rope had been.

"But it could have happened, and I wasn't there," said Farooq.

Sedef grabbed Farooq's hand, pulling him close. Farooq hugged them both, too tight, the small space too hot. Sedef squeaked in discomfort, and they all laughed but did not pull away. Somewhere over Cem's shoulder, the horizon was empty.

## Chapter 10 (Jessica)

The rain was dying down, and from the prow of the ship Jessica could see a collection of giant structures looming out of the ocean, too thick and square to be towers. Beyond these strange buildings, a white coil curved up and around a mountain that must have been Fuji. The coil sparkled with those lights that Jessica had thought were stars, but she could now see that they were glowing windows. Beside the ship floated the woman on the Flood, a smaller, still fantastic, mystery.

"Where does the empress live?" Andrusha called to the woman, apparently blind to her otherworldliness.

She stood, unafraid, small waves lapping at the flat pink board beneath her feet. Jewels lined her ears in alternating colours of blue and pink and purple. They made the curl of metal that pierced her nose seem almost plain, though not as plain as two clear plastic loops that adorned her eyebrow. Imagine choosing to pierce your skin with something gleaned from the ocean!

"The empress lives wherever she wants," said the woman. She sailed her board up close to their ship so she did not have to shout. "She's the empress. *Duh.*"

The final sound meant nothing to Jessica, but its derision was clear.

"How does her hair do that?" Luka whispered to Jessica. The thick wave of white, blue, and pink hair was impressive, but Jessica could interpret this. Most of the married women in the Upper Keep covered their heads.

"It's a wig," Jessica told him. "*Duh.*"

"We need to speak to the empress," said Andrusha.

"Visiting representatives leave their ships in the Greenhouse," said the woman. "Though, I suppose this is *our* ship, isn't it?" She turned to the sailor and began to speak to him in their own language.

"Perhaps we could explain ourselves to the empress?" Andrusha said. The Venetians had come up with a story about seeing the trading ships sink off their shores in the last storm. They were ready to dismiss anything Sora said to the contrary. But the woman was smiling. Whatever Sora had said was not damning.

"What did he say?" asked Luka.

"That the sailors disappeared," said the woman. "Not surprising, with the storms. We thought the ships must have sunk. I would say that it's nice that one made it out, but I don't know if we'll be able to repair this damage. Where are you from?"

"Venice," said Andrusha.

"Did you get your shipments?"

The Venetians shook their heads in unison. Jessica clutched her necklace, massaging the comforting points of the Star of David. Maybe to Sora, with his almost Feral nature, all the sailors *had* simply disappeared. Maybe he had no memory of the riot. Maybe they *would* get away with this... She thought of Hirokai's body sinking below the waves, his kind face twisted in fear and pain, the surprise in his eyes after Jessica had pushed him.

"Well, you should go to the Greenhouse, anyway," said the woman, pointing to a derelict structure covered in wilted vines. "The rest of the representatives are there now."

"Other representatives?" asked Jessica. She had prepared for Fuji and Fuji alone. She had no idea what people from other cities would be like. And she did not like the idea of sailing into the Greenhouse. It looked abandoned, overgrown with greenery. But if they were not the first guests, then a story was already being written. It might not have been a narrative completely within their control, but it was one they were being invited to join.

"Who are the other representatives?" asked Jessica.

The woman stared at her blankly.

"Diplomacy," muttered Luka.

Right. Jessica tried again, in Diplomacy.

"Who are the other representatives? Where are they from?"

"Les Alpes and Kilimanjaro," sighed the woman. "All here to whine at the empress."

Sora eased the ship forward to the Greenhouse. The woman sailed her board parallel to them. *Les Alpes…* That was a beautiful rolling sound. *Kilimanjaro*, like the rhythm of a gentle rain. All these people suffering from the same problems. No one needed to know the Venetians were lying. Tears caught in Jessica's eyes, a stinging mix of guilt and relief.

"Are you okay?" asked the woman. She glided closer, more curious than concerned.

"We're not used to sailing," said Luka. His hand on Jessica's back felt like a warning.

"What can I do to help you?" asked the woman.

"You can convince the empress to send us more food," said Andrusha. "We're starving."

"Starving? Like, you're very hungry? From the trip?"

Andrusha and Luka laughed. Even Jessica managed a small smile.

"We *are* hungry from the trip," Andrusha said. "But everyone in Venice is starving. Your empress will know all about it. From my letters."

"*Letters?*"

The woman did not follow them through the entrance to the Greenhouse, instead delicately balancing in place behind them.

"What's your name?" Jessica shouted back to her.

"Ama," called the woman.

Jessica watched Ama turn her strange little ship around, nothing more than a board and sail between her and the ocean. The movement was so fast, Jessica could barely believe it did not send the woman flailing into the water.

They breached the curtain of vines that covered the Greenhouse entrance. Sora let out a small cry and tugged sharply on a rope. The ship wavered on a dangerous tilt, jerked left, and bumped roughly against a path that was slightly elevated above water level. A small group of people stood there, staring at them in shock. They stopped short behind a large, moored silver-white vessel. Jessica's eyes flitted from the ship to the vines that twined along the curved walls of the cavern.

The silver ship was twice the height of their own, its enclosed interior much larger than their brig, a floating house complete with windows. One of the windows shimmered and Jessica reached over the edge of their ship to touch it. An invisible barrier reflected her hand. She rose onto her toes to try to see her face and pulled back in shock when a completely unfamiliar face appeared through the barrier: blue eyes narrowed; blond eyebrows knit together in a scowl. Then a curtain, far more solid than the rope curtains in Venice, was pulled down.

To their right was another ship, its deck covered with purple vegetation petrified in a sea-salt crust to shard-like stiffness, interwoven with golden braids. Through the waves, Jessica saw that the vessel extended a significant way downwards. She wanted to see how deep it went, but Luka was pulling her portside to disembark. Sora helped them onto the path. The ship shuddered as they left, sinking slowly but steadily into the water. When they were ashore, shaky but secure, Sora rushed to greet the waiting group.

Jessica looked at the curved ceiling, where the vines that grew up the walls intertwined in intricate shapes like coiling eels. She almost tipped over from leaning back too far. The only witness was a nearly invisible woman in a long white coat spraying the vines with mist from an opaque jar. The mist smelled like algae blocks. Jessica swallowed before she could begin to drool. The woman frowned at her and turned away. She had Sora's straight black hair and golden-tinged skin, as did the woman Sora approached. His body was bent in apology, as if he blamed himself for his own disastrous arrival. The two men who completed the group did not look like anyone Jessica had ever seen in her life. As they approached her, she tried to melt into Luka and Andrusha.

"Let me guess," said one of the men. "You also did not receive your algae shipment?"

Jessica had never seen anyone so big, or so dark. His outfit was brighter than any fabric the Fujians ever brought to trade; the long tunic a glossier gold than the braids on the ship; the trousers and sleeves a brighter purple than the petals on its hull. His hair was cut close to his skull but looked like it would grow into curls rivalling her own. His stomach stretched the fabric of his tunic, round like the Feral when they over-ate. A full stomach… It was the most impossible thing about him, more impossible than the gold and purple, or the smile that did not carry a hint of mockery. The man's eyes darted to his companion, clearly concerned by the Venetians' silence.

"Do you know Diplomacy?" asked the other man, before continuing, more slowly, "Where are you from?"

His clothes, from his loose blouse to his tight trousers to his knee-high boots, were made from a spongey material that was trying to pass as white but could not quite lose the faint undertones of pink. His skin was a reverse of that fabric, pink that wanted to fade to white, and his hair, securely tied in a ponytail, was white to the point of translucency. His oddly round eyes were pale blue but glinted like silver.

"We're from Venice," said Andrusha, finding his voice.

"Venice?" laughed the pale man, flashing intensely white teeth. "Should we expect representatives from Neverland or Avalon as well?"

"K2," whispered Jessica.

"Oh," said the man. "Those people—"

"The reason we started the Mercy Experiment."

The woman to whom Sora had been apologizing brushed past to stand between the two men. Jessica saw the sailor scowl in frustration, but he did not follow. The woman was unusual in a way Jessica could not quite explain, and something about her face made Jessica want to tell her all her worries instead of carefully breathing them out.

"I guess that makes them mythical in their own way?" proposed the large man.

"It does make them odd," the blue-eyed man almost agreed. He reached out his hand, and before Jessica knew what was happening, his fingers were stroking her curls. The large man smacked his hand away from her.

"For Christ's sake, Dario," he snapped, "they're not animals in a zoo."

The pale man, Dario, did not seem affected by the outburst. Luka pulled Jessica closer to him, and over the familiar scent of his skin and sweat, she smelled something else, something smoky and sweet. As the large man adjusted his tunic, the scent wafted over to her once more.

"Sora says the sailors disappeared," said the woman, head tilted like she was waiting for an answer.

"Yes," said Jessica.

The woman folded her arms in front of her, letting her hands disappear into her wide sleeves. The fabric was embroidered with a pattern similar to the vines on the ceiling. Jessica was enchanted by the idea that something like mosaics could adorn clothing.

"So, they never came to you either," said the woman. "Unfortunate, but not unexpected. Come, we can make this right. We have not had time to produce a full shipment, but perhaps if we transferred—"

"Shinobu?" interrupted the large man. The woman turned her tilted attention to him. "Perhaps before we discuss this tragic accident, we could offer our newest visitors something to eat?"

Shinobu did not seem pleased at being interrupted, but she nodded. She led them towards a plain white door.

"Of course, Ibada, thank you for your suggestion," she said. "Dario, would you like to invite the other Alpines?"

"My servants have their own provisions onboard," he said, and Jessica thought of the angry face in the window of the silver ship.

Shinobu turned to the large man.

"Ibada?"

"My *friends* went to tour the Algae Plant with Etsuna," he said. "If he has proven as generous as he has been in the past, they have already eaten their fill."

"The Algae Plant?" asked Jessica.

The three strangers looked at her with varying degrees of annoyance and amusement.

"There will be time later to answer any questions you have," said Ibada. "Let's eat first and get you something better to wear."

"Better?" she asked.

Ibada avoided her gaze and gave an embarrassed cough.

"Don't mind Jessica," said Andrusha. Jessica glared at him, but he continued like he did not notice. "She is a... *merchant,* from Venice. This is her companion, Luka. I'm Andrusha, the author of the letters, if you care to know."

Neither Dario nor Ibada seemed to care. Jessica had only heard Grigory refer to her as a merchant, but she rather liked such an official-sounding title. Luka's immediate frown proved that he was not so happy with his own description.

Shinobu's eyes narrowed when Andrusha mentioned the letters. And if she knew about the letters, it was obvious who she must be.

Jessica gave a small bow and imagined she was in one of Shakespeare's history plays.

"My apologies," she said. "We would be very grateful for something to eat, and we are eager to discuss getting an algae block shipment to Venice as soon as possible."

Shinobu, clearly the empress, nodded as she freed her hands from her sleeves and pressed a smooth, circular tile on the wall next to the door. It slid open, apparently without human assistance, to reveal a little room. She walked in, followed by Dario and Ibada, and Jessica ran in before she could count the problems that could arise from entering through a magical door. Andrusha and Luka came in behind her, and the door closed shut, trapping them. The floor began to hum. Jessica manoeuvred herself between the two Venetians.

"Do you always stand so close?" asked Shinobu.

Were they standing so close? It seemed normal to Jessica.

The door opened again. They had been transported. The waterway was gone, replaced by a bright room with warm cream-coloured walls and rows of long black tables. A small group sat at a table at the far end of the room. One of the boys in the group whispered and pointed not-so-secretly at Jessica, his other finger twisting in a mime of her curls. The wide windows that lined the room revealed that they were now high above the water. Jessica's anxiety rose. It wasn't the height, or the magical transportation, but the rows of empty tables that made her squirm. Where were the people? Why were there so few Fujians? Where were the children?

"Jessica? Are you alright?"

Ibada stopped as the rest of the group followed Shinobu to a wall studded with closed windows and a single long shelf at chest height. Jessica breathed in and counted the unanswered questions. Three. She breathed them out.

"How did we get up so high so fast?" she asked. "What was that room?"

"It was a lift," he said, surprised. *A lift*. The room *lifted* them up. It still sounded like magic. "It's… a box that carries you upwards and downwards. I can't imagine climbing stairs to get this high."

Jessica looked back through one of the windows. She supposed this level was about half the height of the Broken Tower.

"It must have seemed like you were trapped in a window-less room," Ibada continued, smiling despite the grim picture he conjured. "You must have been terrified."

Jessica thought about the bodies of children left to rot in the sun after a gang fight, the suckling mouths of the eels.

"It would take more than a box to scare a Venetian," she said.

Ibada considered her comment. He stared at her, an unspoken question in his eyes. But instead of asking, he beckoned her to follow him to the far wall, where he tapped a shiny mounted square. It burst with colour, conjuring strange images.

Jessica gripped her dress, hoping to prevent her hands from shaking. Where had these illustrations come from so quickly? She knew she had magical ideas about Fuji, but she had not expected to be faced with actual magic…

"Don't worry, my friend Fadhila also gets overwhelmed by the number of options," said Ibada, unphased by the impossible display. "Do you want me to choose for you?"

Jessica nodded. Ibada tapped one of the images. It was immediately replaced with a symbol, then disappeared. He repeated the process and walked forward. Jessica knew she was walking too close to him, but this place overwhelmed her, and his unearned kindness made him seem strangely safe. The other Venetians had already picked up trays of food and were making their way towards a table, but Jessica had no urge to leave Ibada's side. She tried to focus on the sweet smell emanating from his clothes, and not her pounding heart.

The door to the lift opened again, and Sora entered. He walked over to the occupied table and started speaking in angry whispers. The only boy who listened had a wide face that sloped to one side.

"This must be all so new for you," said Ibada, guiding her towards the last window. "If you have any questions, I'd be happy to answer them."

She had many questions and was not sure where to start. She settled on the one that probably had the clearest answer.

"What's that smell?" asked Jessica.

"Smell?"

"It comes from you when you move your clothes," she said before hastily adding, "It's not a bad smell. I like it."

Ibada lifted his loose-sleeved arm up to his nose, inhaled, and smiled.

"It's tobacco," he said. "You don't smoke?"

Jessica shook her head, still unsure what caused the smell.

The window in the wall in front of them opened. A quick-moving round Fujian woman deposited two trays in front of them before the window snapped shut.

"That one's yours," said Ibada.

On the plate lay a small pile of tiny clear squares that shook when Jessica lifted her tray but kept their shape. Next to it was a large, soft beige square wrapped in a dry red plant. The crackle of the wrapping made her tooth pang in warning, and she tore it off. She followed Ibada to the table where their group sat. As soon as she joined them, she swallowed her soft beige square in three large bites and listened to the talk.

Everyone assumed that the sailors had died in a shipwreck. The empress planned to send more shipments to Venice. The world here was strange, but food appeared when you pressed a picture, and at least Ibada did not seem ready to kick her out. Everything was going well, but Jessica felt a growing surge of nausea.

It was all too easy. They were going to get caught, their lies were going to fall apart, and then they would have to pay not just for what they had done. They would have to pay for the lying...

"Excuse me, I need to say—"

"Not now," said Luka, grabbing her thigh.

Ibada frowned, clearly unsure if he should intervene. Jessica shook her head. Luka's grip hurt, but his hand felt very far away. Or else her own head was very far away. Either way, she was too hot, and until a few moments ago, the room had seemed wonderfully cool. Luka released his grip and Jessica almost fell against his shoulder.

"Are you alright?" began Ibada, only to be interrupted by the arrival of Sora and the wide-faced boy.

"Makoto, can this wait?" asked Shinobu.

"I don't think so," the boy said, in a slow, slurred speech. "Sora thinks there's been a misunderstanding."

Waves of heat cycled through Jessica's body.

"About what?" asked Dario.

"The sailors," said Makoto.

Jessica knew she should intervene, but she could not lift her head from where it hung towards her chest.

"What's the misunderstanding?" asked Shinobu.

"I'm sure it's nothing," said Andrusha, and Luka tried to hush him into silence, and she wanted to tell them both to shut up, but her mouth could not form words.

"It seems pretty clear the sailors disappeared," said Shinobu. "Is that wrong?"

"It's more how they disappeared," said Makoto. "It wasn't a storm."

"It *was* a storm," said Jessica, surprised that she could speak, unable to stop the words. "But not a storm of rain."

"Jess, shut up," whispered Luka.

"The harbour," Jessica continued, her words running together. "The riot."

"Riot?" Shinobu asked sharply. "What riot?"

"Are you feeling unwell?" asked Ibada.

She was about to answer him, *yes, something was terribly wrong*, but when she opened her mouth, the only thing that came out was a rush of vomit, and then everything went black.

# Chapter 11 (Shinobu)

Shinobu did not know who was more annoyed, herself or the very pregnant Shinku, lying on one of the many beds in the long room, glaring at the new arrival. Shinobu wished somebody would run to fetch a screen from the Vaults to offer Shinku a bit of privacy, but it was years since there had been more than one patient in the ward. Even worse, the Venetian in the other bed had brought a crowd that packed the thin aisle; competing groups of Kilimanjarians, Alpines, and the vastly outnumbered Venetians, every so often cut through by two Fujian nurses. Makoto hovered by Shinobu's shoulder, uncharacteristically agitated, like he wished he could be anywhere else. Everyone was trying to speak at once. Shinobu kept her head tilted with a seemingly friendly ear but was tuning most of it out. Only Jessica's rhythmic retches refused to fade away, echoing through the spacious room, bouncing from the cavernous, vaulted ceiling as the girl threw up on the previously spotless, white-tiled floor.

Jessica fell back on her bed with a groan. Her hair flamed out around her head. Nurse Kazuku put a cold compress on her forehead, an ice pack behind her neck, a clean bowl at her side, and somehow procured a wet rag that she thrust in Yuki's hapless hands. It took the younger nurse a moment to realize she had been tasked with cleaning up the vomit on the floor. When Yuki approached Shinobu, rag out apologetically, Shinobu realized she was standing in some of the mess. She stepped back hurriedly. The other spectators in the ward copied, crowding even closer to the visibly frustrated Shinku.

"Do you all have to be here now?" Shinku snapped, pulling her blanket up over her round belly.

Shinobu knew that she should be tactful and somehow signal to the others to stay quiet about the death of the sailors, but no one gave her the chance.

"The riot was an accident," Luka said quickly, as Andrusha spouted, "You surely can't believe everyone in Venice was involved!"

"Don't you have anywhere to keep the Venetians while you decide what to do with them?" asked Ibada, half-heartedly trying to herd the other Kilimanjarians away from the patients. Dario said, "How do you plan to punish them?"

"Have I done something wrong?" asked Makoto.

The scribe clearly regretted his impromptu role as Sora's translator. His normally carefree face was lined with worry. He pressed back against one of the long windows, as if he might prefer to face the terrible drop to the Flood outside than the tangible anger of the crowd.

"You did nothing wrong," Shinobu reassured him. "You were actually very helpful."

Makoto did not seem to believe her. Shinobu supposed all this shouting was not helping him to believe he had done the right thing. Ibada was trying to quiet a group of Kilimanjarians who claimed a death squad chased the sailors off a cliff (despite none of them having witnessed the riot). Dario's ward, Sofia, was conflating the riot with some tale of a traditional spring rite of sacrifice to the cruel joy of the Alpine servants. In the face of all this chaos, Makoto reverted to a meditation technique that many of the Fujians practiced: repetition of verse.

"*When that I was and a tiny little boy,*" he began. Jessica groaned and vomited into her bowl.

The Shakespeare verse was short. Most of the poem had been lost before the Flood. So now, on top of all this noise, Shinobu had to listen to the same four lines, repeated over and over. Makoto drifted towards Jessica and the empty chair beside her bed. That was meant for Yuki, who turned and glared at Shinobu from behind the fringe of her bright pink wig, as if the scribe was the one who had delegated the nurse her unpleasant task.

"Why should we be punished?" asked Andrusha, though Luka's guilt-flushed face offered less of a protest. "None of us took part in the riot."

"Perhaps it would be best to learn the names of the individuals who killed the sailors, rather than punishing a few token Venetians just because they're here," proposed Ibada, using his large body to block the crowd's view of Jessica.

"Someone killed the sailors?" asked Shinku. She struggled to sit up, her eyes wide with horror. Kazuku ran over to ease her back down and Shinku attempted to push the nurse away, though her bulk impeded her efforts.

"We weren't involved," said Luka.

"You can't prove that," said Dario.

"You can't prove we *were* involved," said Andrusha.

"I could *encourage* you to remember," said Dario.

"If I need to *encourage* anyone to remember something," said Shinobu, "I can do it myself."

Dario laughed. "What will you do? Play pretty music on tinkling bells until they tell you what you want to hear?"

Shinobu ignored the slight. "Do you know who was involved?" she asked Andrusha.

"It was a mob," said Andrusha. "It's hard to pick out individuals in a mob."

"So, you sat by while a mob killed them," said Dario.

"Did Hirokai die?" asked Shinku, forgetting in her panic to speak in Diplomacy. "He's tall, his hair is quite short, he usually sails with his sleeves rolled up…" Her voice was high and breathless. "Did he die, did you see him die?"

Those who could understand did not respond. They did not know the answer, but as Sora had been the only sailor to return, they could guess.

"*With hey, ho, the wind and the rain,*" Makoto muttered, staring out of the large window at the drizzling rain.

"You sat by while the cook poisoned Jessica!" Luka yelled at Dario, and Andrusha spat on the floor. Yuki jerked away from where it fell, and the Alpines closest to the Venetians stepped back with mutters of disgust. "Should you be punished for that?"

"She wasn't poisoned," said Kazuku. "It's an allergic reaction to fusarium."

"I don't believe you," said Luka.

Kazuku looked up at Shinobu, who shrugged. She could take Luka to the Vaults and show him the historic documents detailing the symptoms of a fusarium reaction. But Shinobu did not think it would make him feel better to learn that the allergy was often fatal. The way he kept looking back at Jessica even as he turned his head pointedly away reminded Shinobu of Hirokai and Shinku: how they pretended that they were not looking at each other before sneaking off (despite Shinobu's warnings about crossing family lines). Shinku would face the consequences soon enough. And Luka would learn to live with whatever happened to Jessica.

"We're not going to kill them," said Shinobu.

"If they killed Hirokai, you *should* kill them!" wailed Shinku.

Kazuku patted her hand, which seemed to soothe Shinku for some reason.

"*A foolish thing was but a toy, for the rain it raineth every day,*" Makoto whispered, barely audible above the rain beating harder against the windows.

"You have to do something," said Ibada. His voice was slow, reluctant, and he stared at the growing storm outside. "If you let one community get away with mass murder, you are welcoming chaos. The world has witnessed enough chaos."

"I thought you were on our side," Luka protested.

"I'm on the side of punishing those responsible," said Ibada, looking pointedly out at the water.

Jessica vomited again.

Kazuku was still consoling Shinku, though it was clear Jessica was the one in greater need. Jessica's skin was deepening to a shade that rivalled her curls; beads of sweat left tracks down her face where they cut through the grime of sea travel. The pendant she wore on a chain pierced Jessica's skin, and Shinobu watched a bright red drop of blood slip from collarbone to chest. The sight of the blood made Shinobu lightheaded. She swept over to the girl, pushed back the mess of curls, found the clasp of the chain, and undid it. Shinobu shoved the necklace deep into her sleeve and turned back to the argument, though she was distracted by the weight of the chain, the shape of the star. It was somehow familiar.

"How could any one person stop a mob?" asked Andrusha.

"If your city was mostly full of innocents," said Dario, "there would have been more than one person to stop it."

"Would you have helped the sailors?" asked Luka.

"No, he wouldn't have," mumbled Shinobu, her mind on Jessica's pendant.

"I'm happy to help!" Dario protested. "I would help all the time if I had the opportunity!"

The Alpines in the room went silent and pressed closer together in the aisle. Dario would take out his anger on a few of them later. Shinobu should not have antagonized him.

"We saved Sora," Andrusha insisted.

"You saved one person," said Shinobu. "But five died."

Five people gone, five people who were not Dreamers. The small population of Fuji had suddenly become a lot smaller. Shinobu thought of everyone left. She mentally tied the family lines between them, tested them. Each one broke, too intertwined with common ancestry.

Ibada considered the implications of the loss. "To decimate an entire race is a great crime indeed," he said.

"What are you talking about?" asked Andrusha. "We would never..." He went quiet. Shinobu had a sudden memory of that first letter she received from Venice. *The Upper Keep*:

she remembered that; a strange name. There had been a massacre in the Upper Keep. Shinobu felt for the weight of the girl's necklace in her sleeve.

*A David star?*

"If Fuji does not have the tools necessary to exact an appropriate punishment," said Dario, "the Alpines can take care of it without you ever needing to set foot in Venice." He made it sound as if he were proposing some grand favour.

"*When that I was and a tiny little boy, with hey, ho, the wind and the rain,*" muttered Makoto.

"I can even take care of these three for you now," Dario continued. "If the sickness does not take the girl."

"She could die?" asked Luka. Abandoning his attempts at acting distant, he rushed to her side, kneeling on the white tile still splattered with vomit. Jessica did not notice he was there. Nor did she notice the bowl beside her, instead opting to heave onto her blanket-covered lap. Shinobu expected some sound of agitation from Yuki, but the nurse was staring at the scribe. Waiting. Kazuku and Shinku had gone quiet, too. Everyone waited to see if Shinobu would accept the Alpine's offer. Only Ibada had the decency to look away.

"We will not be needing your assistance," Shinobu said to Dario. He flinched, and she remembered to tilt her head before addressing the group. "We will return these Venetians to their home. And we will never visit K2 again."

"You're going to let us starve," said Luka, not rising from Jessica's bedside.

Shinobu thought she saw Sofia glance at Dario, a hint of concern colouring her usual deadpan expression. But the rest of the onlookers had already abandoned the Venetians. They were unimportant before their arrival, and uninteresting after Shinobu's choice of punishment. Some were looking for a way to leave the ward quietly, some were amused by the continuation of the drama, but only a few seemed as alarmed as Shinobu by Andrusha's rising anger.

"You can't do this to us!" Andrusha cried.

"We're not doing anything to you," she said, her voice low and steady. "Not anymore."

"You're going to let us all *die*?" he asked. "You were just talking about the loss of an entire city being a huge crime!"

"The loss of Fuji is a huge crime, but the loss of K2 will hardly be noticed," said Dario. "You took food and gave nothing. You repaid mercy with death."

"If you push people to the edge, how do you expect us to react?" Andrusha was pleading, desperate. "We asked for help to avoid this kind of violent riot and we were ignored!"

"*A foolish thing was but a toy, for the rain it raineth every day,*" Makoto whispered.

Andrusha was nearly vibrating with rage. The group, sensing further drama, closed around again, trapping Shinobu too close to the Venetians. She stood at the centre of all this attention, everyone hungry for the violence she tried to avoid. Ibada was whispering with his confidant Fadhila, who was trying to pull the younger Kilimanjarians away. Sofia had fled to the back of the group, and Shinobu could barely see the girl's pale face peeking behind Dario's taller frame. Dario himself seemed not to notice his ward, but protected her instinctively, even as his own eyes glittered with excitement, ready to 'aid' Shinobu whether she wanted his help or not. Luka's eyes had hardened even as Andrusha's burned with self-righteous rage. Only Jessica did not seem to be aware of the impending violence. She was not looking at Luka or Andrusha, Ibada or Dario, the Kilimanjarians or the Alpines. No, it was Makoto who held Jessica's attention. She stared at the Dreamer like he was the most important thing in the world.

"You knew what was happening in Venice, and you still let us starve!" Andrusha cried.

Shinobu kept calm, refusing to look caught, refusing to feel guilty.

"What is he talking about?" asked Dario.

"My letters!" Andrusha said. "I sent you letters!"

"Did he, Shinobu?" Kazuku asked in Fujian.

Shinobu had not wanted Ama to worry about the letters. She had not wanted the empress to risk destroying the entire experiment by overworking the already overproducing sōrui-jin. Why should they accommodate the ill-planned needs of a community that would probably kill itself anyway? The information was an obstacle to Ama's happiness that Shinobu had decided to remove without the empress ever finding out. Only the sailors who carried the letters knew about their existence, and they accepted Shinobu's decision to keep them a secret as if the order had come from the empress herself.

"I told you that this was going to happen, and you did nothing!" Andrusha said. "If you want to blame someone, blame the empress, because this is *her fault!*"

No one had heard the empress enter, because no one was paying attention to the lift at the end of the ward. Even Shinobu did not notice her until Yuki gasped and bowed. Ama looked different: no brightly coloured wig or whining voice demanding the gratification of whims that Shinobu had already anticipated. This Ama was not the childish sailor who skimmed over the waves.

The ward went quiet, except for Makoto's muted chants, and the steady brush of Ama's steps as she glided down the aisle between the beds. The long train of her dress followed in her wake. Shinobu knew this dress, solid black fabric cut through with triangle-shaped swaths of gold, but she could not recall Ama ever wearing it. Ama's sparkling piercings had been replaced with demure black studs. Her short hair was smoothed back off her forehead, unadorned, allowing her head to float gently atop her neck that seemed to go on forever as the fabric plunged beneath her collarbone and between her breasts.

Kazuku bowed low, and Shinku did her best to bow from her bed. The Alpines and Kilimanjarians gave sweeping bows and nods of respect, and Andrusha and Luka, almost endearingly, tried to copy them. Shinobu waited for Ama to speak, but the quiet continued, and Shinobu finally realized the empress was waiting.

Waiting for Shinobu to bow. She bent at the waist. Before she had fully straightened, Ama spoke.

"Why did I not receive this Venetian's letters?"

Ama's face was so still, only Shinobu could have known that the empress was furious. She wanted to explain herself – but not here! Not in front of these people: the nurses who were supposed to respect her; the Venetians she had just condemned to death; the representatives she wanted to impress; the Dreamer who had no business knowing her business. She wished for time, for someone to say something, anything.

Then Jessica sang, changing everything.

> *"But when I came to man's estate,*
> *With hey, ho, the wind and the rain;*
> *'Gainst knaves and thieves men shut their gate,*
> *For the rain it raineth every day.*
>
> *But when I came, alas! To wive,*
> *With hey, ho, the wind and the rain;*

*By swaggering could I never thrive,*
*For the rain it raineth every day.*

*But when I came unto my beds,*
*With hey, ho, the wind and the rain;*
*With toss-pots still had drunken heads,*
*For the rain it raineth every day.*

*A great while ago the world begun,*
*With hey, ho, the wind and the rain;*
*But that's all one, our play is done,*
*And we'll strive to please you every day."*

## CHAPTER 12 (CEM)

Venetians lined the rocky curve that formed the harbour. They covered the ramparts and seemed to peek out of every window of every tower. But no one was speaking; they seemed barely to be breathing. This scrounging, fighting mass of humanity stood completely still, waiting for Fujian ships that Cem knew would never come.

Cem sat in the shade of one of the great legs of the Upper Keep. Sedef huddled on his lap, too hot and terribly light. Her eyes were closed; too tired to keep them open. All the children were thinner and weaker, but the strongest showed the most decline.

Roman sat on a boulder, feet sticking out of the shadows, his once-broad shoulders bowed. Bota, who had also kept her gang alive, still somehow looked bright-eyed even with her slick black dress hanging off her shoulders. She sat with her own gang at the edge of the water closer to the harbour, smiling a threat. A few weeks ago, being this close would have been an invitation for a fight, but neither group could expend the energy.

"Do you think they're going to come with food today?" Cem whispered to Roksana. She lay flat on a nearby boulder, anxiously fiddling with the tile shards in her dreadlocks. In truth, Cem did not care either way about her answer. He simply couldn't handle the silence any longer. He could almost hear every grinding tooth. And under it all, a ring-ing in his ears that sounded like a hiss.

"We don't know if they're ever coming back," Roksana muttered.

Farooq slid over to join them, eying the wiry girl with obvious distrust. Roksana rolled onto her side and tossed an arm around a younger girl who pulled closer, despite the heat.

"If a ship does come today, it will definitely have food," said Farooq, his voice grating with forced optimism. "They always bring food."

"Or they might come to kill us as dead as those sailors," said Roksana. "Revenge, you know?"

"Shut up," said Roman, and the children fell quiet again.

Farooq eased himself into the space between Roksana and Cem and leaned against one of the house legs, as if its sup-port was the only reason he had joined them.

"We could try climbing to the Upper Keep," Cem suggested quietly. "They always have pickles."

"It's impossible to climb the legs," said Roksana. She ducked her head in embarrassment. "I already tried."

"But if we *all* tried," said Farooq. "We could get on each other's shoulders, and then maybe we'd be high enough to reach the gulls' nests—"

"It wouldn't be enough," Roman whispered. The other children did not seem to hear him, fully absorbed now in their shared fantasy of hunting for food. Cem untied himself from Sedef's arms and carefully stepped across the uneven rocks to Roman.

"What do you think we should do?" he asked.

Roman did not answer. He sighed and rubbed his face. His eyes were unsettlingly dull.

"There are too many of us," said Roman. "We can't keep you alive if there's no more food. We can't make algae blocks after they've all been eaten. We can't get the gulls to lay more eggs, or the mussels to spawn faster."

Cem looked back over his shoulder. The other children were still plotting, but Sedef was watching. Cem knew that if he left now and rejoined the other children, Roman would not mind. He would probably forget this whole conversation. But Cem felt bad. It was awful if Roman could not understand how important he was to them.

"We don't expect miracles from you," Cem said quietly.

"Everyone expects miracles from their leaders," said Roman. "Maybe they should. Maybe the best ones make them happen. Like the empress's algae blocks."

"Algae blocks aren't a miracle," said Cem.

"Then what is?"

Cem could not answer that. Something impossible, sure, but he did not know what that might be. How could Cem imagine something that was too impossible to already exist?

Roman turned back to watch the harbour. The adults had given up and were making their way back up the ramparts, heading for the cool shadows inside the towers to sleep through their hunger.

"There's not enough," Roman said. "Even if the ships came tomorrow, or next week, there are never enough algae blocks." He spread his hands. He was thinking about all the children, Cem saw – not only his gang, but Bota's too, and the Feral. "You're going to starve. You're all going to die."

"No, we're not," said Cem. Too loudly: two of the nearby Feral, who did not as a rule react to words, looked up from scraping their nails against the algae-thick rocks.

"You're not," Roman repeated.

He did not seem to believe the statement.

"You and Bota keep us all alive," insisted Cem. And it was true: without Roman and Bota, the children would be wild packs, tearing at each other, no better than the Feral. Without them, the fight between Shen and Ghanim would have become a massacre. Cem saw a glimmer of understanding in Roman's eyes, and the older boy looked at the small groups of children huddled in the shadows.

"You wouldn't all be here, if it weren't for Bota and me," said Roman. "There would be only half the number of children left, at most."

Cem nodded, but Roman was watching Bota, standing on the rocks by the water. Nikita sat by her feet, one hand around her leader's calf. Some of the younger members of their gang were playing nearby, pulling strips of poisonous algae off the rocks and flinging them at each other.

"We don't need the blocks," insisted Cem. "We have eggs and mussels, sometimes eels. Look, we're fine!"

And Cem did think they were fine. They knew how to be dirty, and hurt, and tired, and still survive. Because they had leaders who taught them to walk through the muck without crying at each smudge and cut. Leaders who took care of them even though they were disgusting and threw slime at each other. Even when their arms were covered with scabs that healed to scars.

"That's a miracle, isn't it?" Cem said. What could be more impossible than this? Here they were, surviving and all because of their leaders. But Roman did not seem to be listening. His eyes were half-closed, and his head was cocked like he could hear the whisper of some other voice in his ear, and whatever it was saying made him nod in agreement.

Roman opened his eyes. He looked over at Bota and stood up, not even acknowledging Cem as he walked surely across the uneven rocks to approach the girl. Bold of him, Cem thought, to leave the shadows of their unofficial territory, and cross the border into the cloudy light of Bota's unofficial territory. He had to assume that Roman knew what he was doing.

Bota eyed Roman but did not warn him off, perhaps because Roman showed none of the aggression or fear that usually signalled a big fight. Nikita unclasped her hand from Bota's calf, visibly uneasy at Roman's confident approach, but the other children continued to play, oblivious. Cem strained to hear their conversation, but Roman did not speak. He opened his arms wide and wrapped them around Bota.

For a moment, Cem thought Roman was embracing her. His jaw dropped. They did not hug other gang members, and Roman barely touched any of them. Bota seemed just as shocked, her expression muddled by warring emotions of confusion, amusement, suspicion, and anger. The few children watching held their breath; Cem, Nikita... Sedef too. They watched as Roman gripped Bota tighter in his embrace and tipped them both over the rocks into the water.

Nikita screamed.

"You motherfucker!" she cried, scrambling to the edge of the rocks. "Give her back, give her back!"

She flung her arm into the water and immediately yanked it back, shrieking. A latched-on eel came out of the depths with it, and Nikita ripped it off. Blood spurted out in an arc. The eel fell onto the rocks, writhing for a few seconds before shimmying back into the water. Cem turned away from the frothing water as the eels consumed Roman and Bota, white foam turning pink and then bright red.

Nikita howled, not with the empty anger of the Feral, but with wild determination. She lunged forward, into the shadows, and set upon Roksana. She, in turn, screeched and tore at Nikita's hair. Other members of Bota's gang, realizing what had happened, quickly followed suit, attacking whoever was closest. Cem was horrified to see that it didn't matter if the person they attacked was part of Roman's gang, or Feral, or even one of their own. There was no one to call order. No one to set the rules. They were all going to die. They were all going to kill each other.

*Maybe not all of them*, Cem thought, and the voice in his head sounded a lot like Roman. *Probably half. And there might be enough food left in Venice to feed half.*

Cem's stomach sank. Roman could not make more algae blocks appear, but he could make the children disappear. Was that a miracle?

Someone was pulling him up: he almost bit the fingers grabbing him before he realized it was Farooq. When Cem was on his feet, Farooq pulled him further into the shadows beneath the Upper Keep. Sedef ran ahead, and they followed as she deftly led them past slippery algae blooms and gaps where dark water waited below to consume them. The snarls and howls were fading behind them, but this pain would not be sated with one fight. The victors would crawl looking for more victims, hunting anyone who ran.

In that moment, Cem hated Roman, because he had not cared who died to ensure the others lived. Cem was not a good fighter, neither were Sedef and Farooq. When the other children caught them, they were going to be part of Roman's sacrifice.

Sedef stopped suddenly, bringing Cem and Farooq to a halt. At first Cem could not understand what it was that had stopped her. What was this object that had fallen from the sky, that waved its welcome to the lucky people below? But then he realized it was not some impossible and wonderful miracle.

It was a ladder, leading to the Upper Keep.

## Chapter 13 (Shinobu)

Jessica sang and the room was silent. Her final words echoed through the hospital ward, dreamy and light and already fading away to be forgotten.

"Should I fetch paper to record?" Makoto asked Shinobu.

There was no need. Jessica had fainted after reciting the last lines. *Were* those the last lines? She had said them with such finality, even smiling before she shuddered and fell. Quickly, Ibada and Kazuku moved to lift her back onto her bed. Maybe there was more…

The whispered word, "Shakespeare…" travelled down the aisle between the empty beds, greeted with excited nods or confused shrugs. Then other familiar words: Macbeth, Hamlet, and familiar phrases: "*Romeo, Romeo, wherefore art thou, Romeo?*" They tumbled through the ward, inspiring growing excitement or even more confusion.

The Shakespeare plays were supposed to be lost. None of the fragments contained in that lonely shelf in the Vaults were anywhere near as long as the song Jessica had recited. Yes, that was the right word: not *retold*, not *paraphrased* or *analysed*, but *recited*, and Shinobu was struck with the further impossible certainty that Jessica had been reciting *word for word*… Similar words were being shared around the room, but Shinobu knew they were not quite right. She wanted to cry out to everyone to *shut up!* before she completely forgot all the girl had said.

She nodded at Makoto and the scribe rushed off towards the lift, giving Shinobu space to think. *The Venetians had no art, just coloured tiles. None of the sailors ever mentioned a stage or amphitheatre for performances.* It did not make sense. But Shinobu could not argue against reality.

"This doesn't change anything," Dario said, flatly.

"Of course it does," she snapped back. "If this girl knows even the shortest verse of the lost Shakespeare plays, then she is valuable."

Luka was staring at Jessica, then at Shinobu, then back at his friend. It was almost comical. "Her verses are valuable?" he said. "*How?*"

Yes, the verses were valuable, but that was not exactly what Shinobu had said. She had said that *Jessica* was valuable. Ibada seemed to notice the distinction, too. He caught Shinobu's eye, frowning.

"You didn't think that they were worth anything?" asked Ama. The curve of her lip showed some of that impishness Shinobu knew so well.

"Her stories were entertaining," said Andrusha. "We... we liked listening to them. They were worth... an algae block or two."

Dario laughed out loud. "The greatest playwright of Western literature, worth a mere block of the poor man's protein!"

"The greatest what?" asked Luka.

Yuki tugged at Shinobu's sleeve.

"I think Kazuku has everything under control here," said Shinobu, trying to shake out of the nurse's grip.

"But Shinku…"

"How can we even trust that she isn't just making up words?" asked Dario. "That song didn't make any sense."

"Diplomacy sounded different back then," Ibada protested.

"Well, this *song* didn't sound like something one of the greatest playwrights in history would write."

"She's not the only one who knows them," shouted Luka. Some of the Kilimanjarians around him stopped reciting their corrupted version of the song to stare at him. "There are others. In the Upper Keep."

Shinobu swallowed down her envy. She would consider what to do about that later. "Dario," she said, "do you or your servants have fragments? Not guesses, but actual fragments? Preferably written down?"

Dario shrugged, unsure how he should answer. "Maybe Sofia…"

The girl did not look happy to be singled out. "I might have some sonnets in a collection on the ship," she muttered. Several of her companions started laughing.

"Luka, are you from the Upper Keep?" asked Shinobu.

"No," he said, too loud.

"But you know some of the plays, through your companionship with Jessica?"

"I wouldn't say—"

Andrusha grabbed his shoulder. "She's asking if you, a Venetian, might prove to have as much worth as Jessica, from the Upper Keep," he said. "In other words, if Venetians are worth saving, or if they should just save Jessica and let the rest of us die."

At last Luka grasped the point. He nodded to Shinobu. "Yes. I've been to most of Jessica's performances. Enough to recognize... a lot of the plays."

"Luka, go with Dario and Sofia," Shinobu said. "Sofia can share the poems she has, and any other verses she might know, and Luka can let us know if anything sounds familiar."

"He might *lie*," said Dario, and was cut off by a dismissive flick of Ama's wrist.

"He wouldn't dare," said the empress.

Luka nodded and ducked his head, looking small in front of the diminutive woman. Dario began walking away. Sofia hurried to keep up, but Luka's eyes shot back to Jessica.

"It's not like she can go anywhere," Andrusha growled at him. "For once, make yourself useful!"

Luka nodded and headed to the lift, followed by several other Alpines.

"Perhaps the rest of you can take this opportunity to leave as well," said Shinobu, since no one seemed anxious to go. Many people glanced expectantly at Jessica, as if they thought she might break out into another song. "This is a hospital," said Shinobu, firmly. "We have a very ill, very important guest. Not to mention a pregnant woman who deserves privacy."

Several faces flushed with shame. Apologetic nods and sweeping bows were offered to Shinku and Shinobu as the rest of the crowd hurried to leave. Soon the only people remaining in the ward were the Fujians, Andrusha, Jessica, and Ibada. The room felt larger. Shinobu had never felt so small and insignificant under its great arched ceiling.

Andrusha bowed to Ama, more gracefully than his earlier attempt, though his harsh smile was not entirely respectful. "So, you're the empress who has been ignoring my letters."

Ama held his gaze until Andrusha looked away.

"Believe me," she said, "if I have been ignoring your cries for help, it was entirely unintentional. I never received any of your letters. I would not be surprised if they were destroyed."

"They weren't destroyed," Shinobu said quickly. "They're in the Vaults."

Ama did not look at her, and too late, Shinobu realized she had been manipulated into admitting that she knew about the letters. Admitted that she knew where they were, and that she had been keeping this information from Ama. She did not know whether to be proud that Ama had grown into her role or irked that she had been playing dumb as Shinobu coddled her.

"I would very much like to see those letters now," Ama said to her. "If you will allow it, Shinobu."

"I would never dare tell you what you are and are not allowed to do."

"Apparently, you would indeed dare."

Shinobu tilted her head and offered the empress a charming smile.

"I was hoping that you would accompany me to the Coil," she said, switching to Fujian. "And we could discuss the situation before you read the letters."

"I will not be accompanying you to the Coil," Ama replied in Diplomacy. "I will guide Andrusha to the Vaults." She frowned at Ibada, out of place among the Fujians and Venetians. "Ibada, why are you still here?"

The Kilimanjarian bowed. "If you don't mind, empress, I would like to stay here with Jessica."

He offered no explanation, but Ama nodded her approval and then turned to walk to the lift. Andrusha followed, hopping slightly to avoid stepping on the train of her dress. The empress tugged the folds of the train after them before the lift doors closed shut.

Shinobu crossed her arms, feeling uncomfortably lost. All eyes in the room were on her, but this felt different. She did not feel important, surrounded by people waiting to hear her speak. She felt like some piece of art frozen behind a wall of glass, abandoned in the darkest corner of the Vaults, waiting to be forgotten.

There was a slight tug on her sleeve. Yuki was waiting next to her. Kazuku was busying herself at a tap, soaking cool cloths to lay on Jessica's brow. Ibada was sitting by the girl's bed, uncomfortable in the too-small chair, but determined to stay. Shinku, in her bed, was crying quietly. With good reason, now that she knew what had happened to her beloved Hirokai.

"What do you need, Yuki?"

"Could you please ask Ibada to help move Jessica to the end of the hall?"

Shinobu stared at the young nurse and fought the urge to ask: *Why don't you ask him yourself?* He was almost beside them, not even far enough to be blurry in Shinobu's vision and had probably heard Yuki. She had spoken in Diplomacy: he must have understood. But he did not move. He was looking at Shinobu the same way Yuki was looking at her. They were both waiting for her order. As if her orders still meant something.

"Ibada?" Shinobu began but did not need to finish the question.

Ibada stood and gracefully swept up Jessica, and her sweat-soaked blanket, in his arms. He moved down the aisle quickly and placed the girl on the bed closest to Kazuku, who put a wet cloth on Jessica's forehead. It flowed like choreography: Shinobu's orders, others' actions.

"Yuki," said Shinobu. "Why did you want Jessica moved?"

"Shinku's in labour," said Yuki.

Behind them, Shinku's groans became a sharp and sudden scream.

#

Shinobu crouched, a muscle in her back spasming as she balanced Shinku's leg on her shoulder. Kazuku's body was pressed next to Shinobu between the labouring woman's askew legs. Shinobu could not see the nurse's hands and wondered if they had disappeared inside Shinku. She trembled at the thought, releasing her hold on Shinku's leg.

"*Ai!*" shouted Kazuku.

Shinobu straightened up again.

Yuki stood at the head of the bed, trying to feed wraps of fusarium and nori to the labouring woman. But Shinku clearly had no interest in consuming anything.

Shinobu had seen very little in life that looked as painful as childbirth. Only two moments could compare: that time when the Dreamer Masuna fell out of the gathering ship and got caught in the metal net below (his arm was nearly ripped from its socket), and the picture Sora had once drawn of an eel attack in Venice. Black smudges of graphite had stood in for streams of red blood, but there was no artistic substitute for the open-mouthed scream on the sketched figure's face. The picture had at least been silent. Shinku, however, was *loud*…

"Yuki, bring me the swaddling blanket," ordered Kazuku.

Yuki stood shock-still, making Shinobu want to yell. She should be the one supporting this screaming woman's leg, and instead Shinobu was being punished because Yuki could not do her job. Shinobu should be sitting at the far end of the room with Ibada, trying to pretend he wasn't watching, and Jessica, too deep in her fever to be aware of her surroundings.

"Ai!" shouted Kazuku. "The blanket! Now!"

The neatly folded cloth lay waiting on the bed, but Yuki did not reach for it. Her hands, trembling, dropped the fusarium wrap on the floor. "I can't," she said. "I don't want it to come out. I don't want to see it."

"The baby's coming whether you want it to or not," said Kazuku.

Shinku flung her head back into her pillow. A thin stream of blood trickled down her chin... she must have bitten her lip. Shinobu shuddered, and turning away, glimpsed Ibada getting up from his seat. He came to stand next to Kazuku, offering her the blanket. She took it with a nodded *thank you*.

"You may want to leave," Shinobu warned Ibada. "Before it's born."

Ibada returned to his seat at the end of the hall.

"It's coming," said Kazuku. "Yuki, help Shinku sit up."

This time, Yuki followed the order, her face smoothed with resignation. It was a good look on her, Shinobu thought. It gave her the gravity a nurse needed to be trusted by their patient. Even with the pink wig.

A shudder wracked Shinku's body. Suddenly, she laughed. Her laughter was full of the same pain that powered her screams and was so loud it masked her newborn's cries.

"A mermaid," said Jessica, her wondrous rapture echoing around the big room.

Shinobu supposed she could see a slight similarity to the mythical creature: the baby's legs were fused together, its one foot a curled stump that did indeed resemble a thick fin, its wet skin slippery and smooth like the body of an eel. But that was where the resemblance ended. The rest was less magical and more terrible. The baby's arms were shunted and pointed backward, like malformed gull wings. Its heart pulsed frantically and visibly, protected from the outside world by the thinnest layer of skin. Its bladder had no such protection. There were other parts on the outside that should have been inside… Shinobu did not look long enough to identify them. She let her eyes flit briefly up to its face, where all the features spiralled together towards the centre like they had been caught in a whirling typhoon. She could just distinguish two eyes from the merged bulbs staring glassily out at the world. The worst part for Shinobu was the mouth, drooping slightly to the left, a familiar asymmetry in this most twisted of mirrors.

"A mermaid," Jessica murmured again, entranced.

Yuki had turned away to the wall. She was weeping.

"I want to see the mermaid!" cried Jessica, pushing away the covers and trying to rise.

"Get her back in her bed!" shouted Kazuku, wrapping up the baby so that only the face was visible. Shinobu was about to remind Kazuku to speak in Diplomacy, but Ibada did not need a translation. He gently took hold of Jessica's shoulders, guiding her back down, tucking the blanket firmly around her.

"I need to take care of Shinku," Kazuku said.

Shinobu nodded. "I'll take care of the—"

Kazuku thrust the bundle into her arms. She knelt by Shinku, and pressed gently on her abdomen, encouraging the delivery of the placenta. Yuki was still crying into the wall. The baby was trying to cry, but could produce nothing more than a wet wheeze, as if its lungs were not made to breathe air.

*A mermaid belongs in the water.*

"Does it look like Hirokai?" Shinku asked.

"No," said Shinobu. "Not at all."

"Good," said Shinku. "Get rid of it."

Shinobu nodded and walked to the lift.

This was not the first child Shinobu had decided deserved the mercy of a short life. She felt Ibada's eyes on her, his frown and his disgust. Maybe if this happened in Kilimanjaro, his home, not once but over and over, birth after birth of babies you could not bear to look at, he would understand. She had to see this baby as a monster, because when you tried to be kind, to wait and see if they could grow to be like the Dreamers, you were only torturing them.

If Hirokai had been there, if he had not died, perhaps Shinku would have held on to the child, even if only for a few hours. For a few hours, she would have had the pretence of a family, a brief interlude of happiness before reality came crashing down again, and the baby died in confusion and pain.

If Ibada had witnessed that scene play over and over, he would see that this was not a choice made out of callousness, but out of empathy. But all he saw was a woman whisking a baby away to its death, a woman who must look more like a monster to him than the one she carried in her arms.

# INTERMISSION

*Dear Empress,*

*My name is Andrusha. I am a child of Venice.*

*We need your help.*

*For as long as I can remember, we have been hungry. I have spent my whole life looking for food, thinking about food, wanting food. I expect most people live this way.*

*In Venice, people tried to fight the hunger by having fewer children. The idea was that if there are fewer children, then there are fewer people who need to eat, and more mussels and eels for the rest of us. But the families in the Upper Keep continued to grow. They kept having babies, and that made many of the adults of Venice angry. And the Venetians did something that I think was bad.*

*They did not kill everyone. They only killed the women, the ones who were having the babies. They said it would take another generation at least before they started forming their big families again, and by then maybe there would be more food.*

*The Venetians did what they felt like they had to do, and maybe they had to do it, but my friend Luka came back from the Upper Keep covered in blood. Luka thought maybe fifty people died, but I think it was more. His friend who lives in the Upper Keep says it was more.*

*If we don't get more food, it is going to happen again. I
don't know what you do in Fuji to keep your people fed, but
whatever you do, I hope you will help us do it. Please help us.*

*I apologize if my Diplomacy is not perfect. I learned most of
it from Luka's friend.*

*Andrusha*

#

On the path outside the Greenhouse, Ama sat with
Andrusha.

"I did get the first letter," she said. "I remember that one.
How old are you?"

"What?" asked Andrusha.

"You said you were a child," said Ama, the lilting in her
voice playful but accusatory. "You're too old now to have
been a child ten years ago."

"I was thirteen," said Andrusha.

"Do you think someone who is thirteen is a child?"

"There are plenty of children that age, older than that,
even, in the gangs," said Andrusha. "But no, I did not think
of myself as a child. I thought it would make you feel worse
for us if you thought a child was writing."

"You thought the pain of a child would move me more
than a massacre?"

There was no accusation this time, only curiosity.

Andrusha laughed. "Well, there was nothing you could do for the dead. I was still alive. And I was hungry."

"Was that a joke?" Ama asked, still curious.

"No. Yes." He was flustered. "I thought… people feel bad for children. People feel bad about massacres. I didn't know which one would make you feel the need to help."

Ama considered this, tilting her head like Shinobu. "You know," she said, "some people don't even like children. The next time you need help, focus on the massacre. Everyone cares about a massacre."

Andrusha did not correct her.

#

In the Broken Tower of Venice, Borya sat alone on a windowsill. They knew that they did not have to be alone, but compared to Andrusha, everyone else seemed small, tired, and boring. They wondered if Andrusha was sitting alone, too, or if he had better company than Borya. They wondered if Andrusha missed them. Borya did not think that they would mind that. It was nice, to think you were being missed. Less nice to miss someone.

From this height, Borya could not quite see the harbour, but they knew that one of the Fujian ships was still moored there. Borya knew how to sail that ship. If only they could get past the cold stone of fear that formed in their belly whenever they thought about sailing, if only they could breathe through the memory of lungs filling with warm water, they could go wherever they wanted to go. They could sail anywhere in the world.

But what if Andrusha came back and they were gone?

*It's not weak to be afraid of the Flood,* Borya thought to themself.

#

"Can't you do something for the pain?" asked Ibada.

"You think we've done nothing?" Kazuku snapped back.

Yuki raced to Jessica's side, carrying a bundle of cold packs wrapped in linen to protect the girl's skin from the icy compresses. The nurses shoved the material under her armpits, between her legs, on her forehead. But Jessica still moaned, and feebly tried to move the weight of the cold packs off her body. Yuki and Kazuku pushed her hands away and used spare linen to strap the packs against her body.

"Is there anything I can do?" asked Ibada.

"You can stop questioning everything that we're doing," said Kazuku.

Yuki giggled as she wiped sweat from Jessica's neck.

"I feel like I'm taking up space," Ibada complained.

"No one's forcing you to be here," said Kazuku.

Ibada did not argue with her. But he also did not leave.

#

The Station was quiet. The engines should have been growling like distant thunder, the sick-burnt smell of plastic filling the air, but there was not enough plastic to warrant the energy output, so Yana was waiting for the other skimmers and runners to return with their haul before she restarted the processers. Masuna, sitting nearby at the edge of the path, suddenly pulled himself upright with a short cry.

"Did you get nipped?" Yana asked.

When the Station was running, its thrumming vibrated the waters around the building, attracting various sea creatures who seemed to be soothed by the pulsing rhythms. Yana had seen creatures that lived deep below the waves, blood-red squids and anglers with their hanging lights, come up to enjoy sensation. It was a lovely display, a new discovery each time they came back from a haul. But as the shutdowns from lack of fuel increased, the fish used to the vibrations had become agitated. When the Station fell silent, small black fish would nip at anyone unlucky enough to have a hand or foot dangling in the water. If Masuna had been bitten, it was his fault for tempting their ire.

"No, I thought I saw..."

Yana followed his gaze to the surface and glimpsed a large descending shadow that quickly disappeared.

She glanced up at the overcast sky. "Must have been the clouds," she said, and Masuna nodded.

Yana sincerely hoped it was a cloud. She had no idea what something that large could do if it became agitated.

#

*Dear Empress,*

*This is Andrusha again, writing to say thank you.*

*We are so grateful for your generosity. Our lives have been transformed by your Mercy Experiment, as the sailors call it.*

*We learn Diplomacy in groups, what Luka's friend calls "classes". The sailing lessons are also going well. Now that I'm not hungry, I can even enjoy Luka's friend's singing. She's really good. Maybe you'll visit and hear her someday?*

*But I have a small request about the algae blocks. Because we're not so hungry, people have stopped being careful about having children. Last year, I could have told you the names of all the children in Venice. Now, every day seems to bring a new baby into the world, crying and hungry. When they're too old for milk, they'll need algae blocks.*

*We would be grateful for an increase in shipments. If we are receiving the same number of blocks next year, we will start to have the same problems as before.*

*With gratitude,*

*Andrusha*

#

In the Algae Plant, Shinobu tried not to sound like she was whining.

"You can tell that he was trying to manipulate her," she said.

Ama had taken all the letters, but the scribe remembered each one and her fingers itched to lock them away again safely in the Vaults.

"And what were *you* doing, when you kept the letters from Ama?" asked Etsuna.

"Helping her," snapped Shinobu.

Etsuna did not look up from his work, carefully refilling the sōrui-jin's filtration system with juvenile mussels. He should have an assistant. Once, years ago, he suggested inviting children from Venice to work at the Plant. Shinobu denied the request, citing the issues in Les Alpes, how special invitations led to privileged groups and resentful outsiders. It was a good reason, but not the true reason. The children would grow, and stay, and live in Fuji, and cross their lines with Fujians. Soon there would be no true Fujians left in Fuji. Shinobu preferred the idea of no Fujians at all to… imposters? Aliens? Whatever they would be, they would not be Fujian.

"Shouldn't you be helping her now?" asked Etsuna.

But Ama did not want Shinobu's help.

#

In her bedroom in the Coil, Fadhila carefully wrapped up two ebony sculptures of Shetani, the only pieces of Makonde art from Kilimanjaro that she been able to retrieve from the Vaults. She remembered the day the Fujian sailors had begun taking their art, claiming they had better means of preserving it for future generations. To Fadhila, it felt more like a payment extorted in exchange for the "gift" of algae blocks. Fadhila had not travelled with Ibada to ask for the missing shipment of algae blocks, but to steal back what had been taken. Maybe Kilimanjaro did not have the same preservation technology as the Vaults, and a hundred years from now these pieces would fall to dust. But the future generations of Kilimanjarians, including her own son, would never know and love these artworks if they remained on the other side of the world.

Fadhila tucked the parcel in her trunk under a framed photo of her son, Nen. She had not thought that she would be away from him for so long. They had already been here for two weeks, and the journey back would take at least as long. Shinobu had told them that they could leave, that they would get their shipment, but Ibada claimed to be curious about the possibility of the lost Shakespeare plays being recovered. Fadhila thought he was more curious about that sickly actress from Venice.

Fadhila did like Ibada, even when he was lost in one of his fancies. He was often the only one of Fadhila's co-councillors who would approve the more daring reforms in Kilimanjaro. Together, they had adopted a high-rise system not only to increase hydroponic farming production, but to create new habitats for the animal sanctuary, with larger enclosures spreading vertically instead of building past the mountain and over the tumultuous Flood. But now, Ibada's romantic dreams were keeping her from returning to her family.

Fadhila was not worried about being caught for her *theft*. Shinobu was the only one who would notice the missing sculptures, and she was more interested in trailing forlornly after Ama than keeping track of her treasures. But she was worried about Nen. Her husband insisted the boy was just good-natured, but Fadhila did not think his sudden bouts of hysterical laughter had anything to do with his nature.

She wanted to go home.

"This Shakespeare better be worth it," Fadhila told her empty room.

#

*Dear Empress,*

*It has been a few years since my last letter, and I worry that you may have forgotten about us.*

*Yes, we are still receiving the algae blocks, but it looks like you ignored the warning of my last letter and we have begun suffering the consequences.*

*There are too many children and not enough food.*

*By the time the children can walk, or crawl, they are left on their own. Some grow cruel. Some are becoming inhuman. Feral. Frustration grows between those who choose to be careful to ensure couplings will not result in children, and those who do not see the point in being careful when the future looks impossibly bleak. They have lost hope.*

*But there is an easy solution: send more algae blocks. Any increase could offer these children the hope of a future that you once offered to me.*

*I trust you will rediscover the mercy that inspired you before,*

*Andrusha*

#

Sofia sat in the Alpine boat moored in the Greenhouse canal. She had a private room in the Coil, but she always felt watched, if not by Dario, then by whoever he had paid to keep an eye on her. It was better to lock herself into her small room on their boat, the curtains fully shut, with only the soft green light to illuminate her skin.

She held her switchblade, given to her by Dario when she had first been welcomed within the walls of Les Alpes. A strange gift for his new ward. Sofia cut a third red line parallel to the first two she had made on her thigh. She would wait until the bleeding stopped before she went back inside. No one would see the scars under her dress.

It was the fault of those Kilimanjarian girls, the way they laughed in the Coil. They reminded Sofia of her sisters, and she did not want to think about her sisters. She would hear their laughter and then it was like her body was far away from her.

When she cut into her leg, she knew exactly where her body was.

She told herself there was no reason to feel bad, to feel anything. Her sisters were not even suffering anymore. They were dead.

#

The scratch of Makoto's pen stopped, and the Vaults settled into silence.

"It's okay if you forget the rest of the plot," Makoto said to Luka. He was anxious to know if the love potions would wear off, if the faerie king and queen would be reconciled, if the play that the silly actors were trying to put on would go well. But he could sense that something had shifted in Luka.

"Why are we even doing this?" asked the Venetian. "Shouldn't we wait for Shinobu? Or Shinku?"

"What can they do that I cannot?" Makoto said. He saw Luka's eyes flick back and forth as he struggled to put his feelings into words. But the Venetian could not come up with an answer. Instead, he continued to outline a story that did not quite make sense, but that he promised would make more sense if Jessica woke up to tell it the right way.

*Dear Empress,*

*Perhaps you have forgotten about us, but we have not forgotten about you.*

*The population still grows, and we are as likely to see children merely a few years old crawling through the sludge of the algae blooms as we are to see them held in their parents' arms.*

*I almost did not send this letter, because I saw the eyes of my fellow Venetians light up as I borrowed the paper from one of your sailors. I heard the excited whispers as I set my words in ink. The Venetians still hope because you told them help is possible. You told them that they can expect help when you sent those first algae blocks. And we still love, and couple, and hold our children while they are small enough to stay in our arms, because a part of us believes that you will help us again.*

*You may not have been responsible for our suffering when you first reached out with your mercy, but you are responsible for us now.*

*The word "empress" was an empty title when I learned it from your sailors, but I have since come to understand that you were born into a position of power, seen as a leader since your infancy, and treated with a respect that you never fought to earn. There is the assumption that you have power, and though none of the sailors can tell me what that power is or where it comes from, they seem to have complete belief in your superiority. Perhaps your position makes you callous towards our suffering. Perhaps my presumption to continue to write you is seen as an insult more than a plea.*

*But I want you to know that I am pleading. It will only get worse. And as time continues, I know that we will stop seeing you as someone to thank and start seeing you as someone to blame.*

*With the upmost respect,*

*Andrusha*

#

"Did you partake in the massacre?" asked Ama.

She was sailing her wind-board in little figure eights close to the path outside the Greenhouse.

"No," said Andrusha. "Not really."

"Not really?"

"I saw it happen," he said. "From the ramparts. They're high up on K2, some distance from the Upper Keep. Why are you asking? I thought we were trying to figure out how much of an increase in shipments would—"

"So you did participate," said Ama, bringing her sail to a wavering stillness.

"I only watched," said Andrusha.

"That counts," said Ama.

A muscle ticked in Andrusha's jaw. Ama wondered if he was going to yell at her. No one had ever done that before. She was disappointed when he spoke: his voice was calm and level.

"You weren't there," he said.

"No. I wasn't. But you were." She continued to spin her sail languidly. "By the way, I am very powerful. You weren't sure in your letters. But I am. I could save you all right now if I wanted to. Before I finish this turn."

"Do you want to?"

Ama smiled as she finished her turn, and the world stayed exactly the same.

#

Mizutsuki sprayed the leaves inside the Greenhouse. Etsuna had promised that the hormone stimulated growth, but the vines were still fading from deep green to soft yellow. If she concentrated the spray, they recovered, but only for a few days.

Mizutsuki dreaded having to tell Shinobu that the blackouts were only going to get worse. The scribe would consider it some fault in Mizutsuki's work performance, but the truth was the degeneration of the plants was out of

Mizutsuki's control. Maybe if there were more Fujians to work in the Greenhouse who could spray constantly, more plants would survive. As it was, Mizutsuki was glad that there was always more plastic in the ocean to feed the Station, because the Greenhouse would probably stop producing energy within a few months.

#

Ibada and Sofia sat at the edge of the balcony outside the hospital ward, smoking in silence. Every so often, the girl from Les Alpes blew smoke rings that dissipated in the breeze, while the man from Kilimanjaro scowled as he burned through cigarette after cigarette. Kazuku had sent him away, demanding fifteen minutes of peace without his eyes watching her every move around Jessica. Five more minutes to go.

Sofia blew a string of six rings, the most she had managed so far, and gave a satisfied smile. Ibada thought of Fadhila, back in Kilimanjaro, smacking a cigarette out of Nen's hand.

"Are you old enough to be smoking?" he asked Sofia.

"We live in the Flood, Ibada," said Sofia. "I'm allowed to have a fucking cigarette."

They spent the next five minutes in silence.

#

*Dear Empress,*

*I don't know why I'm writing again, as it is clear that you have abandoned us.*

*We are all going to die because of you. We would not have had so many children if you had not given us hope. Why would you give us hope, to take it away again? I wonder if this was your "experiment" all along. It was never an experiment in mercy. It was an experiment in the effects of limited hope. Of revoked hope.*

*I wish I had never sent that letter. I wish you had never responded. But both of us have to live with the consequences of our actions. And soon, you will have to live with the consequences of your inaction.*

*Andrusha*

#

"That last one almost sounds like a threat," said Ama as she lay on her bed. The letters were strewn about the floor, ignored as she watched cartoons on her small monitor. Shinobu fought the urge to pick up the pages as she stood in the doorway. "It would have been nice to know I was getting threatening letters. I could have prepared for this intrusion."

"I was trying to protect you."

"And now Fuji is overrun with foreigners," said Ama. "I've never felt less protected in my life."

"Then send them away," said Shinobu. "You don't owe them anything."

"And the Shakespeare plays?"

Shinobu buried the curiosity that tightened her chest. The Shakespeare plays. The past come to their shore, unexpected, whole, and alive again.

"Not as important as your safety," she replied.

"The foreigners aren't the ones who make me feel unsafe, Shinobu," said Ama.

The empress's attention never wavered from the animated witch and her black cat sidekick on the screen. Ama dressed like an adult now, but still indulged in childish behaviour. Shinobu wanted Ama to be safe, but she could not protect the empress if she welcomed danger.

Shinobu began to pick up the letters from the floor.

"I'm not done with those!" Ama snapped.

Shinobu dropped the pages and left.

#

On the balcony of the Upper Keep, Chava looked down at the Feral as they paced around on their hands and feet. If she closed her eyes, their whines took on a soothing quality. Her own hissing had started a few months ago. At some point, soon, she would no longer be able to help the children who were going Feral to find their kind. She would be one of those wild children, too. She knew it would be better for her father if she went down now, before she was as mindless as the rest of them. She also knew that she would stay in the Upper Keep until her father had no choice but to send her away.

She would at least wait until after Cem had fully changed. He had been slipping for a while now. He was bound to go Feral soon.

#

Jessica was underwater. She knew she should panic, but she was too surprised to do more than look around. She had never seen the world beneath the Flood, and it was proving disappointingly empty, mostly blue around her, mostly black beneath, and an unsettling neon green above. That was probably the surface, but Jessica did not know how to propel her body upwards. She looked into the blue again and was surprised to see that she was not alone. A figure was floating in the water.

It was a mermaid. That much was clear, though it bore only the slightest resemblance to the mermaid in the sailor's illustration. This mermaid was not beautiful. Jessica immediately felt bad for judging the creature. She should be grateful for the chance to see a mermaid. Her father had said they did not exist, and a part of Jessica knew that this mermaid too did not really exist, that she was dreaming, but it was nice to imagine it might be real.

The mermaid beckoned and began to swim away. Jessica wanted to tell it that she did not know how to swim, but her body moved forward of its own accord. She floated after the creature, as if there was an invisible string tying her to its twisted form. She felt no desire to fight its pull.

More creatures began to swim around her in the blue water. She recognized the sock-like fish that had attached itself to Luka's leg on the journey to Fuji, although this one was much larger, and had no interest in attaching itself to Jessica. She saw some eels, but they paid no attention to her. They were wriggling down towards the darkness, and when Jessica too looked down, she saw a large creature, much larger than any of the fish that swam with her. It frightened her, so she stopped looking, though she knew it still swam beneath her, attracting hungry eels and scaring everything else. At one point, the light above her became less harsh, and she looked up to see a vast sting-wave riding the surface, its tentacles drifting lazily down to her. She worried that the painful strands might graze her skin, but the mermaid pulled her down, deeper into the waters.

An object was growing in front of them. All her worries fell away when she recognized it. The Dark Tower. She did not understand how it had ended up under the waves, but she supposed entire cities had been lost beneath the waves.

The mermaid led her through one of the windows into the tower. Once they were inside, the mermaid turned around. Jessica fought the urge to look away from its face. She waited for a sign, any sort of communication, but the mermaid only stared. Finally, Jessica could not bear it any longer. She let her eyes drift upwards.

Someone was standing above the Flood. Their face was terribly distorted, twisted in a way that made Jessica's stomach turn, but it seemed to be a woman. Or, at least, *used* to be a woman: there was something inhuman about the way she was floating, so high above, staring down at her, making Jessica feel small and unimportant and disposable.

It must have been a ghost.

Jessica gasped. The ghost reached one hand down into the waves, and the water itself began to scream. Jessica could do nothing, even if she had known what the ghost wanted. Her gasp had filled her lungs with water.

She thrashed about, clawing at her throat. She tried to beg the mermaid to help her, but only bubbles came from her lips. She groped at her neck for something – but she could not work out what she was supposed to find, and she did not have time...

#

Jessica woke up.

# ACT 2

# A GOOD DEED IN A NAUGHTY WORLD

That light we see is burning in my hall.
How far that little candle throws his beams!
So shines a good deed in a naughty world.

~ *The Merchant of Venice,* Act 5, Scene 1

# Chapter 14 (Jessica)

Jessica thrashed out of her bed, heartbeat thundering, in an unfamiliar room. She stood up, and layers of blankets fell off her and onto the floor. Looking down, she saw that she was wearing a white dress that draped around her body, but threatened to open in the front where a bow was coming undone. She felt naked. Her hands figured out the cause, flitting to her neck to worry at a pendant that was not there. A flash of light from the small bedside table caught her eye: the necklace was there, its chain curled in a delicate pile. Jessica snatched it up and fastened it in place around her neck. She passed the star back and forth along its chain, warming it with her fingertips.

She had no idea where she was, but the clean cream-coloured walls and ceiling looked as neat and precise as the hospital ward. She had no memory of being moved from there. Trying to picture the nurses' faces made her head hurt. She made for the door, knowing she should try to figure out what had happened and where she was, but a portrait on the wall stopped her in her path. The woman in the frame looked exactly like her mother. It took Jessica a moment to realize that it was not art, but the clearest mirror she had ever seen.

Jessica was not pleased with her reflection. She tried to smooth down her curls, but they sprang up the second she removed her hands. She frowned, and the pointed features sharpened further as thick dark red eyebrows knitted together. Most of her face was covered with great splotches of freckles. She was struck with a fear that her entire body had been covered with freckles, but when she pulled the top of her dress open, her neck and chest only showed a splattering of dots. Her arms showed a lighter scatter of freckles that grew thicker the more she pushed her sleeve up, revealing a shoulder that was nearly as splotched as her face.

Jessica gasped and lifted her arms high above her. Her underarms were hairless, smooth. She lifted the hem of her dress and saw that her legs were equally hairless. Someone had removed her hair in her fevered sleep. Jessica crossed her arms in front of her chest, feeling embarrassed and violated. Removing her hair was like… removing her necklace. She shivered and pulled her dress tighter around her. It was cold in this room. She did not like it. She tried to push the door open, but it remained stubbornly shut. Was she being imprisoned?

"*To lie in cold obstruction and to rot,*" Jessica muttered as she tried not to think of prison cells.

There was a small square panel set into the door, shiny and smooth, like the one next to the lift. Jessica touched the square and the door slid open with a soft hiss.

*Magic.* This was a place of magic.

Jessica peered out. To her left and right, a long corridor curved round, dotted in an alternating pattern of round windows and square works of art.

"Are you lost?"

A woman was standing at the far end of the hall. Jessica did not understand how the woman could be so far away and yet her question sounded like it had been spoken behind Jessica's shoulder. She approached far more quickly than Jessica anticipated, her steps silent as she glided up the floor. There was something familiar about her, but Jessica could not quite place her. Her black hair was cut short above her chin and in a straight line across her forehead, as severe as her perfect posture and suspicious gaze.

"I'm not sure where I am," said Jessica.

"You're in the Coil," said the woman. The perfect name for a building wrapped around a mountain. "Where are you trying to go?"

Jessica was too embarrassed to admit that she had no idea. "I'm looking for a friend," she said. "Could you help me find him?"

"The one who sat with you while you were sick?"

That must be Luka. Jessica was touched that he had been worried enough to watch over her. It was very like Luka to act distant when the weather was fine but to rush in when the storms struck.

"Does Kazuku know you left your room?" the woman asked before Jessica could reply. "Should you be walking around yet?"

"It's fine," said Jessica. "I'd just like to see my friend, please."

"Jess!"

Luka emerged from a different sliding door. He ran to her, wrapped her in his arms, and swung her in a large circle.

"Do you still want help?" the woman asked, unamused.

"No, we're fine now," said Jessica as Luka set her down again. "Thank you, though."

"Are you feeling better, Shinku?" asked Luka.

The woman nodded without answering and continued up the tilting floor before she disappeared around another odd corner.

"Was she sick too?" Jessica asked.

"She was pregnant," said Luka. "You don't remember?"

*Yes, of course...* Jessica remembered now: Shinku, lying on the bed, screaming about... *Hirokai.* Hirokai, who had fallen into the water after Jessica pushed him, too surprised to defend himself. Shinku had been screaming about Hirokai, and then... a mermaid? Jessica swallowed down queasy confusion.

"I was pretty sick, wasn't I?" she asked, wiping her sweating palms on her robe.

"Yeah, you were pretty sick," said Luka. "I'm so happy you're awake."

"Were you worried?" Jessica asked, pleased.

"Of course, I was worried," Luka said. "You looked like you were going to die. But now you're here. And standing. And you look so good!"

"You look good, too."

Luka wore a yellow front-tied robe too, but his only came to his knees, while the matching wide trousers he wore beneath flared down towards his feet. His hair had been cut shorter on the sides, but was still long on the top, and brushed back off his forehead. Jessica had never seen this much of his face before in such clear light; clean brown skin, glossy black eyes, and full lips that were now parted in an unabashed grin. And his teeth…

Looking at his startling white teeth made Jessica realize that her teeth did not hurt. Her scalp was not itchy, and her feet were not sore. It was like they had been reborn, transformed from decaying adults into blossoming children.

Jessica snorted a laugh.

"What?" asked Luka.

She held up her arm, letting her wide sleeve fall down to her shoulder, exposing her smooth underarms. Luka reached out the back of his hand, stroking down the smooth skin. Jessica shrieked at the tickling sensation and pulled away.

"Why would they even do that?" Luka laughed.

"Some kind of punishment?" Jessica suggested with a grin. "When I woke up, I thought that room was a prison cell."

Luka's laughter stopped abruptly, and Jessica's heart dropped.

"They know," Jessica said, and Luka nodded. "How much do they know?"

"They know about the riot," he said. "They know the sailors are dead."

"And?"

"What else is there to know?"

Jessica shrugged and hoped she did not look too relieved.

"Oh," said Luka. "They also didn't know about the letters!"

"They never got them?" asked Jessica.

"It's complicated," he said, with a shrug. "I don't really understand what happened, but the empress was livid."

"Are they going to send Venice more food?" Jessica asked.

Luka began to shake his head, then stopped himself. "Not yet."

"What can we do to *convince* them?" she said in frustration. "People are going to die."

Luka was smiling again. Jessica did not know whether to scowl at him or slap him.

"There's nothing Andrusha and I can do," he said. "But maybe *you* can convince the empress."

"And what, exactly, can *I* do about it?"

"Now that you're awake, I know that she would love to hear you perform one of your Shakespeare speeches. Or songs. Or plays. Any of them. All of them."

The *plays*? Jessica stared at Luka, waiting for him to tell her he was joking, but he did not. Talia did say that the plays were famous before the Flood. Jessica had always thought that she was exaggerating to try to engage the other children, who did not enjoy memorizing as much as she did.

"The plays are important?" she asked.

"Important enough that they haven't sent us away, or killed us, because the empress wants to hear you perform."

So, yes, very important. Jessica's palms began to sweat again.

"Well," she said. "I guess we shouldn't keep the empress waiting."

Jessica stood on a platform of pushed-together desks in a makeshift office-turned-auditorium. Faced with the rows of chairs and many expectant eyes, she could not think of a single line from Shakespeare's plays. She looked for an encouraging face, or something that would inspire her, but the spectacle of her viewers kept her jaw clamped shut.

In the seat of honour, Ama fidgeted. She wore a deep green gown layered with triangular skirts stiff as the petrified petals on the Kilimanjarian ship. Jessica had no idea how the material allowed the empress to bend and sit. Shinobu, standing over Ama's shoulder, was more at ease with the pomp and display. She seemed to Jessica like a shadow all in black from her high collar to her straight floor-length hem. Luka had laughed when Jessica admitted that she had thought Shinobu was the empress, but Jessica thought that Shinobu looked more regal than Ama. Though something in the scribe's face unsettled her. An indistinct warning, like a memory from a dream.

Jessica's eyes darted to the scattered watching figures, so pale, with their silver-white and faint-gold hair, and their off-putting pinkish clothes. She looked away. It was easier to keep her attention on the small group from Kilimanjaro sitting at the front. Their phiran-like gowns, which Luka said were called *dashiki* and *iro*, were a mix of bright gold, vibrant blue, and lush purple, and some of the women wrapped their hair up in matching fabric. Luka himself sat at the back of the room, apparently bored, staring out the windows. But Ibada was at the front, right in the centre, looking at her like he had been watching her for years and could watch her for many years to come. It was not much, but all she needed was one friendly face.

Jessica rolled back her shoulders, took a deep breath, and was filled once more with the words of the Bard.

*"The quality of mercy is not strained..."*

She saw the audience, she saw the platform, but she also saw Venice. Not her own K2, though the ramparts and Upper Keep formed the base shape of her imagination, but a magical world of lovers' plots and thwarted vengeance. She let the scene be and focused on the words, the highs and lows of her breath, the sharpness of consonants and the expanse of vowels. And as the words transformed her mouth into an instrument, her heart was pulled along with the rhythm, and the speech became her own. She transformed into something more than herself.

She was used to the Venetians losing interest, especially during a dramatic monologue that did not involve tears or wars and death. But this audience listened, quiet, captivated. The frame of K2 was replaced in her mind with the arching bridges and great monolith buildings of Fuji. As she spoke the final words, Jessica realized how easy it was to forget her home. Abruptly, the euphoria of performing was dampened by a sickening twist of guilt. When was the last time she had thought of her father?

Before she had time to worry, a thunderous applause began, started by Ibada, but the rest of the room quickly joined in. Dario smiled as he clapped, and for a moment his face seemed open, genuine, not nearly as frightening as the silver glint in his eyes suggested. Even Luka smiled: he had no choice but to be proud of her when she performed. She hopped down from the stage, nearly tripping on her gown. Her stumble was caught by one of the women from Kilimanjaro, whose headwrap added to her already substantial height. Usually Jessica felt intimidated when confronted with her smallness, but she still felt large, filled with the Bard's words. She nodded her thanks.

"You can't be done already," Ibada protested, placing a hand on Jessica's shoulder. "Encore!"

She had never heard that word before, but she knew it must mean *more*, from the way he said it with such enthusiasm. Or else it was the heat, pressed through the fabric that separated his palm from her skin, that said *more,* wanted more. Jessica shuddered, happy and confused, searching her mind for a comparable monologue. She was saved when Ama stood up, and the Fujians around her stood too, bowing slightly while they backed away. Ibada removed his hand, and her shoulder felt cold without its presence.

"Beautiful words," said Ama, struggling under the weight of her gown as she approached Jessica. "Spoken beautifully."

"Thank you, empress," said Jessica, bowing in an inexact copy of the Fujians' show of respect.

"Ama, remember?" the empress said. "No need to be formal."

It was hard to imagine their conversation as anything but formal when the other people in the room had formed a loose circle around them.

"I'm looking forward to hearing the whole play," Ama continued. "Such a powerful woman with a great command of language is sure to defeat whatever her foes throw at her. It could be instructional."

"I wouldn't say Portia has many foes," said Jessica.

Ama nodded but frowned.

"Would you be willing to recite for our scribes?" asked Shinobu. She had quietly followed the empress, her persistent shadow. "It is important to record the verses."

"The words weren't meant to be written and stored away," Ibada interrupted. "They're meant to be performed and enjoyed."

"They can't be performed if they are forgotten," said Shinobu.

"I'd be happy to recite for you," said Jessica. "Though it may take some time."

"You're welcome to stay for as long as you like," said Ama.

The empress was distracted, and the words could have been rote, but they still made Jessica want to cry. The empress said she could *stay*… Outside the circle, Jessica saw Luka in whispered conversation with Dario and Andrusha. His eyes were fixed on her, and his expression was cold.

"Thank you," said Jessica, bowing again.

"What did you mean, that Portia doesn't have foes?" asked Ama.

"If you want foes, you need stories of battles," said Jessica.

"Julius Caesar!" said Ibada, and Jessica nodded, surprised. "Stories with kings and armies."

"You know them?" asked Jessica.

"We all know them," said Ibada.

"We know *about* them," corrected the tall woman, approaching Ibada's side. "We don't know the exact words. And the words matter. They lend truth to rumours."

"Fadhila is mad because she didn't want your speech to be good," laughed Ibada.

Fadhila lightly smoothed the fabric of her headwrap with her fingertips, her jaw clenched, and did not respond. Jessica assumed that this meant Ibada was right.

"I'm not quite as prepared to accept your words as *truth*," Shinobu said to Jessica. "But Luka said there may be others in Venice who could confirm the accuracy of your verses. In the Upper Keep?"

Luka separated himself from Dario and Andrusha and came to stand next to her. Jessica's stomach flipped; not at his approach, but at the way all three men looked so smug, so secretive. When men's faces flickered with secrets on the Main, Venetians knew to run.

"There are others who know the words," said Luka. "But no one performs them like Jessica."

"No one performs them as well?" asked Shinobu. "Or at all?"

"No one performs them at all," Luka said, a smile brightening his dark eyes. "But probably because they knew they could never perform them as well as Jessica."

"But if Portia doesn't have any foes, who is the *Jew*?" asked Ama.

Jessica flinched. Abraham's words whispered in her ears: *Every place has its own problems, looking for someone convenient to blame. If you go to other worlds, they'll know they can blame you. They won't stop and wonder if you're Jewish enough. Once they realize hating Jews is an option, they'll hate you.*

She gripped her necklace, hiding the pendant in her palm. Only Shinobu seemed to notice her sudden change in mood. Jessica turned to Luka for help, but he had taken hold of Ibada's arm and was already guiding him towards the back of the room.

"If I can borrow you for a moment," he was saying, "Dario would like to have a chat."

Jessica rolled her shoulders back. *Encore.*

"Shylock is the scapegoat," she said to Ama.

"Shylock?" asked Shinobu.

"Scapegoat?" asked Ama.

"He's being blamed for things outside of his control," said Jessica. "He's being punished for who he is, not what he has done."

"But he has done something very bad," said Shinobu. "He's trying to kill the merchant for his debt. I've read about this work. I know what a *Shylock* means."

Yes, Shinobu was correct, but the most accurate interpretation seemed dangerous when Ama was already stumbling on the word *Jew*. Jessica had a sudden image of a face above the Flood, watching her drown.

"He's a pawn in a game Portia has begun to play with his life," Jessica insisted. "A tragic figure."

Ama still looked confused. Shinobu did not.

"Portia is the hero," the scribe said. "And this is a comedy."

"Maybe it's not so well written after all," Fadhila suggested.

"You can't get the whole plot from one monologue," said Jessica, and Fadhila nodded, reluctant. "And Portia is the hero. That's why it's extra tragic that she is going to these lengths to punish Shylock, when he's the one who has been cheated."

It had always seemed that way to Jessica, so it was basically the truth, she told herself. And they were only words – the Bard's words, yes, but now they were hers, and she could use them as she pleased. No matter how justified Shinobu's mistrust was. It could hurt a lot of people if Ama cast Shylock as Portia's foe and hurt Jessica in particular. Ama did not know that Jessica was Jewish, but so far away from the Upper Keep, she did not feel so "half."

*They won't stop and wonder if you're Jewish enough...*

"But it's a comedy," Shinobu insisted.

"Maybe we should trust the woman who knows the whole story," said Ama.

"You're lying," Shinobu said to Jessica. "Why?"

Jessica was not quite lying. Except about Portia's speech being tragic, and Shylock being blameless. Except about the original point of the play.

"Do you have the full text of *The Merchant of Venice* hidden in the Vaults?" asked Ama. "No? Then wait until you do before you call her a liar. You don't know everything, Shinobu."

Fadhila had slipped away, clearly uncomfortable, while the women argued. Jessica wished she could do the same. She looked over her shoulder, but Luka was gone, as well as Andrusha, Ibada, and Dario.

"It's a comedy," said Shinobu. "She's describing it like a tragedy. Portia's a hero, synonymous with intelligence. She's not making any sense."

"If you don't understand, that's your failing, not hers," snapped Ama. "*Ai*, Shinobu, sometimes I wonder if you actually are a Dreamer!"

It was like Shinobu had been slapped. She turned on her heel and glided towards the door in a breeze of black fabric. A few of the Fujians were suppressing chuckles, and Jessica did not know what was so funny. She wanted to apologize to Shinobu, but it seemed now even more important for *Merchant* to be a tragedy, because she was sure the empress had just given Shinobu an excuse to cast Jessica as the villain. Then, suddenly, Jessica's hands were caught up in Ama's grasp, and she found herself being tugged with surprising force towards the door.

"Come on, Makoto," called the empress, abruptly cheerful. The Fujian with the wide face jogged towards them. "We must talk, and Makoto must record."

Jessica could not follow the sudden movement of Ama's moods, and she thought of the kings and queens in the plays, the dangers of Hal's whims, Lear's insanity, Lady Macbeth's ambition. Her necklace poked into her chest. She did not have a free hand to adjust it, and she thought it might be best not to draw attention to the star, even though she was sure Ama would not know what it meant.

"What do you want to know?" asked Jessica.

Ama laughed and tossed her arm over Jessica's shoulder.

"Absolutely everything," she said.

## Chapter 15 (Shinobu)

Shinobu's hands cramped. She formed fists and then flexed her fingers as the thick muscle of her palm twisted under her skin. She had switched from writing with her right hand to her left when she felt those initial knots beginning to form, but it was too late to prevent the pain. She had left Makoto with Ama and Jessica and followed two arching bridges from the Vaults to the Observatory to escape the endless copying.

The Observatory was walled with glass, broken only by cream-coloured support beams in each corner. Even the ceiling was glass, for observing the stars as one reclined on the pastel ottomans scattered in planned disarray around the room. A large hole cut in a perfect circle in the centre of the ceiling allowed a great ginkgo tree growing in the middle of the room to rise out into the open air. Legend said the tree had been transplanted before the Flood, but Shinobu did not believe this was the same ginkgo as that historical wonder. The authenticity did not really matter, but *knowing* whether or not it was the same ginkgo did. It irked her that she could never be sure.

Shinobu looked up, ignoring the complaints of the muscles hunched too long over a desk. The sky was a solid sheet of dark grey clouds. From this distance, the Vaults looked equally dark and secretive. She could not help but imagine the small crowd still gathered around Jessica in Shinobu's temple.

> "But all my foes will cease to be
> As all my friends will cease to be
> And I will also cease to be
> And likewise, everything will cease to be."

Shinobu whispered the verse to herself: not one of Shakespeare's, but Shantideva's Bodhisattvacaryāvatāra. She tried to relax into the meditation, but her body and mind refused to be soothed. Her fingers trembled, and no matter how hard she squeezed and flexed, she could not control the tremors that made her black silk sleeves flutter.

"Your hands wouldn't cramp so much if you just used a computer."

Only a slight, short increase of Shinobu's trembling sleeves revealed her surprise at hearing another voice in the room. She turned her head to see Sofia sitting cross-legged on a pale pink ottoman that clashed horribly with the peach tones of her leggings and loose jumper. Sofia rested against the window behind her, and though there was no chance of the glass breaking, Shinobu did not think she would look as casual as the Alpine girl if she were the one leaning against that great height.

"We'd have to make written copies anyway, in case there was another crash," said Shinobu. "Though I'm sure Les Alpes would prefer if we uploaded everything."

"It's a shame you hoard the art you've gathered for yourselves," said Sofia, channelling some of Dario's sneer. "It would be easier for us to see the treasures of your Vaults if you uploaded copies to our database."

"Oh, yes, I'm sure you would love to have copies of our *treasures*," said Shinobu, ticking a list off her no-longer trembling fingers. "Our treasures, our conversations, our secrets…"

All internet activity in Les Alpes was carefully monitored. It still shocked Shinobu that the people of High Rock Ridge did not care who read the personal details they shared constantly over social media, or that the Kilimanjarians thought regulations would offer anything more than the illusion of protection.

"I don't care about your secrets," said Sofia, the sincerity of her boredom impossible to deny. "But Dario will probably want me to type up copies."

"No one will stop you," said Shinobu. "Shakespeare's plays are Jessica's, not mine."

*Venice's*, not *Fuji's*. That was what she should have said, but Sofia did not seem to notice. The girl leaned forward suddenly, hugging her knees.

"Hey, don't tell Dario I'm here, okay?" she said, blond hair nearly obscuring her heart-shaped face. "I'm supposed to be listening to Jessica, taking notes or whatever. But…

Well, she was in the middle of *King John*, and the plays can get so long."

"She's still on *King John*," Shinobu said, nodding. "So many words for such convoluted stories." She felt a leap of panic in her throat, mirrored in Sofia's wide eyes as the girl brought her head up.

"But it is art, of course," said Sofia, voice high.

"Oh, yes," agreed Shinobu. "Beautiful."

"The imagery, it's like… visual poetry."

"And the rhythms are…" Shinobu struggled to remember the long word that described the monotonous rhythm that droned through Shakespeare's pieces in verse. "You know… poetry."

"I get tired, with all those words," said Sofia. Curled in on herself, she looked very young. "But Dario wouldn't understand. He likes the plays. A lot. I can't have him mad at me."

Sometimes the representatives from Les Alpes blended together in Shinobu's mind, a mass of pinkish white, accented with flecks of silver. It took effort to look for the small, rare distinctions, the differences that marked the girl who sat at the other end of the room: the hair that was truly yellow instead of white-blond, the eyes that were blue without being silver-blue or white-blue, the skin tinted enough to suggest it could tan if Sofia did not make an effort to cover up and stay pale.

"How long have you lived within the walls now?" asked Shinobu. She tilted her head and gave the girl her most genuine smile. Sofia softened under the innocent display.

"Five years," said Sofia.

"So young to be invited in," Shinobu said. "How very brave."

"Yes," said Sofia, relieved to share, to trust someone. "I was ten. A child. It was like entering a fairy tale."

Shinobu did not fill the silence that followed. Sofia would, when she was ready.

Shinobu could only imagine what it would be like to walk into a world of castles and gardens and underground bunkers all protected by the thick, tall walls of Les Alpes. To be welcomed as a member of the privileged upper class who thrived within the walls, watching films, making art, improving technology that let them float impossibly high in the air or dig through rock, or transport information from touch screens to remote locations. To actually see the other technologies that they kept secret in their Vaults, weapons that could destroy the world one thousand times over, much more irreparably than the Flood. It must have been magical to suddenly become one of those happy people within the thick walls, instead of one of the many less fortunate who lived outside.

People had flocked to the high ground of Les Alpes around the same time others had flocked to Everest and K2. Those who found themselves locked out from that safety and beauty by walls did what they could to survive. The immigrants did not realize how dangerous it was for them to be there, outside the walls, when the community inside realized that they had not prepared for centuries of isolation, and a hunger that outlasted any reserves kept in the vaults. The outsiders did not realize that, for people used to having anything they wanted at the touch of their fingertips, every problem had an easy solution. They did not think how tempting their growing masses – still pounding on the walls to be let in, crowding around the hope of gardens and palaces – would be to an isolated population with no access to mussels or eels or algae blocks, protected from the dangers of the world as well as what was left of its bounty. Like ripe fruit, ready to be plucked.

"I didn't go alone," said Sofia, eventually. "I went to the gates with my family."

"Your mother and father?"

"No. Sisters. Three of us."

"Three golden-haired beauties at the gate," said Shinobu.

"No," said Sofia. "They had brown hair."

By the time the gates opened, the uniform white, pale blond populace inside barely resembled the motley assemblage that existed outside. It would have been easy for them to think that those who lived outside were not like them at all; a little less human, perhaps, and a little more like animals. The crowds outside the walls did not realize that the gates that opened for groups of them, first small and then more and more, were ushering them towards a slaughter. They did not understand until those who lived within the walls replaced their disintegrating clothes with the pelts kept after the feasts were done. The population outside would have run from the sight of those pinkish cloaks, tunics, boots. But sometimes the walls opened to a special few, deemed smart enough, beautiful enough, pale and blond enough, like the lovely Sofia, to be welcomed in, to eat instead of being eaten. And the hope of that better world, inside, kept them complacent outside, waiting for their turn, at the table or on it.

"I guess you're lucky to be pretty," said Shinobu, her voice measured, not bitter.

Sofia laughed, the cruel sound of someone who had survived and would always survive, whatever the cost.

"Oh, my sisters were *very* pretty too," she said. "They had very pretty skin!"

Shinobu did not shudder. She did not tremble. Her sleeves were still.

Those individuals who were not quite pale enough, like Sofia's sisters, kept the rulers like Dario both full and fashionable. When Ama introduced the algae blocks, that kind of farming became unnecessary, but Dario said it was culturally important. What he meant was that it was a better protection from the desperate masses than the thick walls.

As long as people saw that pink-white fabric, they knew they should be afraid.

Shinobu was not afraid of the pink-white fabric. But she decided it would be preferable to listen to Jessica than hear someone laugh about how their sisters died.

"Take as much time here as you need," said Shinobu, smoothing her trousers as she stood. "I won't tell Dario."

"Wait," said Sofia. Shinobu paused, and stared, not tilting her head. Sofia's eyes flashed, unsettled. "Have you spoken to Dario? I mean… has Dario spoken to you?"

"You've seen us speaking," said Shinobu. "You are usually there."

"I mean, about the sōrui-jin," said Sofia.

"What about them?"

Sofia bit her lip. A habit, thought Shinobu, given how chapped the girl's lips were. "He might ask you to see them," said Sofia. Shinobu watched silently as she struggled with how much she wanted to share. "He might ask you how they work. He said… he thinks it looks easy. Easy enough for us to imitate."

Shinobu was under orders from Ama, orders she happily obeyed, not to reveal the secrets of how the sōrui-jin worked. Everyone in Fuji knew that the empress was special, but those engines were proof to the outside world. But there were other reasons for secrecy, valid beyond Ama's desire for control.

"It's hardly easy," said Shinobu. "The mechanisms are quite delicate, and it takes very little to overwork the machines. The population outside your wall would exhaust them to disrepair within days. Besides, the sōrui-jin are only designed to process local vegetation. Who knows if it would even work with the algae in Les Alpes? And if anything went wrong with the filtration system—"

"Don't tell him any of that," said Sofia quickly. "Don't tell him how to make it go wrong."

"What do you mean?"

"He says he wants to know how they work, but I think he really wants to know the opposite. Ama uses them to help people, but if the blocks could hurt people instead… I don't think Dario is curious because he wants to help."

Shinobu nodded, slowly, at the girl who had once lived outside the walls.

"I won't tell him anything," she said.

Sofia sighed and released her chewed lip. She leaned back against the glass, relaxing into the perfect image of careless disdain.

"I came here to rest," she said. "That's all."

"Of course," said Shinobu. "I should return to recording Venice's one contribution to the art world."

A flicker of confusion briefly coloured Sofia's face.

"What about the mosaics?" she asked.

"The what?"

"The coloured tiles," said Sofia. "Andrusha mentioned how the sailors used to take samples for the Vaults. Like the Kanakaria mosaics?"

Shinobu knew about the coloured tiles. She did not think they were much to look at. Most of the samples were fed as fuel to the Station. But something with a name like *the Kanakaria mosaics* sounded very important. Something very important, that she had destroyed.

*And likewise, everything will cease to be…*

"I should go back to the Vaults," said Shinobu. "So many words."

"All that poetry," Sofia agreed.

Shinobu did not pass anyone on the bridges as she went back to the Vaults. She had never seen Fuji this empty and silent. When she opened the doors to the Vaults, the scratch of pens on paper and the tapping on the tablets from Les Alpes were a cacophony in comparison. And over it all, Jessica's voice, too loud. Shinobu could imagine the works in the shelves turning over, made restless by that carrying voice. Perhaps speaking like that helped Jessica be heard over the masses of Venice, but it was too much for indoors.

Shinobu would never say anything. No one else was complaining.

She walked down the steps, not silent, not even quiet, but she could not hear her footsteps over the sound of poetry.

> *"Whoever wins, on that side shall I lose*
> *Assured loss before the match be played."*

Jessica sat on a short stack of shelves dragged out for her by someone who knew that Shinobu would be there later, to drag it back into place.

Makoto was still dutifully scribbling at Jessica's feet, but the space next to him where Shinobu had been was now filled by Shinku. Ama was sitting at the base of the stairs. She turned at Shinobu's hand on her shoulder, an angry pout fixed on her face.

"Shinobu, I'm trying to listen!"

"I know," said Shinobu. "It seems that Shinku—"

"I asked Shinku to record after you left," whispered Ama. She gave Shinobu a dismissive wave. "Do whatever you like. We don't need you here right now."

"But—"

"Shh!"

If Jessica heard, she did not let the conversation interrupt her performance. She gazed somewhere above their heads as her body slipped, slightly but visibly, into a different role, her voice dropping into a lower register as a new character responded. Members of the audience whispered to each other, some repeating the last words Jessica spoke, some comparing notes, but Ama did not shush any of them.

*We don't need you.*

No one else noticed that Shinobu had come down the stairs. No one else noticed when she began walking up them once more, away from the words of Diplomacy in their steady *thunk thunk…* What *was* it called? She did not see Dario in the gathering. She doubted anyone else noticed his absence, or thought his absence was noteworthy, as they all focused their attention on Jessica.

*You do need me,* Shinobu thought. *You don't know it, but you do need me.*

At the base of the Vaults, the audience applauded for Jessica.

"Iambic pentameter!" Shinobu suddenly exclaimed.

"Ssh!" said Ama, but Shinobu barely heard. *That* was the rhythm, that rolling beat throughout the verses! *Iambic pentameter.*

## CHAPTER 16 (CEM)

"You're a stupid girl, Jessica," rasped the old man, hunched over on his seaweed chair. "Your mother always—"

"I'm not Jessica," Cem said.

Abraham stopped speaking. He looked at Cem like the boy was lying. Cem wondered if the old man saw his daughter reaching into the cabinet for the open jar of pickles, if he thought Jessica was the one that had torn off a chunk of jerked gull and brought him the food.

"You shouldn't be here," said Abraham, holding the jerky and a pickle in shaky hands.

"I know."

The old man nodded, satisfied, and began to eat. Vinegar from the pickle dripped from the corner of his lip, into his beard.

No one in the Upper Keep had known what to do with the children when they first crawled onto the balcony. The girl who had dropped the ladder, Chava, had run away the moment they were safe. Cem thought she was worried about getting in trouble with the ghosts, spectres in all black, who had looked at the children like they were the haunted ones. Up close, Cem could tell that most of them were alive. But the streaks of grey and white in some of the people's hair marked them as ancient, as old as any ghosts he had imagined. Cem must have seemed like a dot on a bending timeline to them, a mosquito. If Talia had not stepped in, they would probably have sent the children back down into the chaotic mess that was all that remained of Roman's and Bota's gangs. But Talia had stepped forward, smiling with her eyes even as they could still hear the children and Feral screaming below, and she had taken Cem, Farooq, and Sedef into her home, and given them soup.

Talia asked them questions about themselves, but Sedef said nothing, and Cem only talked about what Roman had done, and Farooq had asked questions in turn, which seemed to make Talia happy. Cem eventually realized she was testing them, but he did not know the right answers. He could not understand at first why Farooq switched to Diplomacy, that fancy language of Jessica's stories, but then Talia opened a great book on her lap with all the stories by the Bard. She made Farooq repeat words to her, while Cem cleaned up their bowls and covered the remaining food, and carefully wiped the soup drying on Sedef's cheeks. He had not realized that he had passed his own test until Talia patted him on the shoulder.

After the sun set, Talia sang them pretty songs over candles. The violence on the boulders quieted, and everyone went out on the balconies to peer below. Talia joined a small group of women, most of them were nearly as young as Farooq and Cem, who nonetheless took up space on the thin balcony like they were the only ones meant to fill it. Cem heard Talia say, more loudly than she had to, that Farooq would be staying with her. One of the women, Abby, a fierce woman with a twisted leg whose limp could not be hidden by her long dress, said that Cem could help Abraham. Abby had two boys clinging to her skirts, one of them holding another baby while Abby rocked his twin on her hip. She was looking round for Sedef, but the girl was gone.

When Sedef climbed back up days later, she told Cem that she left because she did not like the tests. Cem agreed. They were exhausting. He went fishing with some of the Jewish children, and they were horrified when he put his arm in the water to catch eels. They fished for tubers to pickle, quickly plucking them from beneath the great leafy vegetation that grew by the more shadowed boulders and did everything they could to avoid being bitten. It was like Cem had broken the rules, but no one would explain what they were. He supposed Farooq had a harder time: Talia was always asking him questions about the Bard's stories. Though Farooq never complained to Talia, he told Cem that he worried if he got any of the answers wrong Talia would make him leave. Their lives were now driven by the need to prove their usefulness, to give a reason for keeping them safe. Cem knew he could have left with Sedef, but without his gang, he did not know how to survive in Venice Main any more than he knew how to live here in the Upper Keep. At least in the Upper Keep he did not worry about being sliced with a mussel cut by some child without a gang leader who did not care about fair fights. But he understood why Sedef preferred the risk. Why get used to Talia's kind words, the sharp bite of pickles, the distance from the Flood waters, when they could be forced below at any moment? Maybe it hurt less to exclude yourself. Maybe that was why Jessica had always been on the Main...

Cem did like helping Abraham, though. Sometimes. He liked when Abraham's mind was present, and he told Cem stories much older than the Flood. These stories said you could be swallowed by a giant fish and survive to be spat back up again, as long as some distant and powerful emperor wanted you to live. Those stories said that people had come through other great Floods and the world even got better after. That seemed more impossible than being spewed up by a monster, but both stories were fun.

Cem liked helping Abraham until the darkness clouded the old man's vision, and then Cem wished he was doing anything else.

Abraham finished his meal and looked confused, staring at his empty hands.

"Do you need anything before I leave?" asked Cem.

"You haven't been singing, Jessica," said the old man. "If you don't practice, they'll hate you even more. If you're going to put yourself in danger, you might as well—"

> "When that I was and a little tiny boy,
> With hey, ho, the wind and the rain,

> *A foolish thing was but a toy,*
> *For the rain it raineth every day."*

Cem continued to sing as he climbed out of the window. He skipped across the balconies and passed small groups of adults who made room for him. He continued singing even when he knew Abraham could not possibly hear. Singing had no practical purpose, but Talia said not all tools had to be practical to have purpose. He wondered if he pretended to fall asleep next to Talia later, with his head resting on her knee and his eyes shut tight, she would let him stay there. She had before, but he still worried that she would kick him away.

Outside Talia's, some of the children were sitting around Farooq, who was perched on one of the rope handholds. Cem knew the children enjoyed quizzing Farooq. Cem tried to practice the stories too, to be more useful to Talia, but the letters and the words became skewed in his head when he tried to write them down, dissolving into an incoherent hiss. He smiled at Farooq, something he could not remember ever doing below or on the Main in front of a crowd, and he did not feel weak. Maybe it was because, despite the daredevil way Farooq rocked on the handhold, it seemed less likely that he would lose Farooq up here. Caring did not make the children weak; no, it was losing what they cared about. Cem was not really scared of Abraham, who could barely get out of his seaweed chair. But he was scared of the intensity with which Abraham missed his daughter.

When Farooq saw Cem, he grinned and hopped down to the solid floor. When they first arrived, Abby pulled a few of Farooq's teeth, all near the front and centre of his mouth. But Farooq never adopted a tight-lipped smile, was never self-conscious. Cem smiled back. He did not notice Sedef squatting between Ruben and Chava until she tugged at his pant-leg.

"Sedef!" laughed Cem. He crouched to give her an awkward half embrace which left his shirt smeared green and brown with algae slime and whatever else coloured her dress. He did not mind, but Chava hid her face to muffle a giggle.

Chava and Ruben were the only children who did not seem wary of the Venetians. Cem supposed that Chava felt responsible for them, and Ruben felt guilty that Cem had taken over caring for Abraham. Whatever their reasons at first for keeping the boys company, the two Jewish children were starting to seem like friends. Cem had to remind himself that it was not the same as a gang.

"She found some gull eggs," said Ruben.

Sedef looked so proud of herself, Cem guessed that no one had told her that there were many nests at the top of the house legs. They had far more access to eggs in the Upper Keep than on the Main.

"And mussels," said Farooq. "We can prepare them later, if you're free."

Cem thought about Abraham, alone, maybe calling out for his daughter. Maybe calling out for Cem.

"As long as we're not too late," said Cem.

"There's enough to share," said Farooq. He spoke like he was talking to Cem alone, but the Venetians were waiting for Ruben and Chava to request to join them for a small feast. The two children sat quietly, pretending they did not know that the silence was meant to be filled by them.

Cem could not understand. Everyone was starving, and the mussels were here, but the other children would not eat them. Nor would they eat the eels, though Cem did not go fishing anymore. When Cem tried to figure out why, Ruben simply said it was because he was Jewish. Cem guessed that this answer was supposed to explain everything to him, so he did not press for more specifics. Were the Jews more scared of the ocean and its monsters than he was? Maybe they thought the mussels were gross. It annoyed him that the first day he considered this might be the reason, the mussels started to seem a little gross to him, too. But he still ate them.

"There's enough for the three of us, sure," said Cem, breaking the silence.

"I'm not staying," said Sedef. She tied her dress in a knot at her knees. The dress was a gift from Abby, who had been horrified that Sedef did not use more plastic to cover her torso. Cem was surprised that no one had stolen it yet.

"You're leaving so soon?" asked Cem.

"She's been up here for hours," said Ruben. He squeaked as Chava elbowed him in the side.

"It's getting dark," said Sedef. "I need to find a good sleep spot."

"I'm sure Abby would let you stay for the night," said Chava.

Sedef shook her head, and Chava let down a rope ladder for her. Sedef hugged Cem so swiftly he could have believed it was his imagination, and then she was gone, over the edge of the balcony.

"I'm going inside," said Farooq. "Talia's going to let me write the verses on paper."

"That's because your handwriting's pretty," said Chava, like it was an accusation.

"No one lets you write on paper because you doodle," said Ruben.

"Hey!"

"It's true."

Chava pulled up the rope ladder and slapped Ruben's shoulder, not hard enough to hurt, but Ruben fake yelled anyway. Both of them laughed as Chava chased him across the bridges and balconies.

Cem was sure Abby would let Sedef stay as long as she wanted. Abby's face softened whenever Sedef, or Chava, or any of the other girls ran by, so different from the way she smoothed out a scowl when she saw Cem and Farooq. The only boys she tolerated were her own sons, but Cem knew that she especially did not like the Venetians. It made him feel guilty, different, wrong in a way that he could not control, but he did not blame her. Cem was not sure he liked the Venetians very much, either. The best ones were up here or dead.

Farooq hovered by the far bridge, clearly anxious to get to Talia and the promise of paper. "Are you coming?" he asked.

"In a minute," said Cem. "I want to make sure she gets back okay."

"Don't take too long," said Farooq. "I'll wait up for you."

Cem walked along the balconies and across the rope bridges, trailing the girl as she crawled across the boulders. The path that led to Venice Main was straight enough, but that was not the path Sedef was taking. She followed the edge of the water and briefly stopped at the spot where Roman had dragged Bota into the waters, and peered into the waves. Then she pulled herself back and continued her nimble trail across the rocks at a safe distance from the ocean and the eels. Maybe she hoped to see a piece of him left behind, lodged somewhere too deep to float to the surface. But that would not be Roman, any more than an eyelash on Cem's cheek was Cem. Whatever she looked for had been gone the moment it plunged into the waves. The thought that Sedef went to the place where Roman had last stood to look for some kind of comfort made Cem angry. Not angry in a way that made him want to fight, but a worse kind of angry that made him want to curl up and cry. Sedef said Nikita still cried for Bota.

When Sedef left the rocks and scrambled up the steps to the Main, Cem pulled himself back from the edge of the balcony. It must have been drizzling; that was surely why his cheeks were wet. Anyone who saw him stumbling across the bridges from their windows would assume his eyes were red from wiping his face with salt-flecked fingers. When he reached Talia's, and saw Farooq perched on the window ledge, Cem knew he had a thousand good reasons for wrapping his arms around him.

Still, Cem worried that if Farooq asked him why he was holding on so tight, he would only be able to answer with the truth. But Farooq did not ask him. He held Cem as tightly, his warm breath a pleasant ripple through his hair. If Cem kept his eyes shut, and Farooq kept his arms exactly where they were, Cem could still believe that this was the best of worlds, and that it could not be any better.

## Chapter 17 (Jessica)

> *"The quality of mercy is not strained—"*
> *"Let him look to his bond—"*
> *"If you prick us do we not bleed—"*
> *"In sooth, I know not why I am so sad—"*

Jessica had been saying the words for days, repeating the plays, answering questions about the plays, making up stories about Shakespeare, being corrected by Shinobu, negotiating with Shinobu. The scribe was waiting in the Vaults right now, probably with a pen hovering over paper. Ever prepared. Ever ready to record a mistake. And always, always listening.

Jessica could barely remember the dream she had during her fever, but she did recall casting Shinobu as the figure judging her over the waves. Although the dream faded day by day, the idea was now implanted inside her like a warning that this woman meant her harm and could not be trusted.

"Are you planning to get out on any of these floors?"

Ibada's voice snapped Jessica out of her reverie.

"Ibada!" said Jessica. "How long have you been standing there?"

"Only for a few verses," he said, then chuckled when Jessica's eyebrows knit together. "You've been mumbling. Sounds like *Merchant*? An odd version. All out of order."

"Oh. Sorry."

"I don't mind," said Ibada. "It's like a completely different story. No idea how this one will end. And I should be the one apologizing. I was eavesdropping. Which floor are you heading to?"

"What?"

"You haven't pressed the button for your floor."

Jessica blinked. They were in one of the lifts. She did not know which one. She did not remember getting in. She shrunk into the corner, as if her white dress would help her blend into the wall and disappear, though between her blush and her hair, she was probably nearly as red as Ibada's vibrant vest, trimmed with a thick hem of gold.

"Jessica, are you okay?" asked Ibada.

Jessica felt tears pricking at her eyes. She stared upward, unblinking, willing them away.

"I'm tired…"

"You've been working nonstop."

"I have to," said Jessica.

"No, you don't," said Ibada. "In fact, I'm sure Makoto would appreciate a pause to clean up his copies. And Ama is in no rush."

Jessica bit her lip. She needed to remind the empress, and Shinobu, and all of them, why she was here. She needed to prove herself… but right now her head was spinning.

"I suppose I could use a break," she said, weakly.

"Great! Where do you want to go?" Ibada reached for the lift buttons.

"I was kind of hoping to go back to the Coil for a rest."

"Oh," said Ibada, briefly faltering. "Right…"

He pressed one of the buttons. It glowed, flickered, and then went dark.

Jessica's embarrassment had passed, but she felt her blush still on her cheeks. Ibada straightened up, his head nearly brushing the ceiling, but it was not a strain to look up at him. And Jessica realized she rather did like looking at him, knowing he would be there when she looked up, knowing that she would like what she saw. Expecting his voice to cut through the dizziness. A nice voice; deep, like a wave against the shore…

For a brief second, she felt sick, like she had hurt Luka. She had not done anything. But she wanted to do something. She said, "Why were you riding in the lift with me?"

"That's odd," said Ibada.

"I don't mind," said Jessica. "I like it. You're—"

"No, I mean, the lift," said Ibada. "It's not responding. See?"

He pressed the button again. It glowed, faintly, and then went dark. He pressed the rest of the buttons in succession. Some glowed for a second. Most did not glow at all.

"Perhaps they need to be relit?" asked Jessica, wondering how something like that could occur.

"It's not just the light," said Ibada. "We're not moving."

He was right. The lift's usual hum was not there. Ibada pressed all the buttons again, though it was clear even to Jessica that this would not help them.

"Has the lift stopped before?" she asked.

"Mizutsuki was complaining about… Well, not this in particular, but such issues in general," said Ibada. He went to the doors that were seamlessly shut and pulled them.

Jessica watched Ibada attempt to pry open the doors, trying not to find amusement in his uncharacteristic fluster.

"Do you think we should shout out?" he said.

"I don't think that would help," she said. "We should probably just wait. I'm sure someone will notice that we're gone."

Ibada wiped his brow. "Is it hotter?" Sweat was dripping from his temple, but Jessica could still feel the silent breeze that cooled all the buildings in Fuji. "These lifts are too small!" he said. "Why won't these doors open?"

Jessica supposed the lift must seem much smaller to him. But she also knew that it was not the size of the lift causing the problem. On the Main, she once saw a few older members of Bota's gang trap one of their new recruits in a cave, convincing the shrieking child that there was a landslide, that they were trying their best to get them out to no avail, while choking on their giggles. The cave was not small, but Jessica could hear the child get more and more panicked. Jessica had been trapped in a landslide once. It took less than a day for the Venetians to clear the rubble, but to some people it did not matter if help was coming or not. They only saw the wall of stone between them and the outside world. And even though enclosed spaces did not trouble her, Jessica understood what was making Ibada's eyes widen, as he wiped his palms on his tunic.

"Ibada, what problem are we dealing with here, right now? Tell me."

"Fuji has been having energy issues for years now, Mizutsuki said, and she told Shinobu, but now things break in every building—"

"No," said Jessica, grabbing his hands and squeezing them. "What problem are we dealing with, *here, right now, specifically.*"

Ibada opened his mouth, caught Jessica's glare, and closed it again. Jessica felt his hands within hers begin to relax.

"The door is stuck," he said, eventually.

"Good," said Jessica. "Anything else?"

"Um," Ibada considered. "We can't contact anyone to get us out."

"Right. Is that all?"

"Eventually, the malfunction might affect the air—"

"No," said Jessica. "*Right now.*"

Ibada looked at her. His mouth was slightly parted. She wanted to let go of his hands, reach up to the stubble on his cheeks. He was always nearby, but never this close. She had never held his hand for this long before. She knew he was struggling, but she was pleased that he did not want her to let go.

"That's it," said Ibada.

"Ok. Two problems. Is there anything we can do about them?"

"No," he said.

"Good."

"*Good?*" He gaped at Jessica, incredulous.

"Yes. If we can't do anything, those are someone else's problems," said Jessica. "I want you to take a deep breath, think about those problems that are not yours, and then breathe them out."

Ibada looked at her for a moment, his face blank, and then his mouth curved into a smile. He breathed in – and then breathed out his problems.

"What do we do now?" asked Ibada.

"Wait, I guess," said Jessica. "For those problems to become immediate problems, or for someone else to fix them."

"I don't like being contained," Ibada said quickly. "It's never felt safe."

Jessica nodded. "Did something happen? Perhaps when you were a child in Kilimanjaro?"

"No! Not at all…" Without letting go of her hands, Ibada sat down on the floor. She sat down next to him. "Kilimanjaro is very open, so much more so than Fuji. Our bridges are uncovered, and many of the towers are taller than the Vaults, for the hydroponics—"

"Hydro-what?" Jessica asked.

"Hydroponics," said Ibada. "You know? Farming."

"What is that?" Jessica asked, and, when Ibada frowned, added, "It's okay if you don't know the details."

"I *do*, but not in Diplomacy," Ibada said. "I only know the technical terms in Swahili… It's… like flying plants? Air plants. Farming, but the water is in the air."

"Maybe you could tell me more about the buildings," said Jessica, too embarrassed to say she was unsure about the normal practicalities of farming, let alone how plants could fly.

"They're wider than the Vaults, too," said Ibada. "And when you're inside you can see everything that's happening inside, and if the windows are large enough, most of what's happening outside, too. The fishing ships making their hauls, the divers running back up the shore, the children gathering fossils on the sand… Fadhila coming to drag me back to a council meeting. Did I tell you that we were both on the council?"

Jessica shook her head. "That sounds very important."

"It was more important, in the past," said Ibada. "Nobody wants to risk changes when we know how easily the world can break. My work often feels less like helping and more like keeping busy. Maintaining. At least, when I'm not causing problems."

"What kinds of problems?"

Ibada gestured around him. "This collaboration with Fuji is rather new," he said. "Before the Mercy Experiment, we cut off ships before they could even see our shores. The patrols are still out there, now, making sure we stay safe."

"Safe from who?"

"Mostly people who say they've come to help," said Ibada, quietly.

"So, what made the Mercy Experiment different?" Jessica asked.

"Me, I suppose. I saw the ships, and I knew that they carried something to change the world in a way that would mend it instead of breaking it." He laughed. "I was only eighteen! My first year on the council, and I was unsure about everything, but I was sure about the Mercy Experiment. You either change with the world or die with those who cannot. It was like… like Ama did not give me choice."

"Ama was there?"

"Yes. No. Not on the ships."

Jessica did not entirely understand. But Ibada's thumbs were running soft circles in the palms of her hands, and his eyes were dark and calm, and the air was wonderfully cool, so she smiled like it made perfect sense, and Ibada smiled back.

The lift doors slid open. Outside stood Shinobu, with Luka and Fadhila.

"See?" said the scribe. "They're fine."

Ibada pulled Jessica to her feet as he rose. Reluctantly, they separated. The three outside watched them. Fadhila cocked her eyebrow and Jessica dropped Ibada's hand.

"I wanted to make sure you didn't kill her," Luka said to Shinobu.

There was no blush on Luka's cheeks. His hands did not tremble. He did not seem jealous at all, and Jessica was surprised to find that she did not care. As they walked from the lift, Jessica tuned out Shinobu's assertions to Luka that the energy failure was a temporary issue well on its way to being fixed, and instead listened to Ibada, who was telling Fadhila about something he called a "panic attack," and how Jessica had "saved" him. She did not think she had done anything amazing. It was a trick her father taught her.

#

"Ibada's nice to everyone," said Ama.

She had summoned Jessica to her bedroom at the top of the Coil. Jessica assumed that the empress wanted to talk about the plays, but it seemed more like she wanted company while she watched cartoons. Jessica wondered who used to keep Ama company before she arrived, who looked out the massive circular window at the rain-obscured view, who filled the space the Venetian now occupied. Maybe no one. Maybe being empress meant you did not get to have friends.

"That's how he gets people to like him," the empress continued, playing with the curls of her purple wig. She was comfortably splayed across a bed so much larger than Jessica ever imagined a bed could be. Her dress stuck up oddly at the back, pink and black tulle defying gravity, and the ties on her bulbous sleeves looked like they were about to come undone. "Most people are only nice when they want something. Otherwise, they don't really pay attention to other people."

Jessica, cross-legged on a blue-and-silver ottoman, said, "Everyone pays attention to me," and immediately blushed. She hugged one of Ama's stuffed animals tighter. There was a piece of art depicting the creature hanging above the empress's bed, but it looked huge in the picture and so tiny in her arms. The sweet softness of its round grey body and long ears was offset by the perpetual alarm in its wide black eyes.

"Everyone pays attention to me, too," said Ama, laughing. "We're special."

Jessica blushed harder. "I won't be so special when everyone knows the Bard's plays," she said. "Once everyone can learn the words, they won't need to listen to me."

"People don't listen because they want to know the words," said Ama. "Well, maybe Shinobu does. But most of us listen because we like hearing you say them. We like the performance."

"I wouldn't even be performing if I wasn't the only one who knew—"

"We like you," said the empress, laughing in exasperation. "I like having you here!"

"I like being here," said Jessica.

"Good!" said Ama, sitting up, her purple wig askew. Jessica reached out to straighten it, tugging on the smooth artificial hairs of the hard plastic. The empress did not seem to notice the fix. "You're my guest," she said, "for as long as I want you to be. I like you too much to let you go."

When Ama said that Jessica could not leave, it sounded like more than fact. It sounded like a script, written a long time ago, with words and actions and characters that could not be changed. It did not ask for argument, but for the next appropriate line.

"Then I'll stay," said Jessica.

"I know you will," said Ama lightly, turning back to her monitor. "You don't have a choice."

For a moment, Jessica was back on the stairs to the ramparts, alone between the Upper Keep and the Main, with no options, no choices. If her surge of uncertainty was mirrored in her expression, Ama did not seem to notice, distracted by the colourful creatures dancing on the monitor in the corner that were far more entertaining than the silent actress beside her.

## Chapter 18 (Shinobu)

Shinobu stalked through the Coil. She had walked its length up and down again three times. She was not used to having this kind of time to waste; the fact that no one came for help or a question showed how she had been discarded.

She completed her fourth turn at the base of the Coil and began her soft steps back upwards. The rain outside fell in heavy sheets of muted black-grey, blocking the view. It made each piece of artwork adorning the interior seem all the brighter. Shinobu tried to think of them as *her* artwork again. This piece, for example, all gold with black and grey smoke shadows, for years it had had a large tear in it that no one wanted or dared to fix. But with the help of the Kilimanjarians, Shinobu located a colour sufficiently similar that now you could barely see her patch. This piece, a warrior crouched over, a flurry of arrows impaled in her back, face contorted into an angry frown, this had suffered water damage when the base floor of the Vaults flooded. Ama, in the throes of a childhood meltdown, screamed the whole time Shinobu spent repairing it. And still it did not matter how much her hands had mended and recreated these works. They had been taken away from her Vaults on the empress's whim, her desire for pretty things for the Coil. They had never belonged to Shinobu…

It was not *fair*.

The unfairness was the worst. Not the unfairness of how the art had been taken from her, although that was bad enough, but the unfairness of how everyone trusted the Venetian over Shinobu. It did not matter what Jessica said about the plays, however she blatantly misinterpreted the stories. Especially when she misinterpreted *The Merchant of Venice,* trying to villainize Portia and make Shylock a misused victim. Shinobu knew that Jessica was lying, and she did not know why. All she knew was that the girl was hiding something. She was keeping a secret, and her secret was making Shinobu look ignorant because she could not see why the Venetian would lie.

From around the curve of the Coil, Shinobu heard voices, echoed whispers of Jessica's name. She slowed her steps and came to a stop pressed against the inner wall of the Coil, opposite a black-and-white image of a young girl kneeling in front of a dark background. A spiral was twisting deep into the girl's head as if she had been assaulted by a giant screwdriver. Ama usually only liked art that was conventionally pretty, but this picture was satisfying in its own gruesome unreality.

Shinobu studied the circles of the spiral, breathing shallowly and listening to the conversation happening around the curve of the hall, grateful for the visual illusion of the Coil's architecture that kept her hidden.

"I don't know what game you're playing," Luka said, his voice ugly in its harshness. "But you're being cruel, and you look ridiculous."

"I'm not 'playing' any games," replied Ibada. "If Jessica wanted you as badly as you want her, then she wouldn't—"

"I don't want Jessica!"

For a brief moment, Shinobu could only hear Luka's jagged breathing, Ibada's silence, and her own soft breath. Then Luka spoke again.

"I don't *want* her," he said. "I'm trying to look out for her. She's my responsibility."

"Why wouldn't you want Jessica?" asked Ibada. "She's intelligent. She's amusing. She's a captivating performer. It's no crime for two people to want the same woman, but I don't understand why you're lying."

"I'm not," said Luka, but his voice wavered. "I mean, I can't…"

"You can't?" asked Ibada, chuckling. "Is she off limits? Is she something fearsome? Should I be worried?"

Shinobu pressed back more firmly against the wall and tried to tune out everything that might distract her, from the beating of her heart to the dull blinking of her eyelids. *What is Jessica hiding, Luka?* She tried to picture the question burrowing into Luka's brain, carving out its own inward spiral, compelling him to answer.

"Jessica's a good person," he said.

That was not the question Shinobu had asked. It was not the question Ibada had asked either.

"But?" asked Ibada.

"Well, she's *Jewish*."

Shinobu was surprised. Jessica looked nothing like the Jews in the pictures in the Vaults, with their dark hair and darker eyes and skin nearly as pale as an Alpine's. She knew that some of the pictures they had were exaggerated propaganda, and others were based on images of Jews from long-Flooded areas surrounding Les Alpes and the old cities near High Rock Ridge. But even though Shinobu only had a vague idea of what being a Jew meant, something like a religion or maybe something like an ethnic group, she felt that being a *people* required a kind of cohesion. A recognizability to claim one's place in a community. To Shinobu, Jessica did not look all that different from Andrusha.

"Oh," said Ibada. He sounded as lost as Shinobu as to why Luka said *Jewish* as though it answered all questions. "Why does it matter that Jessica's Jewish?"

"It matters because it means I can't want her," snapped Luka. "That would be like wanting... Have you seen pictures of rats? Little animals that used to hide in groups and corners... It would be like wanting one of those. And I..."

Shinobu waited as Luka trailed off. She wondered if he was gathering his thoughts, but then the silence continued, a cold silence which Ibada did nothing to end. Shinobu was glad she could not see the expression on Ibada's face that had stopped Luka's words.

Jessica as a *rat*. Something about that image was familiar, something about her being Jewish, something about the pictures. The image held Jessica's lie. If Shinobu could find the image, she could find the answer, the right accusation…

"Jessica's performances are going to keep the Venetians alive," said Ibada, mildly, "and you're calling her a *rat*?"

"I didn't mean it like that," said Luka, annoyed. "And we'll be able to keep ourselves alive if Dario follows through on his promise."

What did Dario have to do with Jessica? Or with keeping anyone alive? He was not the kind of man to care about that sort of thing.

"You can mean whatever you like, and trust whoever you like," said Ibada. "But it seems clear to me that Jessica should stay as far away from Venice, and you, as she can."

"She'll come back to help with the algae blocks," said Luka. "She has to. And I'm not saying that just because…"

Shinobu could picture Ibada's smug smile.

"Did Dario say where he was keeping the sōrui-jin?" asked Luka with a huffed abruptness.

The sōrui-jin were only in the Algae Plant.

"In my room, for now," said Ibada.

"Show me," said Luka.

Shinobu almost gasped. They had the sōrui-jin. They could not. It was impossible! Shinobu had never given them permission. She wanted to follow them, but something dark at the back of her mind stopped her feet.

Sofia had thought this would happen. Shinobu had never shown Dario how to use the sōrui-jin, but that did not mean he wouldn't find his own way to misuse them on the people outside the walls of Les Alpes. There was no good, or at least kind, reason she could think of that would explain why Dario would involve the Venetians or Kilimanjarians in his plot. If Dario did have a hold of the sōrui-jin, any plans he had to share the technology would result in a mess.

And messes were Shinobu's specialty.

She cleaned up all of the empress's messes. She ensured that Ama's life was easy, that obstacles moved out of her way, and that anything trampled upon in Ama's wake was neatly folded back in its proper place. Shinobu walked out of the Coil, and the doors that shut firmly and smoothly behind her hummed in agreement. Yes, she would clean up the mess. The fallout of this mistake would undoubtedly end with all those affected by it blaming Fuji in general, and Ama in particular. Unless Shinobu could find someone else to blame.

What had those images, that *propaganda,* been for? If she could find those pictures again, maybe she could find a way to put Jessica's Jewishness to good use.

Shinobu walked along the path outside the Coil, steadily drenched by the rain as she made her way towards a covered bridge. Her jacket and trousers stuck to her skin, and her hair fought its high bun. She enjoyed the feel of the rain, the unexpected chill that persisted when she was soaked. She looked out across the vast darkness of the ocean. There was nothing in the distance, nothing that she could see with her limited vision, but she sensed that whatever monsters lurked beneath the waves were content to stay below. Shinobu continued to the covered bridge. The door slid shut behind her. She stripped off her wet jacket and left it in a ball on the floor. She would be back later to clean it up. She doubted anyone else would do it for her.

There was something invigorating about walking along the bridge wearing only her sleeveless blouse and trousers, seeing the contrast between her smooth arms and the embroidered material. The designs were inspired by some of the fashion art she kept in the Vaults. She wanted to look like the women with their kimonos and fans, so poised and sure and beautiful, citizens of not just the past but the distant past, when the Flood was not an imminent disaster, not even the seed of an idea. She knew that the Flood was the result of centuries of ignorance, and then misuse, and then malicious intent mixed with apathy. Those women she admired were as responsible as any of the people who came immediately before the Flood. But the twin blossoms adorning the hem of her trousers distanced Shinobu from this reality. Shinobu reached the entrance to the Vaults and descended into the past.

Makoto was there, transcribing a damaged work from their Fiction collection. "Shinobu," he said. "You look pretty."

"Thank you."

Shinobu stepped out of the lift and put a hand on his shoulder, stopping him before he could leave.

"Makoto, have you come across any documents about *Jews* or being *Jewish*?" she asked.

She knew which records were kept in her own shelves and drawers, the ones related to Judaism as a religion, but they had been crossed and mislabelled decades ago with the documents about Christianity and Islam. Now the three religious texts looked like they were part of one book, and it was nearly impossible to untangle whose myths belonged to whom. And, in truth, she was more interested in finding where those pictures had come from and the stories they were connected to, in finding out what being Jewish had to do with Jessica, and Portia, and Shylock.

"Jews come up near the end of the *Mercy* verse," said Makoto.

"Yes, I know that."

Makoto frowned as he thought. She waited a minute and wondered if he forgot her question, but then his face lit up.

"There's a collection of songs!" he said. "I made up a tune for it: To *life!* To *life!* L'*chaim!*"

"No, Makoto, that's not helpful," said Shinobu. "Is there anything that's not a song? Or a verse? Something that might explain…"

"Explain?"

"Any other text."

"There was a book," he said. "I recorded it because it seemed like fiction, but I wasn't sure, so I gave it to Shinku. She put it with the other history texts."

"Do you know what the subject was?" Shinobu asked. "Or the author's name?"

"The subject was a long word, I didn't know it," he said, shrugging. "But I think it was sorted under 'World War Two'. The author's last name was Frank."

"Thank you, Makoto."

Shinobu began to climb the staircase.

"Shinobu?" Makoto called after her. She stopped and tried to flick the robe-like length of her jacket behind her as she turned and realized she was not wearing it. "I thought… Should I get Shinku?" he said. "Before you go through her things?"

"Nothing in the Vaults belongs to us."

"But... I'm Fiction, and you're Mythology, and she's History."

"You don't need to get Shinku," said Shinobu. "But thank you for checking. Go back to work now."

"I'm going to get supper," he said.

"Then, go enjoy your supper."

"Thank you, Shinobu."

She turned away and continued walking upwards. It did not take long to reach Shinku's floor (no matter what she had said, it *was* Shinku's floor), but she was glad to be wearing fewer layers than usual. The exercise warmed her skin. Maybe she would dress like this from now on, more modern and physically free. Ama would be amused if she cared at all.

Shinobu walked between the stacks, searching through the disparate themes. There was 'The Russo-Japanese War'. There was 'The Haitian Revolution'. There was 'The Monopolization of Entertainment'. She quietly cursed Shinku for sorting documents under themes before author names. 'The Destruction of the Library of Alexandria'. 'World War One.' 'World War Two'.

There were so many more drawers for 'World War Two' compared to the other themes that Shinobu marvelled for a moment that one event could seem so much more momentous than everything that led up to it and everything that came after. Most of the shelves referenced

Japanese involvement, the arena called the 'Pacific' in the pre-Flood Fujian region. But that had nothing to do with the book Makoto mentioned. Shinobu scanned the titles, and, when they offered nothing, the subtitles, and finally found something helpful, not a name or event, but a genre: 'Memoirs'. She opened the drawer, which responded with its friendly hiss, and there at the top, as if it was waiting for her, she found *The Diary of Anne Frank*.

Beneath that, *Night*. Beneath that, *At the Mind's Limits: Contemplations by a Survivor on Auschwitz and Its Realities*.

Of course, she had copied some of *The Diary of Anne Frank*. Mostly to restore the worn photograph of the girl on the front cover. She did not blame Makoto for not remembering the word *Holocaust*. These memoirs referenced this, and other violent acts committed against the Jews. They explained why Jessica had lied about the play, the traumatic past that she was trying to hide, her reasons for being afraid of letting Shylock be seen as the villain he was written to portray. And, if not proof, they were clear indications that Shinobu's interpretation was correct, and that Jessica had lied, and that *Merchant* was not the story Jessica claimed it was.

The difficulty was – they explained it too well. Shinobu could not bring these to Ama. She would turn Jessica into the victim. The others would understand why Jessica had lied but not why Shinobu felt such a need to unveil the painful truth. These memoirs were not useful. Combined with what Luka had said in the Coil, comparing Jessica to a rat, they elevated the performer from celebrity to martyr. Shinobu sighed and thought about her next step.

She could destroy the memoirs. Then no one would have a reason to feel bad for Jessica once Shinobu proved that she was a liar. But the thought of slipping these pages into the water made the scribe's hands shake with disgust. She felt bad enough about destroying the mosaics.

Shinobu picked up all the memoirs and shut the drawer behind her. She spiralled down the steps and, when she reached her own shelves, she hesitated. It made sense to sort the texts under 'Religion'. If they were found, she could claim some sort of authority over them. But she did not want them to be found. And if Shinku noticed they were missing, that would be the first place she would look.

Makoto had said they decided that the memoir did not belong in fiction. It was not fiction. No one would ever look for it in fiction.

Shinobu walked to the far shelf labelled 'Mythology' and deposited the memoirs with the mermaids and unicorns and monsters.

## Chapter 19 (Cem)

"Were those noises coming from the harbour?" asked Abraham.

Cem, climbing through the window, said, "Why don't you go out and see for yourself."

Cem caught the pickle that Abraham chucked at his head and chomped into the vinegar tartness. He checked the state of the pot, and hummed to himself, fitting in the words he could still remember.

"*White as snow,*" Cem murmured. "*Flaxen... Haste and make moan.*"

"Is that from one of the *Henry*'s?" asked Abraham, straining forward to catch the words before they disappeared.

"*Hamlet,*" said Cem. "The girl in it."

"Ophelia," said Abraham.

"The one who drowns," said Cem.

Cem still did not understand why Ophelia made such a big deal about plants. Algae, kelp, it was all wet and warm when it wrapped around your wrist. But Abraham smiled, that small smile adults gave when they were actually sad. It made it hard to tease the old man.

"The noise did come from the harbour," said Cem.

"Did a ship come in? Jessica?"

"No," said Cem, and Abraham slumped back into his chair. "Some of the men from the Main wanted to sink that last Fuji ship. Borya put a stop to it."

"How?" asked Abraham.

"I don't know. I was on the balcony. I could hear about as much as you can hear. I'm just telling you what I saw."

Borya had approached the group of angry men and paused for a few moments, gesturing, perhaps pleading. The men had listened and left. Cem did not know why the men had listened to Borya. He wondered what it would be like to ask for something and have someone do it.

"I can't hear much in here," Abraham grumbled.

The walls were thick. Cem often thought that the walls of the houses in the Upper Keep were thicker than the stones of the mountain, but both seemed doomed to crumble.

"If you're so curious, why don't you go outside to listen?" asked Cem.

"I can't leave here," said Abraham. His hands gripped the chair. "I'm never leaving this room."

"Everyone else in the Upper Keep walks on the balconies," said Cem.

Abraham glared at Cem, silent, as the boy went to the cupboard and checked on their supplies. The desalinator was still rather full but they did not have much jerky left. No one did.

"It'll be good to have more algae blocks," Cem muttered.

"The ships won't come yet," said Abraham. "They'll only come when it's too late."

"That doesn't make sense," Cem scowled. "If it's too late, there will be no one to help."

"No one ever helps until it's too late," said Abraham, his voice sure as his body sagged inwards. "Do you know how many cities fell to the rising sea before anyone tried to move the people who were left to the mountains? Do you know how many people died in those cities? Millions. They knew for years, decades, before the Flood that those cities would drown, but they did not make the people move. They did not do everything they could to stop the waters from rising or to protect the cities from the Flood. They waited, and watched with horror, and then help came, but it was not any help to those who were already dead."

An image of Roman falling into the water flashed through Cem's mind. He wondered if the people who lived before the Flood had waited on purpose for there to be fewer people, a reasonable number to help, but he could not believe that those people had been as thoughtful as Roman. He did not think they had cared about those who drowned, as long as they could get themselves to the mountains.

Cem spat on the floor. "The people who lived before the Flood were evil," he said. "We're different now. People care. The empress cares."

"The empress?" Abraham's expression darkened. He was not fading away, but he looked like he wished he were somewhere else.

"She made food out of poison," said Cem. "She made the world smaller to get the food to us. The sailors said that the wind comes when she waves her arm and the storms rage when she rages. But she doesn't rage at us. She chose to be merciful."

"Do you know why the empress started the Mercy Experiment?" asked Abraham.

"Because Andrusha sent a letter," said Cem.

"Sure, sure," Abraham laughed. It quickly turned to coughs. "But you know the sailors visited before the letters. Looking for art. They saw the way we lived. They saw the bloated bellies of the toddlers crawling up stairs to the ramparts, abandoned, alone. They saw the bodies that lay in the sun, the ridges of their bones clear through their arms and legs, each rib its own step to a jutting collarbone. Do you know what it's like to approach one of these bodies, to see if it's a corpse no longer in need of its plastic dress, or if this figure of death is still breathing and waiting to reach out a bony hand and grab hold of your wrist?"

Some of those images were familiar to Cem, the living corpses of the Feral who forgot not to sleep in the sun, their skin in peeling shreds before someone found them and dragged them into the shadows. But those were rare nightmares. Abraham was talking about these bodies like it had been normal, as if it was understandable not to help, something to be ignored. Like he had experience ignoring it.

"You went to the Main?" asked Cem. He did not think any of the Jews, except Jessica, ever came to the Main. "You left the Upper Keep?"

"I met Jessica's mother on the Main," said Abraham.

"Why did you stop going?"

Abraham stared at him. Cem waited for him to reply with a strange, nauseating anticipation.

"Do you not know about the massacre?" the old man finally asked.

Cem had heard that word before, whispered by the adults on the Main. He knew few details about it.

"Some people died in the Upper Keep," said Cem, shrugging. "I think they fell during a storm?"

"*Fell?*"

Cem jumped away from the venom in Abraham's voice. The man half-pushed himself out of his chair before collapsing back into it, heaving breaths alternating with hacking coughs. Cem wanted to run, but he thought the old man might burst if the boy did not calm him.

"I didn't know," said Cem, trying to make his voice soothing. "I don't know. What happened?"

Abraham's coughing stopped, but his body still shook.

"They came up the ladders and killed us," he whispered. "They decided there were too many of us, and they killed us so there would be more food for them."

"But you're still here," said Cem, incredulous.

"They killed the mothers," said Abraham. His voice cracked. "The wives. My wife. My Dasha. They climbed the ladders we used to leave hanging, because why wouldn't we have made travelling easier between the worlds of Venice? They grabbed the men who traded with them on the ramparts before we understood what was happening, before we could fight. Then they grabbed the women, women who they knew, women who shared recipes to make hard tubers palatable and tricks for making trash wearable with your Venetians, women who had children and husbands and fathers who needed them, and they dragged them out to the balconies and slit their throats above the water. They slit my Dasha's throat while two of them held me down. My face was pressed on the floor where you're sitting now when I heard her stop screaming. I couldn't move. I couldn't run. And why would I? It was done. There was no reason to run anymore. There were other screams that stopped just as shortly. It was over in less than an hour. You came so prepared. You did not waste any time."

Cem shifted away from his spot on the floor, making room for the ghosts he had always known inhabited the Upper Keep.

"Not *me*," said Cem. "I wasn't there."

The old man's eyes turned cold and distant.

"No, Jessica, you were not there," snarled Abraham. "You were playing with your *friends*, the friends who watched your mother die, who you go back to again and again, like there is not blood staining the hands of every single one of them. You were not there, and you will never understand what we went through. But I know why you keep coming back."

"Why?" whispered Cem, curious despite his revulsion.

"Because you're a woman now. Because you could be a wife, a mother. And when they come again, you will die with the wives and mothers. You want to feel that pain, too. To understand," Abraham said, his words rasping, rough. "You should have left me long ago, Jessica. You should have stayed with Luka and forgotten about me. Then you might have had a chance to survive. And I need you to survive!"

"Jessica left for Fuji," said Cem, shivering. "No one is going to kill her there. They don't have a reason to kill her."

"There is never a reason," said Abraham. "But there are always excuses."

He began to cry. Every muscle in Cem's body yearned to run away, but if he did, the old man would be alone, and it was awful to cry alone, worse than crying while someone watched and did nothing to help.

"Abraham?"

"I have been preparing myself to lose her, too, ever since the massacre," said the old man, sinking deeper into his chair, as if he could make himself disappear into the rotting kelp and plastic. "Preparing her, too. When they kill me, she will not miss me, not the way we miss Dasha. But when they kill her, I think I will still miss her."

"No one is going to kill her. They wouldn't. She's…" Cem remembered the way people stopped to listen to her on the ramparts. "She's too good at performing Shakespeare."

Abraham laughed.

"What a stupid reason for not killing someone," he said.

"If there's always a stupid excuse for killing someone," Cem said, slowly, "maybe there's always a stupid reason for not killing them, too."

Abraham did not respond. For a second, when he had laughed, there was a lightness to him, like he could have stood up and walked and it would not have meant anything more than he was curious to see how much jerky he had left. For a second, there was a chance for something momentously normal to happen. But instead, Abraham leaned forward, hands on his thighs, head twisted at a strange angle as if his cheek was pressed against something solid and invisible in the air in front of him. He froze there, and though it could not have been a comfortable position, his body did not tremble. His eyes were wide and terrified. Cem walked up to the chair and waved his hand in front of Abraham's unseeing eyes. It felt wrong to leave Abraham when he was crying, but it also felt wrong to stay here and watch the man in this odd fit.

"I'm going," said Cem. The old man did not respond. "I'll be back. You'll be fine."

Abraham's story did not make sense. None of the children who lived in the Upper Keep were alive when the massacre had happened, and yet they were here. And Talia was here. Abraham said they had killed all the women, but that could not be true, so maybe none of it was true. Maybe it was nothing more than some terrible story hissing around an old man's brain.

Cem left, with one last look through the window at the still immobile Abraham. He considered knocking on the neighbouring houses to see if this had ever happened before, but he doubted there was anything they could do to help.

It was raining softly, and a fine mist hung in the air. Little droplets of water clung to him, and as he moved across the bridges and balconies in and out of the shafts of light that shone from open windows, they reflected the glow and shimmered like something much more beautiful than he could ever be. He nearly ran into Talia as she walked down the path, trailed by Chava and a few of the other children. Some of the water from her full desalinator tipped onto the balcony. She regained her balance, shifting the weight of the jug to her hip.

"Sorry," said Cem.

"Nothing to apologize for," said Talia, waving off his concern. "You look shaken. Is everything all right?"

"We need to get home now," said Chava.

"Then go, you know the way," snapped Talia. "You're a big girl and you don't need me to watch you."

Chava glared – at Cem, not Talia – and the two other children grabbed her skirt as they ran across the bridges. Talia sighed as she watched them go, not nearly so harsh now that the girl was not looking.

"Talia, how come you didn't die in the massacre?" he asked. Talia's face went as distant as Abraham's, but she did not freeze. Cem wished he could pull the words back inside. "I'm sorry. I shouldn't have asked. I'll go."

"I climbed under my house," said Talia. She did not sound upset. She sounded like she was talking about something that had happened in a play, a long time ago, to someone who did not exist. "I went over the balcony on the far side, without the ladder, because they were coming up the ladders and waiting at the top for us to try to run. I held onto the house leg. I wrapped myself around it, and I held tight. I was sure I would fall, but I told myself that letting go was not an option, so it was not, and I did not fall. I stayed there much longer than they stayed in the Upper Keep. By the time I pulled myself back up, they were done."

"I'm sorry," said Cem. "You didn't have to tell me that."

Talia blinked and was back in her body. She shifted the desalinator again, as if the weight was the only thing keeping her in front of him, now, and not back there, under the house, hugging the leg and waiting.

"No, it's good to talk about," said Talia. She sounded unsure. "If I don't talk about it… Well, then I might as well have let go."

"But what about Abby? She didn't die either."

"She jumped off the balcony when it started," said Talia. "She wasn't the only one, but she was the only one who survived."

The adults on the Main said some people fell. Cem realized that that was how they chose to tell the story. That was how they wanted it to be remembered.

"And they did not kill the very young girls," said Talia.

"Jessica was a child," said Cem. "Would they have killed her?"

"They killed some girls her age. They probably would have killed her."

"Why?"

"Her hair," said Talia. "She's noticeable."

"I guess she was lucky to be fine, then."

"Jessica was not fine," laughed Talia. "You think Abraham is odd? Imagine a ten-year-old girl who does nothing but memorize Shakespeare verses. I indulged her. I knew that was her way of distracting her mind from the pain. But it was chilling. It was all that she did. She would walk the balconies, all day, all night, repeating and repeating the words. It did not matter if the rain was pouring or if she had not slept for days. She would collapse on the bridges from exhaustion, still mouthing the words through her dreams. Did you know that she knows *all of the plays*? Every word. That is not normal. That is not the feat of someone who is fine. That is a girl who has been consumed by pain."

Cem thought of a boy throwing himself into the water so that others could survive, letting his pain consume him.

"Was there more food for everyone, after?" Cem asked. "After so many of you died? Mussels, eels—"

"We were *murdered*, we didn't *die*," Talia said, her words sharp though her voice was not angry. Just instructive. "And we don't eat mussels or eels. The massacre did not magically create more food. Only the empress can do that."

It was hard for Cem to listen to Talia. The hissing in his head was growing louder and louder as she spoke. It would be easier to listen to that and forget.

"Are you okay, Cem?" asked Talia.

"Is Farooq home?"

"He is," nodded Talia. "He'll be happy to see you."

Cem ran by Talia without saying goodbye. When he reached the house, he saw Farooq inside, sitting cross-legged, eyes closed, muttering to himself.

> "Why, such is love's transgression.
> Griefs of mine own lie heavy in my breast,
> Which thou wilt propagate, to have it prest
> With more of thine: this love that thou hast shown
> Doth add more grief to too much of mine own."

Cem wanted to go inside and tell Farooq everything. He wanted to relieve the pain thrust upon him by giving Farooq a little to hold. But what if Cem accidentally passed on that hissing along with the pain? What if Cem needed that hissing to deal with the pain? He would not take words away from Farooq.

Cem looked over the balcony. He thought about Abby, looking from this height at the rocks and water below, and deciding it was better to jump. Deciding that she could not survive what was about to happen but surviving, anyway.

## CHAPTER 20 (SHINOBU)

Shinobu had never had to manoeuvre around so many people in her life. Weeks had passed, and still none of the delegations had left. Her body was caught between the exhaustion of having to maintain poise and perfect posture to blend in around acquaintance and newcomer alike, and the stress of the muscle-memory adrenaline kick of being sure she was forgetting to perform some important duty. But the only performance people cared about was Jessica's. Ama brought Jessica with her everywhere, hand clasped around the Venetian's wrist as she encouraged the girl to sing for whatever enthralled crowd they stumbled upon.

Shinobu, striding across the bridge that led from the Coil to the cafeteria, passed a trio of young Kilimanjarians repeating some of Jessica's recently bestowed verses.

> *"Full fathom five thy father lies;*
> *Of his bones are coral made;*
> *Those are pearls that were his eyes—"*

One boy's voice faltered when he looked up at her. He let out a hysterical giggle. Shinobu increased her pace. Even when she was out of sight, the boy continued to giggle, despite his companion's efforts to shush him. She knew that his mirth might have had nothing to do with her, but it fuelled her suspicion that everyone was laughing behind her back. Shinobu turned her anger towards Jessica. Shinobu knew that this verse was as wrong as Jessica's interpretation of

*Merchant.* She had read that poem, a poem in fact written by T.S. Eliot. Did Jessica think that they would not know the Eliot work she had bastardized to fit her own narrative?

There were only two lone visitors in the cafeteria, and neither seemed pleased when Shinobu entered, interrupting their convivial silence. Luka sat near one of the wide windows. He leaned back in his chair, his half-eaten fusarium wraps forgotten, clenched in his grip as he peered over his shoulder at the drizzling world outside. A few tables away, Sofia was poking a raindrop cake with a single chopstick, more interested in watching its clear dome jiggle than consuming it. She had not spoken to Shinobu since their meeting in the Observatory, perhaps afraid that Dario would be suspicious if she started acting familiar with the scribe.

Shinobu walked to the menu displayed at the far side of the room and made her selection from the touch screen. She subtly eyed the visitors. A window slid open and Sumikai deposited a tray with the Venetian-style kimchi made of thinly chopped K2-local tubers. They were displayed in a wide fan and glistened with vinegar and salt: unnecessary for a casual snack, not to mention that tubers plucked from the sewage-like waves of Venetian shores hardly deserved a beautiful presentation.

She brought her tray to Luka's table and gestured at the small bowl of pickles she set in front of her. "Perhaps you would enjoy a taste of something a little more familiar?" Shinobu said, nodding at the abandoned wrap in his lap.

Luka clutched his food closer to his body as he shook his head. "It's not so familiar," he said. "Pickles were mostly traded away. Real Venetians were lucky to get a taste."

"Real Venetians?" she asked.

Luka turned back to the drizzle outside, avoiding the question. Sofia continued to poke at her cake, making no effort to hide that she was listening to their conversation. Shinobu picked up one of the pickles, and though she could have easily popped the small tuber into her mouth, she bit it in half. At the sharp sound, Luka's head jerked towards her.

"There's no one stopping you from having a taste now," she said.

Luka shrugged and took one of the pickles. He ate it piece by piece, sucking on each bite, making it last. Shinobu guessed that he would take as much care licking off the dark flecks of nori that stuck to his sweaty fingers and palms.

"You must be anxious to get home," Shinobu said, nibbling the tip of another pickle. "Back to normal food. Normal life."

"Dario said he would bring us back to Venice when they had a complete record of Shakespeare's work," said Luka. "So, I guess I'll be heading back when everyone's tired of paying attention to Jessica."

"Does Jessica like the attention?" Shinobu asked.

"She likes being liked," said Luka.

Shinobu continued eating her snack, as slowly as she could. By the time she had finished, Luka had still not taken another bite of his wrap, though Sofia had managed to make a dent in her drop cake, marring its perfectly smooth curve with a missing jagged chunk.

"People like Jessica's performances," said Shinobu. "They like the Bard's words. Shakespeare is a legend." She only wished he had stayed that way.

"Some people seem to like Jessica more than the words," said Luka.

"Ibada?"

Anger flashed across Luka's face. "I thought I was the only one who noticed," he said bitterly. "It's a bit much, isn't it?"

"I think most shows of affection are *a bit much*, so I'm probably not the best judge."

Shinobu had never understood the appeal of romance and sex, those urges that made people as smart as Shinku doom themselves to tragedy, unable to resist the temptation of a bad idea. She supposed she did not have a right to judge, since she did not feel those pulls of attraction, but she judged anyway.

"It probably doesn't matter," said Luka with a forced smile. "Jessica doesn't notice it. She's too overwhelmed with attention."

"I'm not so sure."

Luka took a large bite of his wrap and chewed slowly, his eyebrows knitting into a lovely deep V.

"Well, Ibada will be a distant memory when she's back in Venice," said Shinobu.

Luka spat. Sofia looked as alarmed as Shinobu felt at the sight of the thick, wet smudge on the floor.

"Jessica's staying here," he said.

"No. She's not."

Shinobu did not realize how loudly she had spoken until the following silence rang in her ears. Sofia had abandoned her drop cake and rested her chin on her hands as she openly watched them. A single spectator to a surprise performance. Luka shrugged and fiddled with his wrap. Shinobu knew she should do something to put him at ease, but she felt empty.

"I know she was planning on asking to stay," said Luka.

"Planning before she arrived?" asked Shinobu.

A wish, or better yet, a whim.

"Before she arrived," agreed Luka. "And lately. With Ama."

"Jessica told you this?"

"We haven't spoken much since, well, all the excitement," said Luka. He took a bite of his wrap and spoke through a muffled mouthful. "Ama told me."

Ama wanted Jessica to stay. And Jessica had always planned on staying. And everyone was talking to each other, and no one was talking to Shinobu, let alone listening to her, and why should they? Why should they listen to everything that Shinobu knew when they could listen to everything the actress invented instead?

"Are you okay?" asked Luka. "You look..."

Shinobu tilted her head. "I'm fine," she said. "Jessica can't stay."

Luka sucked the nori on his thumb, exactly as Shinobu had predicted he would.

"Can't?" asked Luka. "Or you won't let—"

"She *can't*," Shinobu repeated. Luka flinched. "Fuji is for Fujians. We decided that long before the Flood. It's how we've survived."

"For Fujians," said Luka, nodding. "I mean, I noticed, I just never thought about why."

"Our doors were closed when entire countries were being swallowed by the ocean," said Shinobu. "We're not going to let someone in after all these years because they're entertaining."

"But the empress said—"

"Ama was probably being nice," said Shinobu.

Sofia laughed. By the time Shinobu turned to look at her, all of the pale woman's attention was on her drop cake, but a smile still trembled at the corner of her pink lips.

"The empress does not strike me as the kind of woman who is nice just to be nice," said Sofia, her voice quieter than her laughter. "Perhaps she realized that if the Venetian knew she would be kicked out as soon as she had shared all the plays and verses that she knew, Jessica might have found herself slower to remember all the words."

The explanation encouraged Luka, and even made Shinobu feel better.

"Jessica won't be too happy about that," said Luka, though he sounded happy enough.

"It'll be better for her, when you take her home," said Shinobu. She hesitated, tried to read the reason behind the man's upset, then took a risk. "I'm sure she would go if you told her to go. I'm sure she would listen to what *you* want."

"I don't care what she does," Luka said, agitation unsettling his beautiful face as he lied. "I don't want her to be disappointed, that's all. She's spent so much time living out fantasies, I think she forgets she isn't in one of her stories."

"If she knows you want her to go back with you, I doubt she'll be disappointed."

Shinobu was not sure if the Venetian heard her. She was sure Sofia did.

"Where's Dario?" he asked. "I should tell him that she's coming. We'll have to prepare the ship for another passenger."

"Sofia, take Luka to Dario."

"I'm not done," said Sofia, and pointedly nibbled another miniscule piece of cake. "Dario's in the Algae Plant. The pretty Venetian can find him there."

Luka's head snapped up at the word *pretty*. He looked at Sofia, and his posture changed to something as performative as Jessica's speeches.

"I know I've been there before," said Luka. "But I could use some help finding the way."

He looked hopefully at Sofia, who pushed a thin strand of blond hair over her ear, so pale it seemed to disappear. The Venetian's attention on the teenager unsettled Shinobu. The Alpine girl was not much younger than Jessica, but she was still undoubtedly a child. Shinobu could not tell if Sofia did not notice the intent in Luka's expression and did not react in order to discourage this attention, or if she simply did not care.

Sofia put down her chopsticks but did not move from her seat. Shinobu realized that she was waiting for the scribe to tell her not to take Luka to Dario, or to ask to come with them, or to demand why Dario was in the Algae Plant at all. Shinobu kept her face blank and said nothing.

Makoto shuffled in from the bridge that led to the Vaults, a stack of papers hugged close in his arms.

"Shinobu?" he asked. "I need help."

"You shouldn't carry so many papers at once," said Shinobu. "You wouldn't need help if you practiced forethought."

"It's not that. It's some of the verses. I know them from before, but differently. Look," said Makoto. He dropped the stack on the table beside Shinobu, but there were too many papers, scribbles, extra notes in shorthand, to decipher what distressed him. "It's the spot."

The papers were covered in ink spots. So were his sleeves.

"Makoto, I need to help our guest," said Shinobu. She nodded towards Luka, who seemed more amused than annoyed by the intrusion.

"But, Shinobu, it's wrong," Makoto said. "It's *changed*."

Sofia pushed her plate away with a breathy sound of disgust. "Come on then," she said. "Onwards to the Algae Plant."

It took Luka a moment to understand she was talking to him. The door at the far end of the room was already sliding closed before he jumped up to follow her, Shinobu and Makoto already forgotten.

"It's the spot," said Makoto again.

"Which spot?" Shinobu asked, forcing her voice to be calm. "The papers are covered in spots."

"Washizu Asaji's spot," said Makoto. "The damned spot."

*Throne of Blood*. Shinobu frowned as Makoto thrust one of the papers towards her. The speech was familiar. The scene was famous. She felt sick. She had listened to the entirety of *Macbeth* during one of Jessica's recording sessions and had not recognized it as the same story because… it wasn't as *good*. They did not even have the film in its entirety, and sometimes the audio had no matching picture, and sometimes pieces from earlier or later scenes seemed cut and blurred together, but it was such a good film. Everyone in Fuji liked that film, and she now knew two versions of this tale, and she thought that *Throne of Blood* was better. But Shakespeare was supposed to be the best…

She could have told herself it was because Jessica was twisting the Bard's words, but she did not think Jessica was making up everything. She did not believe that the Venetian was clever enough to conjure up hours upon hours of speeches. As Shinobu thought of each convoluted plotline, each disguise that would have fooled no one, each longwinded speech, she realized that she simply did not like Shakespeare's plays.

Maybe everyone who claimed he was great was wrong. But Shinobu feared that, maybe, she was too close to being a Dreamer to understand why he was great.

## Chapter 21 (Jessica)

"But the important part of *Coriolanus*," said Jessica, "is fighting against a corrupt system, no matter what you lose at the end."

"But he died," said Ama. "Brutally."

"Yes, but he died as a hero, because he became a better person."

"Did he?"

"Die as a hero? Or become a better person?" asked Jessica.

"Both," said Ama. She was getting bored. "Neither. Whatever. Makoto, could you get us some snacks? I want snacks."

From Jessica's position, head hanging off the edge of Ama's bed, curls trailing on the floor, it looked like Makoto was walking on the ceiling.

"No fusarium!" Ama shouted after him, giggling. Jessica joined her giggles, as if the empress had referenced a joke, and not the time Jessica nearly died.

"What would *you* like?" asked Makoto, pausing by the door.

"Daifuku mochi," said Jessica, and Makoto left to bring her what she wanted.

A thrill ran through Jessica. She spoke, and people listened, and they did not ask questions. There may have been dubious morals in the original texts, about women and outsiders, but not when Jessica seasoned the words with commentary. And what she said was taken as fact. She was an authority. It was strange and intoxicating.

Ama, perched on an overstuffed pillow, hopped down. She pulled off her pale blue wig and pushed away part of the wall that smoothly slipped to the side, revealing a larger collection of wigs.

"How does it do that?" asked Jessica.

"How does what do what?" asked Ama.

"The wall. How does it move, when you touch it?" said Jessica, and the empress laughed in the way that Jessica had learned meant she would not answer because she did not know.

"You're still so naïve," said Ama. "It's lovely."

Jessica knew that when it came to how the technology of Fuji worked, Ama was equally naïve, and tended to lean on the answer that her family made it a long time ago. According to Ama, her family pulled the Coil from the ground fully formed. Doors opened automatically because her family demanded that they open. Any technology that satisfied their whims was less important than the whim itself. Ama thought she had the room at the highest point in the Coil because she wanted it, not because other people let her have it.

When Jessica pushed for specifics of *how* the magic that existed throughout Fuji might work (the screens that flashed any food choice you could want, the windows that turned dark when you wanted to nap, the cool air that circulated through every interior), Ama would throw up her hands and suggest that Jessica ask Shinobu.

"Tell me about Ibada," said Ama. "What's he like?"

Where had *that* question come from? Jessica imagined Ama's mind as a chaotic mosaic of mismatched tiles, each one fighting for dominance. Perhaps this subject had come from a conversation they had days ago.

"He's very kind," said Jessica. "Friendly. Welcoming. I don't know why you're asking me. You've known him much longer than I have."

"I meant more, *what's he like in bed*, but you don't have to tell me if you don't want to."

Jessica sat bolt upright. "I'm not, and we haven't!" she sputtered. She rolled her shoulders back and took a deep breath. "I *mean*… I don't know what he's like in bed. If you're curious, maybe that's something *you* should pursue!"

She meant the last part as a joke and did not understand why she was immediately angry at Ama at the idea. But Ama waved away the words, tossing her long wig to the ground in favour of a short, spiky pink one.

"I'm not interested in men," said Ama. "And I'm occupied enough with Yuki and Sumikai. I've never met a man who was half as pretty as either of them."

"Luka's pretty," said Jessica, the words out of her mouth before she could regret saying them.

Ama shrugged. "If you like that sort of thing," she said. "I didn't really notice. Why are you smiling?"

Jessica could not help it. She and Andrusha had been so sure Luka's beauty would endear them to the empress, and Ama had not even noticed. They could have left him behind. In Fuji, Jessica was the Venetian who mattered. "No reason," she said.

"Maybe Luka is a *little* prettier than Ibada," Ama conceded, though she did not sound convinced. "But Ibada will miss you if you go. I was going to make you stay for me, but maybe he could be more persuasive."

"I need to be convinced?"

"Luka said you were leaving with him and Andrusha on the Alpine ship."

"I was unaware of these plans," said Jessica, frowning. "I guess he forgot to tell me."

"It does seem like he forgets that you are friends," said Ama, shrugging. "Or else he thinks you're so close he doesn't need to talk to you."

"Am I supposed to be leaving?" asked Jessica, uncertainly. She *had* shared all of the Bard's plays. Maybe that was all they wanted.

"No, you're supposed to *want* to stay because I want you to stay," said Ama, opening a new part of her wall to reveal jackets piled on top of jackets. "That's much better than me having to *make* you stay. But you should probably talk to Luka because he definitely thinks you want to leave."

Jessica stood up and lurched for the door. "I'll be back."

"What about your mochi?" Ama called after her.

Jessica curved down the coiling hallway, sliding her star pendant back and forth along its chain. She knocked on Luka's door, and swallowed her surprise when Dario opened it.

"Pardon me," he said, slipping past her into the hall. "I enjoyed your performance last night. Titania's monologue was very illuminating. I think I actually laughed."

"You did. She had just been drugged," said Jessica. "It was a very embarrassing situation for her."

"Later, true," said Dario. "But not at that moment."

"Excuse me, I need to speak to Luka."

Jessica left Dario behind her and entered Luka's room. The Venetian jumped up when he saw her and immediately tried to cover a large crate next to his bed with his sheets.

"What is that?" she asked.

"Is anyone in the hall?" asked Luka.

"Dario."

Luka's shoulders slumped in relief. He pulled back the sheet and beckoned to Jessica.

"Look at this."

She had meant to confront him immediately, but curiosity mixed with the pleasure at being called close, so she approached, quiet and cautious. He opened the lid of the crate.

Jessica was not sure what she was looking at. Something large, metal and heavy. Something that Luka could not have carried to his room alone. Something he was trying to hide. Whatever it was, it had put him in debt to Dario and made him nervous.

"What did you *do*?" asked Jessica.

"It's a sōrui-jin," whispered Luka. "We're bringing it back to Venice. We can make our own algae blocks and we won't have to depend on Fuji."

"You're stealing it."

"There's no reason for us not to have one!" Luka shut the box again. "We could probably sneak up another and keep it in your room."

"I'm *not* going to help you steal from Fuji," said Jessica. "The empress has been so kind to us—"

"To us, yes, but what about Venice?" asked Luka, grabbing her arm as she turned to leave. "She ignored Andrusha's letters for years!"

"Shinobu hid them from her!"

"You believe that?"

"I do," said Jessica. Luka let go and sat back on the bed. Jessica's arm throbbed where he had grabbed her. "Why did you tell Ama I wanted to leave?"

"The Fujians won't let outsiders stay forever, no matter how amusing you are," said Luka. "It's smarter to leave before the empress gets tired of you, while there's a ship that's willing to take you back to Venice. Besides, don't you want to make sure the Upper Keep gets algae blocks?"

"Why don't you just make sure that the Upper Keep gets its own sōrui-jin?" asked Jessica. Luka did not look at her. "You could, but... you're not going to do that, are you?"

Jessica realized she was worrying the star on her necklace. She dropped her hand.

"You're not going to get away with stealing from the empress," she said. "I'm sure someone has already figured out that the sōrui-jin are missing."

"Etsuna thinks that they broke and were scrapped for fuel in the Station," said Luka. "He'll find out the truth eventually, soon maybe, but Ibada, Dario and I have been covering for each other. It's not just Venice. Ibada is taking two back to Kilimanjaro. Dario has, well, I don't know how many—"

"Oh, well if *Dario's* doing it, it must be a good idea," said Jessica, rolling her eyes.

"It's not a *bad* idea."

"Do whatever you want," said Jessica. "But keep me out of it. I'm staying here."

"Shinobu will make you leave," said Luka. "She hates you."

True. The scribe was always glaring at her, ever since she knew that Jessica had lied about *The Merchant of Venice*. And Shinobu had her own kind of power in Fuji. If she wanted Jessica gone, Jessica knew that, eventually, she would be gone. But why did Luka look so pleased?

"Why do you want that?" asked Jessica, heat prickling across her skin. "I told you I needed to get out of Venice, and you said you would get me out, and you did. You knew I wasn't planning to go back. I don't need anything else from you. I don't need you anymore."

Luka reached for her, his face contorted with anger. Jessica hit him before she could think about what she was doing. He leaned back, shocked, one hand pressed against his cheek where Jessica's hand had struck him. Her palm tingled but the pain had not yet set in. She wanted to apologize but bit back the urge. When someone tried to hurt you, you hit back. Her father had taught her that. He also taught her that it did not mean they would not try to hurt you again. Jessica held herself tall, refusing to let him think she was afraid. Because she was not afraid. She was powerful.

"Is that what you're mad about?" asked Jessica, the words escaping on a breathless laugh. "That I don't need you? Did you think I would be helpless here? Or did you think I wouldn't have any friends, because who would be friends with me besides you?"

"You've always needed me," said Luka. He held his ground, but warily. "I saved your life."

"You stopped me from seeing my mother die," said Jessica. "And I appreciate—"

"No, I saved your life!" shouted Luka.

"What are you talking about?"

"I knocked on your house leg that morning to get you to come down," said Luka. Jessica nodded. She tried so hard to forget that day, but she did remember something bringing her down the ladder, calling her away from the Upper Keep before the sun rose. "I made sure that you weren't there when the Venetians came."

"Wait," said Jessica. "You knew it was going to happen?"

"Yes. And I saved you again, when it started, and you tried to go back up. You wanted to get back to your family, and I held you back in the shadows where they couldn't see you."

Jessica remembered his arms over her; she remembered them often. She thought those arms had shielded her. But now she could feel those arms, like bars over a cell, holding her down. Keeping her away as the blood fell from above.

"If you had told me, I could have gone up for my mother."

"There was no time for that," Luka said.

"I could have told everyone," Jessica said. "We could have tried to run…"

"I only had time to save you."

"I could have saved my mother!"

"You would have died too!" Luka shouted.

He sat on the edge of his bed, every muscle in his body trembling with anger. "You can't survive without me," he said. "You would kill yourself doing something stupid. Like trusting the Fujians. Shinobu hates you. Ama will get bored with you, and then she'll want you out. If you don't leave with me now—"

"You'll make me?" asked Jessica. She rubbed her hand, but it did nothing to ease the pain. "You can't. I don't want to go back to Venice."

"Then I guess I'll have to wait here with you until you do."

Jessica left the room. She passed by Dario, still in the Coil, but he did not stop her. Jessica wondered if he had overheard.

She could feel Ama's grasp on her wrist still, like a promise that she would never get tired of her, but now that feeling was intertwined with the memory of Luka beneath the Upper Keep. Every hand that had clung onto her was like a weight, pulling her down, drowning her. Jessica broke into a run. The colours of the paintings blended together as she sped past them, until she could not tell whether it was the windows or the frames that held the image of a monster breaking the surface of blues and greys washed together in violent swirls. By the time she found sanctuary, her eyes were burning and the chain of her necklace was choking her, but all she wanted to do was keep running.

# Chapter 22 (Cem)

"Hey, Cem!"

Abraham did not rouse from his sleep at the sound of Farooq's voice. Cem checked to make sure the old man was still breathing, then hopped out to the balcony. Farooq was waiting for him with three other children. For a moment, Cem did not recognize them, but then the hissing in his head receded, and he realized they were Sedef, Ruben, and Chava. These lapses were happening more frequently. It would be a problem soon, but it was not something to think too hard about right now because all four children were holding algae blocks.

Cem caught one that Farooq threw to him, and immediately munched on the slippery substance. Algae blocks meant that Venice was not going to starve. So why did the other children not look happy?

"There's something strange on the Main," said Chava.

"A ship arrived," said Farooq. "Andrusha's back."

"And Jessica?" Cem asked.

"No," said Farooq. "He's the only Venetian who returned with them."

"The Fujians brought him back," Cem said, deciding immediately that he would not tell Abraham.

"No. Different people," said Sedef. "White people."

White? Maybe it was a ghost ship. But why would ghosts bring food?

"Were they the ones that brought the algae blocks?" Cem asked.

"Yes," said Sedef. "And they brought something they say is better."

Cem spat over the edge of the balcony. Chava giggled. She did that whenever Cem or Farooq spat.

"A white man is putting on some kind of show for it," said Ruben.

"I don't think it's a show," said Farooq. "At least, not like Jessica's. Someone should check it out."

The other children looked at Cem, expectedly.

"You and I could go?" Farooq prompted.

Cem nodded. It would not be safe to be alone on the Main, let alone when it was full of ghosts, and they were the two who had grown up there. But Cem thought it was a bad sign that Sedef did not feel comfortable spying on the white people and wanted to leave the work to the older boys.

He followed Farooq down the ladder.

"I'll take care of Abraham while you're out," said Ruben before Cem had gone too far.

"Bring him some blocks," Cem called back. He did not say that Abraham had already had a meal today. Let him have two.

They did not run into any other children on the boulders. There was a new ship moored in the harbour beside the weathered Fujian trading vessel, unfamiliar, but beautiful: the colour of light grey clouds sparkling with sunlight. It was like an idea of a ship, from some fantastic story. Cem wanted to touch that smooth hull, but Farooq was already scrambling up the steps to the Main. Cem did his best to memorize every glinting point of the vessel before following Farooq, although he could feel the memory disappearing into the now near-constant hissing inside his skull.

Farooq stopped suddenly on the ramparts. He looked upwards. Cem saw a wall of backs on the open balcony of one of the towers, framed by a trefoil arch. An accented, musical voice floated down to the boys. No one stopped them at the door like they used to when they were part of the gang. Cem and Farooq ran up the stairs, past the adults whispering in anxious conversations. They were oblivious to the boys, who joined the back of the crowd, blocked from moving further forwards. The words of the melodic voice were now easily heard, though the speaker remained hidden. There was a rumbling sound like a small, constant cave in. It must have been part of the show.

"The trays can be cut into blocks. There are tools for even cuts in Fuji, but you can use any sharp object to do it."

A few of the Feral were huddled in the stairwell, including Nazli. Cem had not seen the girl since Roman freed her from Grigory's cave. She seemed as fine as any of the Feral could be and made no sign that she recognized Cem.

"The algae's poisonous," said Zehra, her growl unmistakable though she remained hidden somewhere in front of them. Many voices grumbled in agreement. "Aren't the blocks poisonous?"

"Not after they are… sent through the sōrui-jin," said the man, his melodic voice faltering.

"Sent through?" asked a man. "What does that even mean?"

His words were met with the rough thwack of several people spitting, and the crowd murmured, unhappy, untrusting.

"I'm sorry," said the musical voice. "I don't know the words for engine parts in Diplomacy."

"We don't have to know *how* it works to know that it *does* work. The sōrui-jin makes algae blocks. We can make our own food now."

Cem recognized Andrusha's booming voice. The man's confidence seemed to calm most of the crowd, but one agitated figure moved to the side of the group. The way she shifted, uneasily, as she separated herself from the crowd, made Cem far less sure of Andrusha's statement than the other Venetians.

The girl had light blond hair and the whitest arms he had ever seen. She looked up with round eyes the colour of blue sky. She was wearing a dress made of a muted pink and unfamiliar material. She bared her teeth at Cem; he thought she might have been trying to smile but had forgotten how. The rumbling stopped suddenly, and the girl's eyes darted towards the focus of the crowd's attention.

"It's broken," said Zehra.

"It needs to be…" the man searched for the right word. "Exchanged."

There was a scraping sound, like mussel cuts on stone. Some of the crowd moved forward, some leaned back, and the shift of bodies created pockets of empty space. Cem slid forward until he was at the front of the crowd. He shivered when he saw a white man, even paler than the girl. He wore the same pink material, but on his nearly translucent body, it looked blood-stained.

This man stood behind a large box constructed of several smaller boxes that were fused together and held aloft by black legs affixed at each end. He had lifted a thin metal sheet off the top of the central box with long sea-spray fingers and tilted it forwards, towards the crowd. It turned without separating, locked on some hinges that Cem could not see, filled with a familiar black and grey striped mass: mussels. The man gave the box a rough shake and the mass fell to the tiles. Many of them had grown together, but a few pairs and single mussels clattered and skidded towards the crowd. Several of the spectators had to jump away to avoid getting cut.

Andrusha was standing over the display, smiling, triumphant, acting like the hero of Venice once again, though it seemed to Cem that the white man was doing all the work.

"The mussels need to be exchanged with new ones, um... *clean* ones," the white man explained, although Cem did not think the mussels that had fallen from the sōrui-jin looked particularly dirty. "You need a single layer at the bottom of the sōrui-jin to start. They'll grow on their own, and the engine won't run until there are enough for it to work properly."

"How will the sōrui-jin know?" asked a man at the front of the crowd.

"It's been imbued with the empress's magic," Andrusha announced.

"It reacts to the weight change," said the white man.

The Feral from the stairway had slipped into the crowd to gather the mussels. Cem knelt and snatched up two. Someone hissed near his ear. He hissed back and the small figure darted away. Cem untucked his shirt and wrapped the mussels in the loose material, hiding them away from any greedy eyes.

"Taking a gift back to your keepers?" whispered a voice.

Cem snapped his head back. Borya was behind him, laughing quietly.

"They're mine," Cem hissed. "And I'm not… *kept.*"

"Of course you're not," said Borya. They stood with confidence, as if their jutting collarbones and hollow cheeks were a choice and not the result of slow starvation. "You managed to escape from here," they said. "Not as good an escape as the Jew girl managed, though. She sailed away and sent us these white monsters."

"Ghosts," said Cem. He clamped his mouth shut, but Borya nodded.

"You know, I could sail away, too, if I wanted," they said. "But it wouldn't be any better. I asked Andrusha. He said the children died in Fuji, too. He said the empress was silly."

"Why are you here?" asked Cem.

"What?"

"If you could sail away, why are you still here?"

Borya shrugged. "There's nowhere I want to go."

The image of Andrusha's red beard mixed with thoughts of trade and violence, gifts and abandonment, sailors coming to Venice, Borya sailing away… What was that Jew girl's name? Was she someone's daughter? Cem desperately wanted to crouch and scramble and hiss. He wanted to bite Borya's hand. He needed to stop panicking or else…

"Are you all right?" The white man's voice was still musical, but laced with a sharpness that made Borya retreat into the crowd. Cem snapped back to himself. He could see a few of the Venetians still standing around the sōrui-jin with Andrusha. Andrusha's eyes were on the white man. He looked helpless, although his smile remained fixed on his face. He was responding to the Venetians' questions, but Cem did not think he knew the answers. This white man probably knew, but he did not have the words for them.

"Thanks," said Cem.

The man bent down. Cem supposed it was his way of trying to seem friendly, but there was nothing friendly about those round pale eyes.

"I'm happy to help," he said.

From behind Cem's shoulder, Farooq said, "Is that why you're here?"

Cem had not heard him approach. He felt the heat of Farooq's body close behind, but he could not look away from the white man's face.

"I'm here to make sure no one in Venice starves," said the man.

"I thought that was the empress's job," said Farooq.

"And I decided she wasn't doing a very good job."

"So, did you come to help," asked Farooq, "or to show the empress that she was doing a bad job?"

A muscle twitched in the white man's jaw. "I came to help."

"The empress has been ignoring our letters for years," said Farooq. "Why are you helping us now?"

"Can't you just be happy that he brought the algae blocks?" Cem hissed at Farooq.

The white man reached out a hand, and for a moment Cem thought he was going to grab him. Instead, he merely ruffled the boy's hair.

"It's good to want more than just algae blocks," said the man, his voice soothing. "It's good to question the motives of others. I understand your friend's distrust, especially with new people."

He smiled past Cem at Farooq.

"It's not because you look…" Farooq started, and then stopped and blushed.

The man was not listening. He reached for Cem's sleeve, as if to admire the design. Cem was wearing a tunic that Abby had given him after his own plastic ties finally broke. It had belonged to one of her older sons. The boy's initials were embroidered on the sleeve, in the middle of a six-pointed star.

"Would you do me a favour?" the man asked. "Make sure that some of these algae blocks get to the Upper Keep? I heard there might be difficulties..."

"We already did," said Farooq.

The man nodded and his expression softened. Cem thought that he seemed nice. He had brought food. He was even talking to two unimportant boys while Andrusha was clearly taking the credit. But still Cem found himself fighting the urge to run away, to hiss, or scream. Something about this man was not right…

"What are you wearing?" said Cem. He immediately regretted his question. The man's eyes flicked up. He looked almost fearful.

"It's a local fabric," he said, hardening into cold amusement.

"Not plastic?" asked Cem.

"No."

The hissing in Cem's head was almost overwhelming. The man's hands were on his shoulders, trying to steady him as he swayed, but Cem jerked in his grip. Suddenly the man's pale companion was by his side, gently removing those long fingers with the mere suggestion of her touch.

"Dario," she said. "Let him go." Her voice rang with a similar melody, but hers was a sad kind of song.

"I don't know why he's so upset, Sofia," Dario said defensively. "I was being kind."

"New honours come upon him," said Sofia. "Like our strange garments—"

"Cleave not to their mould but with the aid of use," Farooq quickly replied, cutting off her quiet voice. The girl stared at him, her eyes widening.

"Our little actress was telling the truth," Dario said. "We should go to the Upper Keep, make copies for Shinobu. Bring back proof."

"It would take too long," said Sofia. "If Shinobu wants proof so badly, she should come here and get it herself."

"But it could be a gift," said Dario. "An apology of sorts."

"I want to go home."

Dario sighed. All his hard amusement was gone. "We should help the Venetians set up the engine." He turned to the boys, nodded, and then fixed his pinkish shawl around his head. There was something familiar about it. Clouds of blood in the water.

"The redhead," muttered Cem.

He did not know what he meant, some hazy memory, but Sofia looked upset. Before he could explain, she dragged Dario back to Andrusha. Farooq grabbed Cem's arm and pulled him away. Cem, his hands still hiding the mussels against his chest, struggled to keep his balance as they ran down the stairs, across the ramparts, and to the boulders past the harbour.

"Why'd you take them?" asked Farooq. "We have food."

"I thought the old man might want them," said Cem.

"He won't eat them."

A rope ladder fell down. Cem, still cradling the mussels, followed Farooq up. Farooq was right. The old man did not eat mussels. The old man… He had a name, and it was not *father*, but that was the only word Cem could grasp onto, through the *hiss*…

Ruben, Chava, and Sedef were waiting for them on the balcony.

"Was it a show?" asked Ruben.

"No," said Farooq. "It was a machine that makes algae blocks." He walked along the rope bridge that led towards Talia's home, and Chava and Ruben followed, speaking all at once, a series of questions that rapidly turned to noise. Sedef did not follow them, instead sliding by Cem to get to the ladder and the world below.

"Stay for dinner?" asked Cem.

Sedef shook her head. "It's getting dark," she said.

Cem unwrapped the mussels. "Here," he said. "Take them."

"Don't you want to eat them?"

"I shouldn't, up here," said Cem. He was not sure if that was true, but Sedef grabbed the mussels and disappeared over the edge of the balcony. The hissing was still there, quiet and constant, but Cem felt better. It felt good to be able to help someone.

## Chapter 23 (Shinobu)

Somewhere in Fuji, Ama was screaming. Shinobu could not hear it, but she could feel the tantrum that rumbled throughout the city like an earthquake. It shone in the eyes of all the trembling scribes. The vibrations of Ama's anger penetrated the silence of their plugged ears as they entered the Rice Farm where Shinobu was torturing Luka.

It was not the flashy kind of torture Dario would have employed. The soft bells, small gongs, and water-light chimes that the rotating procession of scribes brought in and out every few hours could have been soothing. But it was constant.

The Rice Farm, far from the central Coil, was usually noisy. The harvesting machines, now turned off, thundered as they scraped through the man-made ponds. But the building was soundproofed. The squealing and cracking of metal against metal did not offend any ears outside, nor did the unceasing murmur of bells. Nor the Venetian's infrequent screams. When Ama was calmer, she would remember this. She would be grateful. It was helpful for Shinobu to remind herself of that as she too suffered through the ringing and the screaming.

Luka sat in front of her, secured by a wide belt to a bench welded into the wall, ankle tied to ankle, wrist tied to wrist behind his back. His eyes flicked to her, then to the scribes who sat further away, instruments balanced in their laps.

"Why did Dario take the sōrui-jin?" Shinobu asked. Her throat was sore from three days of questioning.

"He wanted to save the world." Luka leaned towards her, and the belt cut into his stomach. He winced in pain. Shinobu sighed. She was tired, Ama was angry, and the ringing of the bells was vibrating her teeth. "Dario wanted everyone to be able to make their own algae blocks," said Luka. "He wanted to help the people starving in Venice, share the technology."

"What a wonderfully altruistic plan," said Shinobu. "You should have said it was your idea. Or Andrusha's. Then I might have believed you."

Luka had been quick to blame Dario, an immediate confession on the first day. It would have looked as though he was enthusiastically cooperating if it had not been such an obvious lie. At least, it had seemed obvious three days ago.

"I told you what Dario told me, that's all I know." Luka's voice was strained. "If you don't believe me, I don't know what to tell you."

"Tell me what Dario is going to do with the sōrui-jin."

"He's going to help people!" groaned Luka. His body sagged gently to his side, head lolling towards his left shoulder, before his fluttering eyes snapped back open. He pulled himself upright. "He's… He's going to… Who? Who are we talking…"

"Dario. What is he planning to do with the sōrui-jin?"

"I told you," Luka said. "Why is that so impossible for you to believe?"

The bells rang. Shinobu's head throbbed. "Because he wears human skin, Luka," she said. "The Alpines wear human skin. They kill the poor, and they eat their meat, and they turn their skin into cloaks and boots."

"I know," said Luka.

"You know?" Shinobu asked, almost laughing, almost hysterical. "You know, and you're telling me that you trust him? You don't think he's going to find a way to keep hurting people. To abuse Ama's gift?"

"He's not going to hurt people. He's going to feed people."

"So, he's trying to increase their livestock," Shinobu said, settling into the sense of it. "Increase the people who depend on them, that they can take from and kill, who then fear them. Worship them. Hate them."

"No," Luka said, loud despite the obvious pain it caused. "He knows what he has done. What Les Alpes has done. He told me what happened to Sofia's family. He's always tried to help her, but it wasn't enough. He'll try to help the whole world, and it will never be enough, but he *is* trying. He's trying for the same reasons that make it impossible for you to believe him. He wants to make up for what he's done. I don't know if he can, but if his guilt will feed Venice, I don't care."

"Feeding Venetians doesn't make up for a culture of cruelty," said Shinobu.

Still, she understood guilt, that weighted bundle that would not sink quietly into the Flood. She understood that, as impossible as it was, Dario might try to ease that burden. Sofia had said not to trust him, but the girl had her reasons to hate Dario and the rest of the Alpines who lived within the walls. Revenge could be as impossible as redemption, but Shinobu understood the pull of that, too.

"I don't know," whispered Luka. His voice was failing after his outburst. "We wanted to help people. I… I don't know anymore. I'm sorry. Please. I want to sleep…"

He was probably telling the truth. Shinobu meant to tell him that they were done, but she had another concern, one that might not have mattered to the world or to Fuji, but which mattered to her.

"One last question," said Shinobu. Luka looked up, hope flashing in his eyes. "Why is Shakespeare important?"

Luka's surprise seemed to melt away some of his pain. "You're the one who told us that he was important," he said. "We didn't even know until we got here. I just thought the stories were fun."

"You know the stories better than I do," said Shinobu. "I knew about them. I knew their reputation. But I listen to them, and…"

"And?"

"And they're nothing more than stories!" said Shinobu. "And some of them are copies of stories we already know. They're set in a time that's nothing like the world we live in, not even like the world before the Flood. A world that existed centuries ago, but people kept telling them, and performing them, and describing them as the most amazing stories ever told, describing Shakespeare as the greatest writer… I believed them. But I don't hear it! I don't understand why these stories, written so long ago for people who don't exist, for a time that does not exist, should matter to us. Why Shakespeare matters. Why those who know his words matter."

The gongs and the bells echoed around the walls.

"They weren't written for a certain time or people," Luka said, frowning as he searched for the right answer. "The pieces of them that place them in a certain time aren't important. It's what the stories mean. The truth behind the words."

"So, I'm supposed to believe Shakespeare was a genius that lived during a particular moment in history where he could recognize these timeless truths and make up these stories that are supposed to matter, and which keep mattering…"

"I don't think so," said Luka. "I don't think he made them up. The stories are *timeless*. I'm sure that there were lost twins, and abandoned sorcerers, and betrayed rulers long before Shakespeare. And their stories continued long after

Shakespeare's world died, and will continue long after our world dies, too."

"You don't think he made up the stories?" asked Shinobu.

"I think he made up the words to the speeches and songs. But the original stories? No. I think he wrote them down, with his own little changes. He recorded them. Like—"

"Like a scribe."

Luka nodded.

Shakespeare was not simply an entertainer, or a writer, or a poet. He recorded stories, histories, truth, for future generations. He was a *scribe*… And that was the most important work of all. The preservation of stories for the future. Not the performance of them. And certainly not the performer.

"Will you let me go now?" asked Luka.

"Where's Jessica?" said Shinobu.

"I thought you said that was the last question."

"I changed my mind."

Luka hesitated a moment. "She went home," he said. "Back to Venice, with Andrusha and Dario."

"Why didn't you?"

Luka's head had fallen towards his chest. He was crying again, twitching with each strike of the gong and shuddering in time with the tinkling chimes. He had not cried since the first day, when she had been so sure he was lying about Dario. Her mistake. Luka had actually been quite helpful. Shinobu nodded at the scribes, who stopped their instruments, and, with relief, got to their feet and raced out of the room. Shinobu was left to untie her prisoner. Once she was alone with Luka, she reached into her sleeve and pulled out Jessica's necklace.

When Shinobu had seen the Star on the girl's nightstand, she had considered hiding it in the Vaults with the memoirs, but she had not liked the thought of keeping it with her treasures. It was a piece of the actress, and Jessica's decision to leave it behind did not change that truth. She pressed the necklace into Luka's hand; he immediately clutched the metal in his fist so hard that Shinobu wondered if he was trying to crush it. If so, he was wasting his time. The necklace was stronger than it looked.

#

Shinobu followed the path of fallen paintings Ama left in her wake as she raged through the Coil.

"Those sōrui-jin were *mine*!" the empress's voice echoed around the curving hall. "*Jessica* was mine!"

Shinobu picked up one of the pieces lying haphazardly in the middle of the floor. It was the glaring warrior riddled with arrows. She leaned it upright. She left the spiral-headed girl where she had fallen, precariously propped against the curving wall, as though she was deciding whether or not to give in to gravity. Chaos suited her.

"Shinobu!" Ama shouted, sustaining the last vowel with a whine.

Shinobu hurried to the empress.

Ama was waiting for her at the base of the Coil, struggling with a larger painting of two very startled dragons. She hoisted the creatures into the air and threw them to the ground before running her fingers through her short hair. It stuck up at wild angles. Her piercings glittered in the neon lights, and for a moment a frightening image flashed into Shinobu's mind, of Ama's wild hands tearing out each of her jewelled piercings, blood pouring from the wounds across her face. Shinobu rushed forward and grabbed the empress's hands in her own. Ama frowned at her, crowding the piercings in her brow.

"Let go of my hands," she said.

"Stop hurting the art," said Shinobu, but she released Ama.

"This is *your* fault," said the empress, her voice no longer panicked, but measured and cold. "The sōrui-jin. Jessica. I know it is."

Shinobu kept her face blank.

"Where's the Venetian?" asked Ama.

"Which—"

"The only one that's left!" said Ama.

"Luka is in the hospital ward."

"Is he sick?" asked Ama. "He's probably faking it."

"He's recovering," said Shinobu.

"You didn't do anything Dario would do?"

"No," said Shinobu. "But he still needs time to recover."

"Where's Jessica?"

"She went home."

Ama nodded, then turned and left the Coil. As the glass door slid shut behind her, Shinobu could see the wind buffeting her wide pink sleeves. A storm was coming. Shinobu considered staying behind and hanging up the pictures, but the sight of Ama's little body nearly billowing away made her quaver, and she followed the empress. Ama was already stepping into the safety of a covered bridge, but not the one that led to the hospital.

"Where are you going?" Shinobu called out over the screams of the wind. "We know where the sōrui-jin have gone. We know that Dario is responsible."

Ama did not reply. It was like talking to an illustration, but Shinobu could not stop trying for an answer.

"Even if Dario isn't being malicious, we can't expect all the cities to use the engines responsibly," she said. "They'll work them until they break. They'll use the wrong algae. They'll need us again when everything goes wrong. They'll realize they cannot save themselves without you."

Did Ama turn her head? Maybe slightly, but she kept moving forward, over the Greenhouse, to a second covered bridge.

"We still have sōrui-jin," said Shinobu. "We can keep making blocks. We can be ready for the day when they come back for help. Then they'll appreciate you even more. And we'll be able to help them more when there are…"

*Fewer of them.*

The empress wanted to save everyone. Ama had not been able to save everyone before, because there were too many of them to save. If the men failed to share the sōrui-jin properly, as Shinobu was sure would happen, then there would be a manageable number of people left. Ama could save the whole world, exactly as she wanted.

They were approaching another covered bridge, one that would take them to the building at the farthest edge of the city: the Station. Even the bridge reeked of the melting and burning plastic that was consumed within for fuel. Shinobu held her sleeve over her mouth and nose, but the smell made her eyes water. The bridge curved down sharply and deposited her on the flat path that bordered the Station.

Shinobu slipped her glasses out of her sleeve pocket. The murk of the ocean took clear shape and form. The waves lapping at the lip of the path were not vague threats but solid and sure. And so *high*… The ocean's surface was nearly the same height as the path. Had the Flood risen further?

Shinobu followed Ama around the corner of the building, towards the working entrance for the gathering vessels.

"Ama, this isn't a good idea," said Shinobu.

"You don't know what I'm thinking!"

The skimmers and runners were readying themselves for another expedition to harvest the plastic trash that littered the vast ocean. They looked up from where they crouched working on the deck of their gathering vessels. Most of them jumped up to bow deeply. The others gaped. They were never graced with the appearance of the empress, and the head scribe too rarely visited.

"Is something wrong with the Greenhouse?" asked Yana.

"No, it's fine," said Shinobu.

She let the *for now* remain unsaid, though the runner nodded like it had been spoken.

Ama was frowning at the bulky and slow gathering vessels. They were nothing like the trade ships, now all lost or broken.

"How far can your vessels travel from Fuji?" asked Ama.

"As far as they need to go," answered Yana before Shinobu could interject.

"As far as Venice?" asked the empress, her voice too pleased.

"They've never had to travel as far as K2," said Shinobu.

Yana and the runner Yousuke glanced at each other, and Shinobu wondered if she was wrong. It was probably a good thing, for the world, if they had to venture so far for dense collections of plastic. It meant the oceans were getting a little cleaner. But it was not such a good thing for the continuation of the Station, which needed a readily available supply of plastic.

"We've gone as far as the Everest Crater," said Yana. "Well, once. It overstressed the ship. We had to feed it to the Station when we returned."

"It's not safe," Shinobu said to Ama. "It's not a good plan. You can't ask them to take such a risk while you wait safe at home."

"I won't be waiting," snapped Ama. "I'll be taking the risk with them."

"What did you say?" asked Shinobu.

The gathering vessels had much less room below deck than the trade ships. Shinobu could not imagine Ama in that small brig built to shelter the workers.

"We will go to Venice, and the rest of the cities around the world, and we will get our engines back," said Ama. "And Jessica. I'll need at least one runner and one skimmer. Probably two of each, to keep the vessel in working condition."

"What about the Station?" asked Yana.

"It'll be fine with one pair to maintain it," shrugged Ama. "That's what the Greenhouse is for, anyway. They were each made to complement the other's work."

Yes, they were made to be backups in case the other energy source failed to perform to standard. That did not mean that you planned for one of them to fail by displacing the majority of the workers.

Ama had positioned her hand in a manner she thought was discreet over her nose and mouth, but the rancid odour of rotting sea creatures stuck inside ancient plastic containers, the salt-sick smell of the seaweed half-dried in the sun, and the musk of humans who spent their lives rummaging through trash was too much to be blocked out. The empress's eyes were watering; Shinobu's too. Hirokai had been a runner before Shinobu transferred him to the trading ships. He lived among this garbage for years, yet he still complained about the scent of the ramparts of Venice. If Ama could barely stand the stench of the gathering vessels, she would never be able to handle going to K2.

"You can't go," said Shinobu.

"You can't tell me what to do," said Ama.

"I can advise you. You used to trust my advice."

"View this as an opportunity to earn back my trust," said Ama. "Bring your copies of the plays. Check them for accuracy in the Upper Keep. Wasn't that always your plan? This will be a good chance to prove that you're still useful."

"I interrogated Luka," Shinobu insisted. "I found out who was responsible for stealing the sōrui-jin. I found out where Jessica is. I think I've proven my usefulness."

Ama was not listening. "You two…" she said, pointing.

"Yana," said the runner. "And Minato."

"And you two…" Ama gestured to Masuna and Yousuke. They did not offer their names, looking to Shinobu for guidance. "You will join our journey to K2. We will leave tomorrow morning."

It was too soon to adequately prepare for such a long voyage. No one protested.

"We will meet at dawn at the Greenhouse," Ama continued.

Ama never woke before dawn. She sometimes did not go to sleep until after the first light had just begun to rise over the horizon.

"I will have everything we need for the journey," Ama said, then she paused to consider. "Mizutsuki and Kazuku will help."

They would help, and they would not argue.

"Clear out anything from the vessel that you do not need," the empress ordered. "Make sure there is room enough for the six of us."

"You don't need me to go with you," said Shinobu, panic rising in her throat. "Any one of you can check the accuracy of the plays without my help."

The ocean looked so large, containing a myriad of horrors she had only heard of, and never wanted to see. Ama smiled cruelly – someone who knew exactly how powerful they were, staring at someone who could not refuse them.

"I'm sure you would love to be left in charge of Fuji," said Ama. "But your job is to serve me."

Shinobu's job was to serve the dead, to preserve their voices, to save words and art and information for future generations. But the empress walked away before she could begin to protest. Shinobu was left as the sole object of attention for an audience that knew this was a terrible idea, but there was nothing any of them could do to stop it.

## Chapter 24 (Cem)

For the past few days, Sedef's moans of pain had echoed through the misty air of the Upper Keep. Cem had heard her when Sedef was climbing up the ladder, a surprising amount of noise for someone who had always been so careful about keeping quiet. Her skin was too hot when Cem grabbed her arms to help her hoist her tiny body to the balcony, but she did not sweat. She was dry, and her lips were cracked. Foaming drool slipped from the corner of her mouth.

She was an easy target. Cem's first instinct had been to hide her, before some other child saw her. But his mind was full of the strange hissing fog… He was sure they were back in their gang, and that one of Bota's followers would attack Sedef. Farooq found him trying to push the girl through the window into Abraham's home and he talked Cem back to reality, convincing him to take Sedef to Talia.

Through the un-curtained windows, Cem watched Talia tend Sedef. The woman kept a scarf over her face, covering her nose and mouth. She rinsed her hands with boiled water, left to cool, before and after touching the girl. Ruben said those were measures to protect people from getting sick, old tricks from before the Flood. They seemed to work. Talia was fine. But Sedef was getting worse.

"The fever should have broken by now," whispered Chava. She stood with Cem and Farooq, away from the window, though she was clearly drawn to the sounds of Sedef's moans.

"Has a fever lasted this long before?" asked Farooq.

"Yes…" said Chava, but she drew out the word, hesitant. It was a response that invited a question, but Cem did not want to hear the answer.

They moved back from the window as Talia climbed out. She scanned the worried faces, very few of whom had the decency to pretend they were on their way somewhere else and not waiting to see if the girl had died yet. When she caught sight of Cem, she walked over to him, pulling down her scarf in the open air.

"You found her like this?" she asked.

Cem tried to answer, but his tongue refused to cooperate.

"No, she found us," Farooq said. "She climbed up to us."

"Did she get into anything strange? Eat anything new?"

The boys shook their heads. There was nothing new to eat. There was nowhere strange to go.

"She was fine the last time I saw her," said Farooq.

"When was that?"

Cem jumped to his feet, jostling Farooq.

"It was after the white man came!" he shouted, the words finally forming. "She saw the ship arrive, and the sōrui-jin, and D... D..."

"Dario," said Farooq.

"But shouldn't I be sick, too?" asked Cem, the man's name already slipping from his mind. "If it has to do with him?"

"Maybe," said Talia. "Not necessarily. Do you know if he's still here?"

"No, he's not," said Farooq. "All the white people left."

Talia frowned as she thought. "Find Andrusha," she said at last. "This may be a sickness brought from Fuji, and if he knows what it is, he may know what to do about it." Her voice dropped to a whisper, as if she was talking to herself: "Though it could be anything. The symptoms seem like a flu, but it's not behaving like a flu..."

"I'll go," said Cem. He felt Farooq following him and stopped. "I'll go alone."

"But—"

"Watch Sedef for me," said Cem. "If she comes around, she'll want one of Roman's nearby. It won't be so scary for her."

Cem wished Roman was here. He had a way of making his gang members feel better when they were injured or sick. Cem knew that Roman could not come now to help Sedef, but he could not remember why.

"You'll be safe," said Farooq.

Not a question. Cem nodded.

Talia went back into her home, still mumbling questions she could not answer under her breath. Chava was whispering one of the Bard's soliloquies quietly to herself, one about muses of fire, but trying to make sense of the speech made Cem's head hurt. Easier to let the words fade away behind him as he descended to the boulders.

When his feet touched solid rock, he was enveloped by the quiet of a day not yet started, with no one to fill it with whispers. The quiet was wrong, and he did not know what to do about that, so he started walking and hoped he would figure it out.

A small group crouched in the shadows near one of the last house legs: a collection of Feral. One of the girls had bright tiles woven through her long dreadlocks, a process that would have been too time-consuming for the distracted minds of the wild children, so she must have changed very recently, despite being at least as old as Cem. When the group saw him approach, they scattered deeper into the darkness. They left a pile of unopened mussels behind, bloody from their prying hands.

As he made his way up to the ramparts, quiet settled over Cem's shoulders like a shroud. The day was starting, and no one was coming down with desalinators. Cem thought he heard whispers above him, but it was not the growing cacophony of trade and fighting. He shivered and hugged his arms but kept walking up.

When he first heard the moaning, he thought it was his conscience telling him to go back to Sedef. But as he walked higher, the moans became clearer. They were like echoes, voices overlapping; Cem wondered if another person was sick and had crawled away to hide in a cave, howling, lonely and abandoned. But some of the echoes sounded softer: some had the lower timbre of a baritone voice; some shushed like waves; still others cawed like gulls. These were the moans of people, many people. Cem reached the top of the ramparts, sure of what he would see, but shocked all the same.

The sick lay on the tiled floor, three or four next to each other, thrashing and panting and moaning. Their mouths foamed more than Sedef's, and their eyes did not seem to see him, even when he walked over one man to distance himself from the dangerous drop to the harbour. From the thick seaweed still wrapped around his foot, Cem recognized this man as one of Grigory's friends. The smell coming from the wrap was nauseating, and Cem knew that whatever was inside had rotted to the bone. The man's breaths were shallow, and there were long intervals between each dry inhalation.

Some Venetians wandered among the sick, jugs of water held in the crooks of their elbows. They brought the water to the lips of those who could still drink and splashed it over the feverish bodies of those who could not. Some of those walking about looked sick themselves, and they stopped every few steps, as if they had forgotten what they were doing. He recognized Zehra, though she seemed to drink out of her jug more than she offered it to the suffering. Cem tucked his head down and rushed by her, but Zehra did not notice him. She walked as if she was in a dream, with a kind of careful confidence. Cem did not see Ecrin. He had never before seen them apart.

The awful moaning was overwhelming. The Venetians who tried to help, knowing that they could not, were bad enough, but the worst part was all the space. There was so much space to move between the crying and dying. The living walked odd patterns in no particular direction, with no need to weave or find paths. Every pocket of emptiness was a body that used to be there, a person who used to fill it, but was gone.

A thin woman, obviously sick though not yet immobile, was leaning over one of the bodies. Her hand was resting on the man's still chest. The woman reached under the corpse's arms and pulled it to the side of the ramparts until it hung halfway off. She gave the body a sharp kick, and it fell the rest of the way to the water below. The woman spat after it, wiped her hand over her mouth, and ran her fingers through her hair. Her long golden hair.

Nikita.

She looked older now, an adult. But it was not just her age: it was the way she moved with the other adults, disposed of one, accepted a sip of water from another. She was an adult because she was not part of a gang. And Cem was not part of a gang anymore, either. He could not remember why, but he hated it. He wondered if, without their gangs, he and Nikita were still on opposite sides, still at war. A verse filled his head, too beautiful to be quieted by the hissing.

> *"Suppose within the girdle of these walls*
> *Are now confined two mighty monarchies,*
> *Whose high upreared and abutting fronts*
> *The perilous narrow ocean parts asunder."*

Nikita's head jerked up and she glared at him. Cem had not realized he had spoken out loud.

He hopped over a few moaning bodies to get to her, careful not to come too close to the drop, and careful to stay more than an arm's length away. He did not know if she would try to fight.

"Nikita," he said, "what happened here?"

"What kind of stupid question is that? We're sick. We're all getting sick. Are none of you sick in the Upper Keep?"

"No, we are," said Cem hastily. "Sedef…"

Nikita spat near Cem's foot. "Sedef, and almost everyone else."

"Is there anything to do to fix it?" asked Cem.

"Why should I tell you?" Nikita snarled. "Did you know Roman was going to kill Bota? Did you all plan it together? Did you laugh as you climbed up that ladder while the rest of us ran and fought and died?"

"I wouldn't have… I would have stopped that… I think."

Memories threatened to break through his confusion. *Bota was dead.*

"You didn't, though," said Nikita. "And now she's gone."

"It's not my fault," said Cem.

"It's somebody's fault. It has to be."

"Why?"

Nikita twisted a long strand of hair around her finger. "Because then there's something I can do about it."

"There's nothing you can do to help Bota," said Cem. "But Sedef… She didn't do anything wrong. Please, Nikita, does anyone know what's happening? Where's Andrusha? Talia thinks he might have brought it and might know how to fix it."

"Andrusha?" Anger flared in Nikita's eyes. "No, he got sick, too."

"But he brought it," Cem insisted, suddenly sure. "Where is he?"

"Borya said he left with the white man."

Cem remembered Andrusha standing over the sōrui-jin, taking the credit for the white man's gift. He could see that shock of red hair so perfectly, although in his memory the man was standing in the harbour, not in the tower. There was something wrong about that, but the red hair was too distinct for Cem to accept he was misremembering. He knew Andrusha was to blame for all the people that died, and all the people that would die, and now he was too far away to help the people he had hurt.

"Thanks, Nikita," he said. "I'm sorry. About Bota."

Nikita shrugged. "If she hadn't died then, this sickness would have got her. Same with all the kids who died after. They'd all be dead now, anyway."

"No," said Cem. "If Roman and Bota were alive, they would have known what to do. They would have found a way to help us survive."

"You don't look like you need help surviving."

Cem did not have time to reply. Some of the adults had noticed them talking, and he could see curiosity in their eyes that he did not want to feed. He rushed away towards the steps to the harbour. He did not slow down until he reached the Upper Keep's shadows and banged on the nearest house leg. A ladder was dropped down for him and, as he made his way up, he thought about the cries of the dying on the Main. He thought about Nikita's question, and its hidden accusation: *Are none of you sick in the Upper Keep?* Sure, Sedef was sick, but she came from the Main.

As Cem pulled himself onto a balcony, meeting Farooq's quizzical expression with only silence, the quiet from the homes filled him with dread. There was no echo of moaning here, no more space than there was before, no bodies to give to the eels.

So many people were dying on the Main. And no one from the Upper Keep was sick.

## Chapter 25 (Jessica)

Jessica knocked on the golden door. After a brief hesitation, and some muffled coughs, Ibada's voice called out.

"Come in!"

Jessica entered. Inside, Ibada reclined on a plush gold chaise longue, smoking a hookah.

Large portholes dotted Ibada's room. Each time Jessica saw that view, she had to remind herself she was not drowning. She was not stuck in her nightmare, gasping in danger with an unusual mermaid. She was inside a beautiful sub-hybrid ship, en route to Kilimanjaro, completely submerged and yet safe from the water and the monsters that swam there.

Beneath the surface-level deck of the ship, the interior extended several floors downward into the ocean's depths. Criss-crossing stairs and ladders made the contained space feel immense, and simultaneously displayed and hid rooms of various sizes waiting under her feet and around each corner. It was chaotic but controlled: chaos by design. Despite the whirlwind of purple and yellow walls, lights that glowed through bulbs of pressed flowers, and doors that opened downward and upward as often as they opened inward, the ship never dissolved into the random unpredictability of Venice. Sailing under the waves, her old home seemed impossibly far away, and getting more distant every day. Jessica let the memories fade into dull images of muddy black water and faded pastel walls, allowed this fantasy of gold and sub-hybrids and flower lights to slip effortlessly into place as her new reality.

When she ran to Ibada's room in the Coil, he was happy to accept her offer to come to Kilimanjaro to perform. He was so happy that Jessica felt almost guilty. He did not understand that he was doing her a favour rather than the other way around.

Jessica watched the creatures swimming outside the ship. She took a deep breath to ease her anxiety. Something bright red with multiple tentacles propelled itself through the waves by one of the windows, and she tried to reassure herself that she was safe inside the sub-hybrid. But an even larger monster could be glimpsed swimming further away in the distant darkness, reminding her that nowhere in the ocean was safe.

"Beautiful, isn't it?" asked Ibada. He placed his hookah behind the chaise longue and waved away the smoke. Jessica had already explained that she did not mind his smoking, even if she did not care to join him. She enjoyed how the scent of tobacco followed Ibada throughout the ship and followed her, too, after she had spent time with him.

"Or not," said Ibada, and Jessica realized she had been staring at him, silently.

"Sorry," she said.

"Don't worry about it. It's a mesmerizing view."

She almost told him that she had been looking at him, not at the view outside, but she was sure he already knew.

"Sit," he said, gesturing at a small round ottoman opposite him. "Is everything all right?"

"Yes," she said, taking her seat. "Well, no, but it has nothing to do with you. Or the ship, or my rooms, or the food. It's all lovely."

"Now that we've exhausted the incorrect answers, can you tell me why you're not all right?"

"I think I might be a terrible person," said Jessica.

Ibada leaned forward, resting his elbows on his knees, propping up his chin and contemplating her. "I think you're wrong," he said. "Could you explain why you think that?"

Jessica fidgeted with the edge of her dress. She had left the clothes she wore in Fuji back in the Coil, not sure if taking them would be considered stealing. She could not find her dress from Venice, and finally learned from Yuki that it had been incinerated in the Station as trash. Fadhila came to her rescue, offering one of her own dresses, "To borrow, not keep." Jessica was not nearly as tall as Fadhila, and had to tie the extra pale green fabric that would have pooled onto the floor in a knot by her calves. Ibada watched her play with the material and did not rush her to answer.

"It's complicated," said Jessica.

"Try to explain as simply as you can," said Ibada.

"I hate my father."

It felt real as she said it, but not quite like the truth, and not quite like a lie, and not quite what she was trying to explain. Ibada nodded, more curious than agreeing, but also not condemning her, which was a relief.

"You thought you were talking to him while you were sick," he said.

Jessica flinched. Her hair bounced against her bare shoulders, and immediately tangled in the thin straps holding up her dress. "I didn't know you came to visit me."

They had not known each other then. She had been the silly girl confused by a touch screen who became violently ill.

"I was with you… a lot," said Ibada. He was holding something back. "It sounded like you were arguing with him."

Jessica tugged some of her tangled curls free. "We argued a lot," she said. "But that's not why I hated him. And it's not really hate. It's…"

"Complicated," said Ibada.

Jessica nodded. Being so far away from the Upper Keep made it difficult to remember why they had fought so much. In a room whose windows offered underwater views, with strings of flower petals hanging from the lights high on the ceiling, and the hum of the ship causing them to shudder and spin as if they were caught in the process of falling, it was hard for Jessica to think about her life in that dark single room. To remember the sound of Abraham's voice, and the smell of the piss, and the other curtains shut against her.

"It's not my father so much as my family," said Jessica.

"Your mother?"

"No, she's dead."

"I'm sorry," Ibada said.

She shrugged away his concern. "It was a long time ago…"

After a moment, Ibada said, "Do you want some tea?"

Jessica frowned and her anxious fingertips flitted across her collarbone. "Why?"

"Because we've established that you hate your father, or your family, you lost your mother when you were very young, and we still haven't got to why you think you're a terrible person," said Ibada. "Which makes me think that we might be here awhile. And if we are going to be here awhile, I, at least, would like some tea while we talk."

Ibada did not wait for her response. He leaned back and lifted a small device, a *phone*, from his side table.

"A pot of tea, please," he said, relaxing again as he hung up. He smiled at her. "You don't need to look so frightened. A phone can't jump up and bite you."

Jessica pulled herself upright. She knew it was a strange kind of communication, and while she liked the idea of speaking to someone anywhere on the ship, she did not like the idea of others listening. Fadhila had rolled her eyes as she explained how no one could hear unless the button was pressed "on," but Jessica thought the small black square looked malicious enough to listen whenever it wanted, and the long wire that connected to the wall was too eel-like to be trustworthy.

"Is everyone in Venice your family?" asked Ibada, and she jerked her eyes away from the phone. "Is that what you mean by family?"

"Just the Upper Keep," said Jessica. "Kind of. I'm only half. Half-Jewish."

"Okay."

"Jews are…"

"You don't have to explain Judaism," said Ibada with a hushing wave of his hand. "And I already knew that you're Jewish."

Jessica clutched instinctively at her neck, but her fingers only found a few of her curls. "Who told you about the Upper Keep?"

"I don't know anything about any *keep*," said Ibada. "There are Jews outside of Venice, you know. Many in High Rock Ridge. Some in Les Alpes, too, but…"

Ibada looked out the window at the now empty under-water view.

The door to the room opened, and a young woman in a grey and white striped iro and buba entered, carrying a tray with a large silver teapot and two matching cups. She set it on the table and left without looking at Jessica.

Jessica had never thought there might be Jews in other parts of the world. She had never thought to ask, and if anyone in the Upper Keep had known, they had never bothered to tell her. She was not sure if this new knowledge made her feel better or worse. She supposed that would depend on whether these communities were people who would welcome her, or shut her out.

Ibada handed her a cup steaming with bright red tea. The first sip burned the tip of her tongue.

"Your father wouldn't be happy that you chose to travel with me," Ibada said.

Jessica snorted then coughed as she nearly choked on her tea.

"Why?" she asked. "He doesn't even know you."

"From what I've heard, Jewish communities are pretty tightly knit. You should probably be travelling with a Jewish man, travelling to other Jewish communities." Ibada raised his eyebrow, trying to convey something that Jessica could not decipher. "Choosing me, that choice, is that why you think you're a terrible person?"

"You don't understand," said Jessica, clutching her teacup, letting it burn. "You don't know what I did."

Hirokai, floating, half-consumed by eels, his expression more baffled than pained... She had killed him. She needed to get away from Venice, from her father, from the Upper Keep, from the anger and pain because she could not handle it anymore, and Hirokai had died because of that. There were supposed to be consequences for actions. But the confession caught in Jessica's throat, tightening her chest, and her breath quickened into desperate gasps.

"Jessica," Ibada said, voice low and calming. "I know that whatever you're thinking, it's upsetting you. You don't have to tell me what it is. But ask yourself: Is there anything you can do about it? Right now?"

Jessica shook her head.

"Well then," Ibada continued. "You need to take a deep breath, count your problems, and then breathe them out."

Jessica's giggle faltered, but she followed his advice, her own advice. She was still afraid that there was a price yet to be paid, but Ibada was right. The tension in her chest eased as she breathed out. There was nothing she could do about any of it. Whatever confession she could have shared, whatever consequence she might have met, Hirokai was gone, and the sailors were gone, and there was nothing she could do to bring them back. She could only live with the choices she had made from the moment she had pushed Hirokai to her decision to flee from Fuji.

She had not realized that she was choosing Ibada when she had decided to run away to Kilimanjaro. But that was what he had said. *Choosing me.* That was the choice Ibada thought she had made, and he had accepted her request to come with him. What did that mean? The answer seemed obvious and impossible.

"Why did you visit me when I was sick?" asked Jessica.

It was not quite the question she wanted to ask. Instead of answering, Ibada rose from his chaise longue, closed the small space between them, and kneeled beside her. He reached out his hand, fingers close to the stray curls that cut across the left side of her face like a frayed curtain over her eye and cheek. He paused, fingertips hovering next to the strands, until Jessica lifted her own hand and guided him the rest of the way, and then her red curls were twirling around his fingers.

It was not the first time someone had caught onto her hair. She would often feel little tugs as she pushed through the crowds on the ramparts, perhaps by mistake (her curls had a life of their own), but more likely driven by a curiosity that could not be controlled. When she snapped her head away and glared out a warning to the culprit, they would have already disappeared. But Ibada did not pull away, and Jessica did not want him to pull away. Her empty cup slipped out of her hand and onto the floor, landing with a soft thud on the plush purple rug, but she could not move her eyes away from Ibada's face to see if it had cracked. A blush burned her cheeks, and words tumbled from her lips before she could think of the right thing to say or conceal.

"I don't usually choose to be with people," said Jessica, forcing away an intruding image of Luka, smiling, laughing… "I mean, my choices are about me. I'm not the kind of person to end up with another person, so if I gave you that idea, I'm sorry. I'm… I'm an in-between kind of person, not more, if that's what you thought, or wanted."

"My choices are about me, too," said Ibada, humour in his voice, although he was not smiling. "And who said anything about ending up with someone?"

*Shakespeare*, Jessica thought, but did not say it out loud, already feeling like an idiot. That was how it worked, wasn't it? You found someone at the beginning of the play, and at the end you either married them or you died. Or they died. Or everyone died. Jessica knew that in Venice couplings were as frequent as they were impermanent, much more relaxed than any play, legend, or fantasy. But the idea of a casual coupling, with a real person, had seemed more impossible for her than witch prophecies or shipwrecked sorcerers.

Ibada had not come any closer, had not touched her anywhere but where she had guided him. Jessica considered pushing him away. Not because she wanted that, but because she did not know what else she should do. She had no idea what happened next.

"You could end up with someone, someone wonderful, and be happy," said Ibada. But Jessica did not believe him. "And you could also be happy in the meantime."

*Could* she? She had never wanted to be happy. She hadn't really thought of happiness as a goal.

"I can be happy…" said Jessica. It was meant as a question, but she said the words as if they were true. She was so used to her words being lies, performances, that saying this made her not want to believe it. If this was a performance, she needed to do more than stare at her captive audience. It was not the audience's job to act. They waited for Jessica to act, and Ibada was waiting.

She usually had so much time to practice before performing, time to whisper words over and over to herself until they were perfect, to choose moments of highs and lows, to find emotion behind difficult phrases. But this performance was completely new. As her lips pressed against Ibada's, she was sure she was doing everything wrong. As his tongue slid across her teeth and deeper into her mouth, her jaw dropped in surprise, and she was sure she was doing things wrong that she did not even know she was doing wrong.

She braced to feel a pain in her back tooth, prepared for the embarrassment of having to explain to Ibada that he needed to be softer, but there was no pain. There was nothing crawling in her hair to worry about as Ibada's grip tightened. Her own hands and fingertips were smooth as she pushed up his dashiki and explored the skin beneath. When she closed her eyes, she could still see her body that she had left behind in Venice, the decay, the scraps of flesh peeling from her hands and the black and yellow spots that had dotted her teeth. But she was not that woman anymore. She was not dying. She was here, and very much alive, and determined to enjoy being alive, no matter how much her ever-fretful mind told her there must be something to worry about. Surely there was something still offensive about her, in the thin line of her lips or the extravagant redness of her hair. There must be something so revolting about her that made everyone turn away from her, she thought, even as Ibada showed no desire to turn away.

Questions and problems screamed in her mind, too chaotic to form into coherence. With Ibada's mouth on her mouth and one of his hands reaching through the curls to clutch the base of her neck and his other hand guiding her hip up to follow him with shaky steps before pressing her back down against the chaise longue, there was no time or opportunity to breathe any anxiety out. Something still coiled deep in her stomach, but was somehow not so unpleasant…

Ibada released her mouth only to bury his face where her neck met her shoulder. His lips and teeth caught as much on curls as on skin, and instead of taking the moment to breathe out, she bit her lip and let the chaos build. Ibada's hand left her hip to push up the length of fabric that had become unknotted. His hand returned to her thigh and slid up farther, but he stopped abruptly. She opened squeezed-shut eyes to see him watching her.

"Is this all right—" Ibada began. Jessica grabbed his hand before he could finish asking and guided it higher.

Ibada never looked away from Jessica's face as he touched her, and though he did not ask her anything else, Jessica found herself nodding, her curls twisting into a wild mess as the desire grew. This was not anxiety. This was nothing like anxiety, and it was not so unfamiliar. She realized she was whispering a steady, encouraging verse.

> *"Take him and cut him out in little stars,*
> *And he will make the face of heaven so fine*
> *That all the world will be in love with night—"*

There was more, much more that she wanted to say, but the speech became reality: her vision was in darkness then burst with stars. All the verses in her head were silenced, and she released all the chaos and worry and everything she did not know and could not control, not on a breath, but on a wordless cry.

## Chapter 26 (Shinobu)

The wide rectangular hulls of the gathering vessels contained a constantly whirring mass of machinery, metallic teeth chewing plastic to pulp. Shinobu would have preferred to lie between two great grinding gears and let her body be pulped in turn than stay exposed to the storm for a second longer. She wished she could join Ama below deck in the little cabin with their squished-together bunks and barely enough room for two people, let alone six. The limited space had been made even smaller by the addition of stacks of Shinobu's Shakespeare records, several wigs that Ama did not want Yuki to steal, and the bulk of the empress's wind-board, which she refused to leave behind.

Shinobu's bun had been torn loose in the wind, the clips now lost to the ocean. Thick wet strands of hair clung to her cheeks, across her face, and wrapped around her neck. At least her glasses were safe, secured firmly by her misplaced hair, even as the wind and rain tried desperately to tear them away. A large wave crashed over the deck, and, for a moment, Shinobu's entire body was submerged. She clung to the side railing and a startling image assaulted her: Shinobu, not wrapped in her hair, but in kelp growing from the distant ocean floor like arms, pulling her down into its embrace. Even when the wave had passed and Shinobu was free to gasp, the strands around her neck felt like a deadly promise.

*Full fathom five—*

"Shinobu, to the port side!"

Yana's cry cut off the verse before Shinobu could become completely lost.

Shinobu realized that she was curled completely around the railing. Yana and Minato were near the starboard side of the prow, pulling seaweed-wrapped debris from the engine that was struggling to grind it down. Shinobu imagined the whining gears working against too much input, the clogged machinery, and saw the release of steam as the rain hit the overworked engine. If the engines did not consume the trash, the gathering vessel would not move forward, and if the vessel did not move, they would never get out of this storm. Even when it passed, they would be stuck in the open ocean. To the portside of the prow, Yousuke and Masuna struggled with another dredged-up mass. There was a third engine at the stern, but it ground to a halt when the storm began and a wave upended a portion of the metal skimming net into its jaws.

"Shinobu!" Yana shouted again, her voice clear and strong despite the wailing of the storm.

Shinobu pried her fingers loose from the rail and crawled across the deck. The skimmers and runners all stood so sure, eyes wide and frightened but bodies practiced, not ignoring the storm but doing what must be done. Yousuke and Masuna did not pause in their constant digging, hands close to the blades of the engine. Shinobu hid her head from the storm and followed the rail along the portside of the deck, reaching blindly with her left hand to grope her way forward to the second engine. She was too terrified to feel ashamed.

> *Of his bones are coral made*
> *Those are pearls that were his eyes...*

The top of Shinobu's head bumped gently against the covered back curve of the engine that hid the wide chute which transported the shredded trash into the ship's stomach. *Hull.* Stomach. She pressed her hands against the metal and pulled herself to her feet.

Masuna was helping Yousuke with a burden that looked like kelp... but kelp should not be so hard for the engine to chew.

"There's something stuck underneath," said Yousuke. He was closer than Yana, but harder to hear. The wind caught his voice and carried it far away. "Try to pull it out. It won't go through."

Shinobu wiped some of the blur from her glasses with her sleeve. She did not want to reach into the dark bundle, but she stuck her hands underneath the kelp and grasped for whatever she could find. She felt something long and slick, and she pulled hard.

There was a moment of resistance as the engine refused to release its half-chewed prize, and then something tore. The stuck pieces were swallowed, and the rest of the obstruction came loose in her hands. A spray of blood joined the rain on her glasses. With a sharp cry, she tossed the offending creature over the boat. *Eels*. The beast's infamous mouth had been torn away, but Shinobu was sure it was an eel. They were rare in Fuji, but they infested the waters around Venice, where fish were scarce and humans plentiful. The ship must be close to Venice…

The kelp was tugged out of Yousuke's and Masuna's hands into the engine.

"There is something wrong with that wave," said Masuna.

Shinobu thought he meant the wave breaking over the railing that tried to knock them off their feet and brought in its wake the longest continuous piece of soft grey plastic Shinobu had ever seen. Yousuke and Shinobu gripped handfuls of the wispy material and shoved it into the engine. Masuna did not help them. He seemed frozen in place. He pointed past starboard, past where Yana and Minato struggled with their own engine. In the dark distance, Shinobu saw the outline of towers, solid black against the blue-black of a storm-ravaged sky. Those must be two of the towers of Venice, the closest one the abandoned Dark Tower, and that further one… She could not remember the name, but she knew it was not abandoned. It was connected to land, to K2. Her chest heaved with relief.

Yousuke dropped the plastic sheet and clapped his hands over his mouth with a moan. He was not looking at the towers. He was looking at something closer, something horrifyingly familiar.

Now that Shinobu was wearing her glasses, she could see the shape of the monster that had arisen in Fuji much more clearly than before: its pointed face, fat neck, and the thrashing body (almost as large as their gathering vessel) that breached the surface of the Flood and crashed back down. A sturgeon, but impossibly large, the largest fish Shinobu had ever seen. Some of the historical records in the Vaults warned that the fish had been growing as the Flood rose, but they never warned how big. And the sturgeons in illustrations did not look quite like this. Their bodies were smoother. They had whiskers, yes, but whiskers did not writhe. Those things growing out of this monster could not be whiskers. They were more like tentacles, too many tentacles, each moving with a mind of its own. As the monster's body crashed into the water, a few of the tentacles were knocked off by the impact, showering down upon the Fujians' ship. One of them fell at Shinobu's feet. She picked it up before it could be sucked into the mouth of the engine. An eel. The monster's entire body was covered in feasting eels, and now the dislodged creatures were flopping on the deck, their mouths constricting and opening like dilating eyes. Revolted, Shinobu kicked one. It thrashed its body towards her, but its mouth did not have time, or the proper angle, to latch onto her.

Masuna was not so lucky. He had wrapped the loose fabric of his trousers up by his knees, to protect the clothing from being pulled into the chewing gears of the engine. It was a sensible precaution, but it left his lower legs bare. One eel latched onto his left calf, its body pulsing. His right leg was covered with eels, sleek body blending with sleek body. Yousuke fell to his knees to tear the eels off Masuna's body. Shinobu told herself the rain made it look like there was more blood than there actually was. She knew that she should probably help, but she moved back to the rail to hug the metal again. Yousuke shouted at her, but she could not hear what: the wind was picking up, screaming in her ears. She looked over to Yana and Minato. None of the eels had got them. Yana's voice was stronger than the storm.

"Go to the empress!"

Ama, yes! Ama was all alone, below deck, and the hatch was shaking violently, ready to fly open.

As she stumbled across the deck, Shinobu felt like she was floating far away from her body. She ignored the chewed-up eels that Yousuke was pulling from the engine and the screwed-up expression on Minato's face as he tried to help, slipping and sliding. She ignored Yana's voice, suddenly shrill, because she needed to get to Ama… She was so close now. If she reached out her arms, she could unlock the bolt on the hatch…

It dawned on Shinobu that Yana was not crying out to her to save Ama. She was crying out to the scribe to save herself.

There was a tremendous shudder and a metallic groan. The hatch was no longer in front of her, but above her, and Shinobu was sliding away from it. The ship was tilted completely on its side. Shinobu turned her head to see the great bulk of the sturgeon's body roll away. The ship immediately righted itself, and Shinobu, propelled upwards, was briefly airborne before falling back down, hard, on the deck.

Something grabbed her. Shinobu's muscles tensed, but it was only Yana. The runner kept her body flat, close to the deck, pulling Shinobu with her as she scrambled forward. New trash had been dredged up in the confusion, including an ancient plastic net that had wrapped itself around their legs in a manner of seconds. An eel, too, was trying to attach itself to Yana's leg, but its grip was weak, its teeth unable to pierce the dense, waterproof fabric of the net. But Shinobu was not wearing the outfit of the skimmers and runners. She was not completely covered. She looked down at her arm and saw two eels suckling at her flesh. They did not hurt at all... Yana grabbed them both in one unforgiving fist and tore them away. *That* hurt. Shinobu shook her head, wiped her glasses on an equally wet sleeve and scanned the deck for the other Fujians.

Many more eels were flopping onboard and something wide and solid like the beam of a sailing ship had lodged itself into the starboard engine. This showed no signs of life, although the portside engine was still whining away, swallowing trash with determined persistence. Shinobu could not see Masuna or Minato. They were not on deck. She caught a glimpse of Yousuke near the very edge of the prow, sprawled in front of the railing. His shirt had ridden up his back. Several eels had latched onto his skin, and two were protruding from his neck. Shinobu pulled against Yana, trying to go back for him, but the runner tightened her grip as she forced the scribe towards the hatch.

"We need to get below now!" Yana shouted.

Shinobu could not tell if Yousuke was dead. She did not think he was. She did not think the eels would still be sucking so enthusiastically if he was dead. Shinobu dug her heels into the deck, and the tangled net halted Yana's progress.

"We can't lose anyone else!" said Shinobu.

"We've already lost too many!" Yana grabbed Shinobu's shoulders and turned her away from Yousuke. "It's done, Shinobu! There's nothing we can do! We're done!"

Shinobu knew this was true. She had known for so long… There was nothing to be done for the future of Fuji. There was only this horrible present on a ship floundering on the edge of yet another dying community. A shadow fell over the deck, blocking the rain and the wind. Yana screamed. Shinobu saw the sturgeon rising in the air, preparing to crash down yet again. Yana grabbed the scribe and leapt towards the railing, her strong arm and the tangled net forcing Shinobu to fly with her, before the monster fell onto the space where they had been standing. The ship tipped again, and Shinobu and Yana were pressed against the rail, bodies thrust under the water. But it did not feel like water. It felt like eels, an ocean made of eels, all wriggling and swarming under them, fighting each other as they struggled to feed.

The sturgeon rolled off the ship again. Shinobu and Yana were tossed up and collapsed in a heap on each other. There was an eel on Yana's face, another on her hand, and Shinobu grasped at them. Yana's hands were moving quickly, each sharp tug bringing a new wave of pain to Shinobu's body. She had to get to Ama, get below the deck, find the hatch…

But when at last she found the hatch, it was open. The metal cover had flown open.

Shinobu had a horrible vision of Ama lost in the waves, among the eels, desperate, her mouth open in a silent scream filling with water. Then she saw the bright pink sail of the empress's wind-board, forced through the hatch, tugged but not torn as Ama threw herself out into the storm. The empress floundered for a moment before catching her balance on the violent ocean surface. And she sailed away, leaving Shinobu behind.

Shinobu felt Yana's hands on her, guiding her to the hatch, pushing her down into the hold. She saw a flash of pink as Ama abandoned ship. Abandoned her. And then Yana closed the hatch, and Shinobu saw nothing more.

## Chapter 27 (Cem)

"The storm is coming," said the ghost in the corner.

Cem did not know why he had chosen to sleep in a cave occupied by a ghost, and not a very smart ghost at that. The storm was here. Rain crashed outside the window. Did caves have windows? Did rain have feet? The raindrops sounded like ten thousand feet. Maybe he was hearing the echo of sounds not yet made, a flood of people who had not yet climbed up the ladders. They were not on the rocks now, but they would come in time. They were sick and they were scared, and the rain could not keep them away forever.

Cem did not like this ghost. It had grey in its beard and its throne smelled rotten. But despite his urge to skitter away, he did not want to leave the shadowy figure alone.

"What are we going to do?" asked Cem.

"You're going to survive," said the ghost. "It's the most and least we all can do."

"But what about you?" asked Cem. "If they're coming—"

"There is always a storm. There is always a Flood. And there is always a reason to die. It's harder to survive, but we figure out how to do it, anyway. And if you spend enough time surviving, it'll get easy. The little pains you leave in your wake become easier to bear. You don't get as old as me by being kind."

"When I'm as old as you I'll be dead."

Old age had always terrified Cem. It was being a ghost, a living ghost, something that should have died but refused to disappear into the darkness. Cem realized that this ghost was not dead, of course he was not. He lived here and was still very much alive. Cem was supposed to take care of this ghost. He knew there were other people that he loved that he also needed to care about. And the hissing in his head told him to take care of himself.

The rain beat harder on the balcony. It sounded red, like something that could pour out of a neck. Cem hugged himself. He had seen blood in the waves before when someone was pushed in. The waves were red, the corpse was red, and that figure, the pusher, red, red, red. Cem closed his eyes.

"I don't know what to do."

"Leave," said the ghost. "Abandon me. Survive. Make sure that you survive."

"Why?" said Cem.

The ghost laughed, the sound dissolving into watery coughs. "You don't need a reason. Survival is for anyone who figures out how to do it."

"How am I supposed to do it?"

The ghost stared at a point far away from the cave and the storm. "You need to become selfish," he said. "You need to decide that your survival is worth a sacrifice. And you need to figure out who that sacrifice is."

The hissing exploded in Cem's mind. He hunched over, nails scratching against the floor. The ghost watched him writhe. Part of Cem's brain told him to stand before he forgot how, and another part told him to run before he remembered too much. Bota had fallen into the waves, wrapped in the embrace of another body. Someone who mattered. A sacrifice. A death that meant something, that let more people survive, people like Cem. Cem, who had figured out how to survive, who had lived and adapted. If he died, it would not matter. He was not important. The hissing calmed a little at this truth, and his acceptance of it, and Cem was able to pull himself to his feet.

Whoever he was willing to sacrifice had to be important.

The ghost's head drooped to the side. He was drooling into his whitening beard. No one cared about this ghost. No one checked this cave except for Cem. This spirit did not matter enough to sacrifice.

"I'm going to survive," said Cem.

"Get out of here."

"What?"

"I needed your mother, but I don't need you," shouted the ghost. "You're nothing!"

Cem did not remember having a mother. A mother was a myth, the kind of story told by someone standing high up on the ramparts, fearless above the drop. An important person whose hair fell like blood.

"I'm nothing," agreed Cem. But if he stayed here, he was going to disappear, and he was not ready to be a ghost. So he crawled out of the window, pushing aside the rope curtain. "I'm going."

"Good," said the ghost.

Outside, the rain hurt as it struck Cem's head and shoulders, but he resisted the urge to crawl back inside. The ghost's continued ranting made it easier to move further into the storm. "Get away from me! As far you can!"

Cem pressed on through the rain, crossing balconies and rope bridges, letting his muscle memory guide him where his body wanted to go in a world that was strangely unfamiliar. As the rain raged above him and below him, Cem imagined reaching a level of Venice so high it was up in clouds, the world and the monsters far below him. He groped blindly out with his left hand and his fingers touched a windowsill. He pulled himself through the window, inside, and immediately crouched on the floor, ready to bite and spit at any other Feral who had found their way into this small haven. But there were no Feral here.

Farooq was there, sitting next to a small bed, where Sedef lay still, eyes closed. Farooq and Sedef. Cem remembered them. He cared about them. He jumped to his feet and watched Sedef's little body, waiting until he could see her chest rising and falling in desperate pants before he let himself breathe out in relief. He stripped off his soaked tunic and hung it on the back of a chair before he crouched by the foot of the bed. He hoped he had not hissed when he landed in the room.

"Where's the woman…" he said, but he was not sure who he was asking about.

"Talia went to check on Abby's brother," said Farooq. "She had a bad feeling. I think she's stuck there now."

"I think the ghost had Talia's bad feeling, too," said Cem. "Something's coming. Something bad."

Farooq frowned at Cem, and Cem wondered what he had said to warrant this concern. He was sure he had said words. He would not have had such a headache forming if he had forgotten how to make his tongue work again. The hissing would have been out instead of trapped in.

"What's coming?" asked Farooq. "What's bad?"

Cem remembered bodies on the ramparts, so far below. An angry girl with golden hair, Bota's favourite, kicking a body into the harbour. Another body for the eels, more blood in the water. A riot was coming.

"No one up here is sick," said Cem. "No one but Sedef."

"I'm a little better, now."

Sedef's voice had always been quiet, but now it sounded like a whisper of a memory of someone, a sad memory that you tried to forget. Cem leapt to sit beside her. He grabbed Sedef's hand; Farooq was already holding the other. Her hands were hot and dry, like rocks on a too sunny day.

"Do you need anything? Something to eat?" asked Farooq. "Talia left broth. It's probably cool now, but—"

"Do you know how you got sick?" asked Cem. Farooq shushed him, but Cem knew this was important, more important than food, for their survival. "Did the white man do something? Maybe to the algae blocks?"

Pale blue eyes flashed in his mind, and long fingers that needed to be pried from his shoulders. A man who was a monster... but that was Grigory, and this man was nothing like Grigory. He smiled with a full mouth of pointy teeth and covered his head in blood-red skins.

"I don't know," Sedef said. "I heard Talia say that she thought it might have been Andrusha. That he brought back something from the empress. A punishment."

"Why would the empress send a punishment with Andrusha?" asked Cem.

"So people would blame him and not her," Farooq proposed. "But if it's a punishment, why aren't they punishing the Upper Keep?"

"Because the punishment will come later when the Venetians realize none of the Jews are sick," said Sedef at the same time Cem said, "Because the Upper Keep was already punished before, when it rained blood."

They were quiet again and listened to the rain assaulting the roof.

"More people are going to die," said Farooq. "Even if everyone gets better. They'll want someone to blame."

"Or the Fujians will come and kill whoever didn't die from the punishment," said Sedef.

"There won't be many people left to kill," said Cem.

"And everyone left will kill each other, blaming whoever is left because they're there," said Farooq.

Cem turned his head to the ceiling and tried to picture the clouds above. Tried to believe that some powerful figure was looking down at them. Someone who could save them with the wave of her hand, who could help if only she wanted. Someone who lived far away and high above the pain who could pull them up to be with her.

"I wish there was a ladder to the clouds," he said. He did not mean to say it out loud. He waited for Farooq and Sedef to laugh, but they did not.

"I wish someone could wave a magic staff and fix everything," said Farooq. "*I have bedimm'd the noontide sun, call'd forth the mutinous winds, and 'twixt the green sea and azured vault set roaring war...*"

"I wish the riot never happened," said Sedef.

The riot. The riot happened, and the shipments stopped, and the Venetians left, and the white people came, and everyone got sick. But it had all started with the riot…

"The riot!" Cem shouted. "I know who's to blame for the riot!"

"You do?" asked Farooq.

"Well… I *knew*."

He remembered red, blood in the water, but also red on the head of the person who pushed that first sailor. When he tried to focus, two faces flashed in his mind: Andrusha, and Jessica. They blended together, two people, but only one pair of hands reaching out, and he could not make sense of it. Cem hissed through his teeth. He did not understand why Sedef gasped and clapped her hands over her mouth, why she looked like she was about to cry. Farooq did not look like he was about to cry. He looked the way he did after a child died in a fight. As if he was breaking inside but would not let that stop him from living. Farooq grabbed a piece of paper from a stack on top of a small chest in the corner of the room. He picked up a bottle of ink and carefully filled a pen.

"Tell me whatever you remember, while you can still remember it."

"What are you doing?" asked Cem.

"I'm writing a letter."

"We don't know how to write a letter."

"I know how to write a speech," said Farooq. "I've read enough of them. I can make whatever you say sound official and important. Like Shakespeare. Tell me everything you remember, and whoever reads it will be able to figure out who's to blame."

"We have no way to share the letter," said Cem. "It'll be too late by the time they come from…"

"Fuji?" suggested Sedef.

Cem nodded, though he was no longer sure what the word meant.

"We do have one of their ships, though," Farooq said.

Another memory cut through his mind, sharp and sure. An angry face.

*You know, I could sail away, too, if I wanted…*

"Borya can sail!" he shouted. "They said they could sail if they had somewhere to go. A reason. This is the best reason."

"Who should we send the letter to?" asked Sedef.

Her face was still flushed, but now it could have been with excitement.

Farooq grabbed more papers from the chest.

"Whoever we can get the letters to," he said. "Everyone we can get to read them. Everyone around the world."

#

*Hear me, now, oh world-wide listener*
*And know the pain of sickness, rot of death*
*That ravages the Savage Mountain here*
*And may have brought hot death to your fine shores.*
*This sickness has its root in one sure evil*
*An isolated action done in haste*
*A single person's hand who wrought our deaths*
*By starting wild riots on our rocks.*
*This villain hides somewhere on land or waves,*
*Travels in ships, or sits in quiet comfort,*
*While suff'ring plagues the victims of their crime.*
*This monster cannot hide forevermore*
*But waits to face a coming punishment.*
*Look for the sign of evil, go and find*
*The one to blame: the redhead of Venice.*

# EPILOGUE

Shinobu had told Ama that there was no art in Venice, so the empress assumed that they must have gotten very lost along their way, or else that terrible and thrilling sea monster had thrust their ship off course. The tower where she took shelter was so full of art, Ama could have been back in the Vaults. And this was only the base. A staircase wound upwards, hugging the walls, promising even more treasures on the upper levels.

Ama lay on the first few steps of the staircase, her body aching, coughing up sea water, skin thrumming in pain. She tried to distract herself with the beauty of the strange stone sculptures around her. They were great hybrid beasts: giant men with long beards and longer wings, women who were part human and part bird and part snake, lions that could fly with flat humanoid faces. The figures had been pieced together, not only in the way the artists had intended with their depictions of monstrous hybridity, but through renovations that must have occurred after some massive destructive force broke them to pieces.

The statues were cut through with cracks like jagged scars that had been fused back together again, each imperfect part finding its way back to an approximate whole. It reminded Ama of certain pottery in Fuji, broken pieces reconnected with liquid gold, but no precious metal shone in these fixed cracks. The pieces wore their pain plainly, told it clearly, even in their resolute silence. Even then,

Ama would not have been able to fully understand their suffering, the sacrifices and ugliness that marred anything that survived disaster, if that pain had not been mirrored on her own skin.

When she first scrambled onto the staircase, she thought the steps were buzzing with electricity, setting her skin on fire. But when she found the strength to lift one arm, to turn and examine a burning leg, she saw bright red lines criss-crossing on her flesh. There was a similar burning cut across her neck and face, and she could only imagine the grotesque designs that had scarred her as permanently as each of her piercings. She remembered her board cutting through what looked like great bubbles of foam at the tower's entrance, and thin strands like silk wrapping over her as she was knocked off her sail and forced to swim to her current perch.

A sting-wave.

They had sounded so lovely when Shinobu described their gentle *shush-shush*. But the marks they left on Ama's skin were ugly. She was not supposed to feel pain. She did not like it. Pain burned. Pain turned the beauty around her into ugliness.

Something glittered golden on a platform above the empress, promising a beauty that remained unscarred. Ama stood up, gritting her teeth against the sting-wave burns on the bottom of her feet. She teetered for a moment on shaky legs, then stumbled up the winding staircase, past platform after platform of patient, silent, pain-wracked art.

"I'm not afraid of heights," Ama whispered to herself. Her voice sounded loud and rude in the Dark Tower. "I'm not afraid of heights. I'm not afraid of heights."

Ama collapsed next to the glittering sculpture: a man made of gold. He sat cross-legged with one hand raised, a soft smile on his lips, oddly familiar and comforting. Ama laid her head against one of his knees. She pretended that this cold body was Shinobu, chilled from hours in the Vaults. Ama's mouth trembled with the urge to ask for a story, one about the monsters beneath the waves – great serpents illustrated with blue and gold bodies, dragons that swam with wild manes and even wilder eyes, sting-waves that covered the ocean surface like a blanket, bumping against the borders of surviving communities with their shush-shush-shush. *Shush-shush-shush*, Shinobu would whisper from the end of her bed. *Shush-shush-shush* echoed the words of Shinobu's stories as Ama dreamed of clear jelly bodies and embracing tentacles.

> *Once, there was an emperor's son, who was forced to become a commoner...*
> *Once, there was a schoolgirl, who was looking for a magic crystal...*
> *Once, there was a prince, who was kept hidden from all the pain in the world...*

Ama sat up and stared at the familiar statue. Yes, it was the Buddha… Shinobu had joked with her about his story, in her own dry way, outside the Greenhouse, while she was making copies of her precious *Rebecca*. The Buddha had been exposed to the suffering of the world, and despaired, but then saw a way through. He left behind him a call to ease the suffering of the world, one that must be answered by exceptional people. Ama had tried but she had not really understood suffering. She remembered wanting to feel it, a desire disgusting to her now that she really knew what pain felt like. Pain burned. It cut you in pieces. The empress willed herself to feel the confidence she had once possessed, the knowledge that everything would be okay in the end, because she could make it so.

"I can do anything."

Ama had always known this was true. It was why Shinobu had tried so hard to control her tantrums before the empress broke more buildings or caused more storms. It was how her family had pulled the Coil out of the ocean and wrapped it around Fuji. It was why the world had Flooded, not the initial flood caused by arrogance and ignorance, but the flood of ink that a distant emperor of her line spilled over the map of a civilization that did not deserve the earth it tortured. Selfishness and chaos started the destruction, but that emperor made the impossible Flood. He forced the waters to rise because he had the power to do so. This power thrummed through the line of Ama's ancestors and filled her being. It could destroy whatever she wanted to destroy and help whoever she wanted to help.

"I am a god."

How many times had she told Jessica, Andrusha, visiting delegations, that she was powerful, the bearer of magic? She was used to the smiles, the dismissal: *Silly Ama!* She did not care. *She* knew it was true. She never felt the need to prove herself to these little people, so insignificant, clamouring for her help and attention. But she had still given them what they wanted. She had given algae blocks. She had given her time, and her mercy, and all she got in return was this pain.

"I can stop all suffering. I can save the world."

Her statement sounded hollow and false when heard only by stone creatures who did not care about algae blocks, or works of art, or beautiful words. Outside of the protective walls of Fuji, thrust into the darkness with scars written across her skin, Ama was suddenly aware that her goal was impossible.

Was this how everyone felt? Everyone in all the world? No amount of algae, or art, or words could ease this pain. No practice reaching towards transcendence – that weightless, selfless existence she barely touched when she leaned so far back on her wind-board, somewhere between two worlds – could remove that burden from humanity. The Buddha was wrong. He had not relieved the world's suffering through his empathy. Ama knew better now, better than him, better than the silly hopeful girl she used to be.

Ama could not make the world better. The world was the best it could be.

She reached her hands over the edge of the platform and felt for the Flood, physically so distant, and yet she could sense its soothing waves in her veins, under her skin. The waters were far below her, but her mind slipped back into that place between sky and ocean, skimming along the surface, her hair tilting close to the water, to disaster, teasing the inevitable plunge into darkness… She rode that sense of selflessness all the way down to the tower's foundation. She felt for the depths of the Flood outside the tower and all across the world. She felt for its power, and its weight, and its inevitability. She felt for its want, and, *oh yes*, it wanted to help, too. She felt for the water and grasped it tight. She pulled the Flood towards herself, and the water began to rise.

#

On the northern fishing shore of Kilimanjaro, Nen stood, toes in the sand, as the divers fled the unsettled ocean. He had been waiting for his mother's ship, for Fadhila, but by now he should have known that the ocean never offered what you expected. His friends in school all knew that the ocean did not act the way it was meant to. Though their teachers charted histories of climate change and information denial, the facts still did not add up to the destruction of their world. This impossible sight of the water rising to cover his feet and then his ankles as fishermen tore off their wetsuits and raced past him to solid land – it made sense in the way that it did not make sense, in the way nothing made sense when you looked at it head on and accepted the absurdity. Nen began to laugh and he could not stop, hysterical, yes, but sure that this was the only reasonable response.

#

Venetians screamed on the ramparts, but Borya did not care about the sick and dying. They had run down the spiralling stairs of the Broken Tower as the building rocked, dropping its delicate zoon dubs in crashes of splintered wood. Its structure had held together long enough for Borya to bound down the constantly shifting steps that threatened to toss them off in a far bloodier splintered landing. When they had reached the walkway, Borya saw all the towers on the ramparts sway and groan with snaps and cracks – but the buildings did not fall. The towers were more secure than the boat tossing in the bucking and rolling waves in the harbour far below. The last Fujian ship was on the brink of capsizing.

Borya pushed past those who ran upwards and those who had frozen on the steps to the harbour. They leapt from the tiles, teetering for a moment on the bucking ship before they remembered… *That* rope, that was the one to pull, and that one there was the one to secure, and then the ship's balance would recentre… And it did. The ocean still rose, with purpose and violence, but Borya was not scared. They were not scared of the ship. They were not scared of the water. Their hands gripped the ropes, ready to fly, somewhere, anywhere, as soon as someone told them where they needed to be.

A large flat ship unlike any Borya had ever seen before pushed a steady path through the unsteady waters. Something that looked like a plank used to construct the towers of Venice had pierced through one of its large engines. Another engine was releasing a hiss of steam, but the ship still managed to stay afloat. A flash of movement caught Borya's eye, and they saw a boy waving high in the Upper Keep, a stack of something precious clutched close to his chest.

#

The first few floors of the Vaults were already completely flooded. Shinku tried to absorb some of the calm radiating from Makoto as she opened drawers and grabbed anything that seemed important. Makoto hummed a silly tune about constant rain that did not seem so silly now. Shinku scrambled for anything she could hold that was sorted under Religion, and then ran to Mythology, and then, in a drawer where they did not belong, she saw a stack of books that were *hers*. Not *hers*, but they belonged in History, and she protected history. Shinku grabbed the entire stack, the memories of Frank and Améry and Wiesel, adding them to her ever-increasing large bundle. She did not know why her books had been taken from her, but she knew that someone was trying to hide them, and she had a feeling that meant it was incredibly important for them to be seen.

#

From her bedroom window in the southernmost tower, Sofia saw the water far beyond the wall creep its way upwards, covering meagre rows of crops one after the other. It hardly seemed real… She was too far away to see the people in the fields, but she knew that they would be running to the walls of Les Alpes, pounding on the gates, desperate to be let inside to higher ground. She did not have to go downstairs to know that no one inside the walls would open the gates. She sat immobile on her window seat, safe in the tall southern tower, but she could not stop hurting herself. She did not realize how deeply she was cutting into her skin until Dario tackled her to the ground and wrenched the razor from her fist, his hands slippery with her blood.

#

Beneath the ocean, Ibada watched the sea creatures flee together, great schools of disparate fish. Panic rolled their bulbous eyes as they were forced to unknown destinations by currents that Ibada knew should not exist. Something was happening to the Flood. He thought about waking Jessica, but she was wrapped in the sheets, a smile playing at the corner of her mouth. She looked like she was dreaming. She looked like she was happy. Ibada did not want to ruin her happiness, so he watched the exodus of the fish, alone.

#

When Abraham heard the people outside screaming, he dragged himself from the chair Jessica had made for him.

He pulled himself out onto the balcony, wincing as he went, but it was worth it to see the waters rising. He did not understand why Talia was yelling, why Chava had fallen into hysterics, why that boy from Venice Main was waving wildly for help. This was the help.

The Flood had risen again, like it had done before. That Flood was hardly the first time the world had ended in a rush of waves, and there had been plenty more floods between then and now. Yes, everything was about to get worse for everyone, for a while. There was nothing they could do in the face of a disaster caused by forces so much stronger than them, so completely out of their control. It was far too late. And help always came when it was too late. In these rising waters, Abraham saw destruction, yes, but he also saw hope for change.

Abraham hoped that towers would fall that could not be rebuilt. He hoped that precious possessions would be lost that could never be regained. He hoped that people became angry, and that their anger would move them to action, even if that action was climbing higher than they thought they ever could. He hoped that things would get even worse so they could finally get better. He hoped that Jessica was safe, that she would survive, that she could use her talent to be something good. After everyone had crawled through their pain, they would need something good to remind them how much could survive disaster after disaster.

Abraham laughed until he could no longer hear the people around him crying. Small hands that were not Jessica's (but if he closed his eyes, could be) tried to pull him back into his home and patted his back to comfort him, but Abraham did not need to be comforted.

Everyone was acting like it was the end of the world, like there were no more stories to tell and no more words to be spoken. But he could hear a voice far away singing a foolish song of the wind and the rain, about when the world began, and he did not want to miss seeing everything begin again.